PRA

*All Americ*

**BY DAVID HAYNES**

"A wildly funny, realistic look at beauty pageants, sibling rivalry, self-esteem, and growing up. Highly recommended."
—*Library Journal*

"It is a wonder that David Haynes is able to inhabit the female persona so completely, crossing gender lines to raucously spoof beauty pageants, sibling rivalry and TV shows in what is one of the [year's] smartest books. . . . [His] most sure-handed work to date."
—*Chicago Tribune*

"With this hilarious tale of a woman's emotional collapse and unlikely means of recovery, Haynes adds to his growing reputation as a distinctive and versatile humor writer. . . . Deneen [is] the wise, irreverent and brutally honest girl-friend every woman wants."
—*Publishers Weekly* (starred)

"Deneen Wilkerson is the most amazing creation yet in David Haynes's distinguished line of memorable female characters. Wise, wicked, sexy and moving, *All American Dream Dolls* is a smashing novel that proves once again that Haynes is one of the best—and the truest—chroniclers of black lives today."
—*Black Media News*

"Haynes was picked as one of *Granta*'s top 20 U.S. novelists under 40, and with characters and voices like these, it's no wonder. . . . This book's magic lies in the narrator's voice."
—*Booklist*

"[Haynes's] energy and wild-eyed good humor make him one of the most underrated fiction writers alive."  —*Salon*

"A frequently hilarious noel, with consistently on-target punchlines and an eye for real people."  —*Kirkus Reviews*

"Sometimes Deneen is as sharp and witty as Savannah from *Waiting to Exhale*. . . . Do Terry McMillan's fans have a big, warm Oprah-style hug waiting for Deneen?"
—*St. Louis Post-Dispatch*

"[Haynes] breathes a welcome freshness into his main character. She is quirky—and not only when her mental health is failing. In this way, Haynes strikes out from the *Waiting to Exhale* formula."  —*Newsday*

"Haynes [has] talents as a truly comic writer and observer of pop culture."  —*Washington Post Book World*

*All American Dream Dolls*

# DAVID HAYNES

# All
# American
# Dream
# Dolls

A Harvest Book
Harcourt Brace & Company
San Diego    New York    London

Requests for permission to make copies of any part of the work should be mailed to: Permissions Department, Harcourt Brace & Company, 6277 Sea Harbor Drive, Orlando, Florida 32887-6777.

The characters and events in this book are fictitious. Any similarity to real persons, living or dead, is coincidental and not intended by the author.

Library of Congress Cataloging-in-Publication Data
Haynes, David, 1955–
    All American dream dolls / David Haynes.
      p.    cm.—(A Harvest book)
    ISBN 0-15-600572-7
    1. Mothers and daughters—Fiction.   2. Sisters—Fiction.
   3. Beauty contests—Fiction.   4. Afro-American women—Fiction.
   5. Saint Louis (Mo.)—Fiction.   I. Title.
PS3558.A8488A79   1998
813'.54—dc21   98-15056

Text set in Meridien
Designed by Will Powers

Printed in the United States of America
First Harvest edition 1998
E D C B

*Thanks to the Ragdale Foundation
and the Virginia Center for the Creative Arts,
where much of this book was written.*

*All American Dream Dolls*

# One

I was on my way to what I hoped would be *the*
romantic vacation of my life, off to Door County
for a whole entire week of sweet sane rest. More rest. I needed
more rest.

You know Door county, don't you? It's that cute little
finger of Wisconsin that sticks up into Lake Michigan like
a pointed penis. Littered with quaint country inns and cute
shops and scenic vistas, everything there practically drips love
and happiness. I was in the car, Calvin driving, traveling east
on I-94. We'd been on the road for about an hour when
Calvin, who I'd been messing around with for the previous
eight months (a post-college record!), dumps me. I tell you
this sad story by way of explaining how a person such as
myself could end up spending the better part of the summer,
of what on the surface seemed a competent adult life, living
in the guest room in the basement of her mother's house.
Athena Deneen Wilkerson, a college-educated, hardworking
professional woman. Advertising phenom, friend of the earth,
an owner of major appliances. Yes, this happened to me.

Katrina, who introduced me to Calvin in the first place,
warned me that he was a chump, but I didn't trust her. She
is the sort of person who tells you she has a great guy for
you, and then a few days after you go out with him for the
first time tells you what a chump she thinks he is. If he was

such a chump, why did she introduce us in the first place? Either she wanted to see me fixed up with a chump (maybe), or else she really wanted him for herself and, for whatever reason, was having trouble putting out the right bait (probably). So, she introduced us, and, as happens in such stories, one thing led to another. I'd rather not get into that part—the dodging and feints, the courting and wooing. Those performances led eventually to my taking a week of the months of vacation they owed me at Waltershied, Williams and Caruthers, packing my things, and tooling along the interstate in Calvin's painfully conservative 1996 Toyota Camry Sedan. The radio was playing that perfectly awful "I Will Always Love You" as performed by Ms. Whitney Houston herself. Now, don't get me wrong: the sister's got great pipes. But to me this song has always sounded as if somebody let the rocker down on the cat's tail. I can't stand this damn song. So what did I do? Me, a person who has been asked at baseball games to please speak rather than sing the words to "The Star Spangled Banner," I opened my mouth and I started singing along with her, like it was me in the movie who'd just had all that good white-boy loving. One thing me and Ms. Houston have in common: if you can't sing it right, girl, sing it loud. I looked over at Calvin. I expected him to be cringing and covering his ears. He stared straight ahead, as if Whitney and I had been leaning across the back fence exchanging recipes instead of engaging in a soulful duet. No expression on his face at all.

So, I resumed looking out the window. Looking back at me was some of that fine Wisconsin scenery. You know how exciting that is. Look: a tree. Look: a billboard. Look: a herd of buffalo. A herd of buffalo!!!

"Calvin," I said, "There's a herd of buffalo over there."

He didn't say anything.

"Did you hear me? What is a herd of buffalo doing in the middle of Wisconsin?"

"I think we ought to break up," he said.

I guess I don't have to tell you that such is not the answer to the question about what a herd of buffalo is doing in Wisconsin. I swiveled my head over in the nigger's direction to make sure I'd heard him right. "I beg your pardon?" I said.

"I think we ought to break up," he repeated, and I said, "Oh."

I guess he couldn't have been more direct, could he? Still, it left me sitting there on my vacationing behind with a whole lot of questions. Like: Why? And: Why are you telling me this now? And: If that's how you feel, why is your car still going seventy-one miles an hour *away* from the city where we both live? But, you know how sometimes you get the feeling that in the play you are performing everyone but you has somehow missed their cues, that whatever your next line is supposed to be isn't readily apparent? Yes, I had fantasized a whole lovely story about our trip. I had imagined such charming sentiments coming from my mouth as: "Wisconsin sure is beautiful in the summer," and "Don't you just love the way the waves break over the rocks," and "Why don't we stay right here in this bed all day long." I had not imagined that on my romantic vacation I would be responding to bullshit like this. And, while I consider myself to be both mentally quick and verbally agile, at the moment the best I could come up with was that pathetic and thinly aspirated, "Oh."

Calvin kept driving. As if all he had done was announce the score of a Timberwolves game. I sat there trying to cook up a more appropriate response.

The thing is, when you are in a car traveling somewhat

over the legal speed limit, dressed in a cute summer outfit (in my case, an adorable Hawaiian print shirt I found at Lane Bryant—liana leaves and orchids in the most delicate earth tones you could imagine; and white tennis shorts, cinched in the middle with an old Boy Scout belt), with a man who has just dumped you and who also, as it happens, knows a lot of personal information about you, such as the location of various moles on your body and the specific brand names of the feminine hygiene products you use (who happens to have a whole routine of not particularly funny jokes about "things with wings"), I think it is vital to respond appropriately to being unceremoniously dumped. The unceremonious part is important. Maybe if he had hired a brass band or some out-of-work actor in a gorilla suit to present me with the bad news, I'd have had a more cogent reaction. As it was—presented with this sound bite as coolly as if he were asking me to try a new brand of mustard—I was unsure how to respond.

One might, I imagined, begin weeping. Silently would be nice—though my preference has always been for full-throated out-and-out wailing. There is much to recommend this approach, the first and by far the most important advantage being that men are completely incapacitated by tears. Tears are to men what kryptonite is to Superman: they have the capacity to turn the most intelligent rational he-man you know into a sniveling wimp. My previous relationship, Robert—the Black Ninja Sumo Monster—had an attack of conjunctivitis that he claims was caused by *my* crying because he refused to escort me out of a kick boxing match at the St. Paul Civic Center. It was our second and last date. I'll not speak of his crazy butt again. Still, for the most part, I am not a crier. It's a cheap trick—lazy, demonstrates a lack of ambition—and must only be used for the most dire emergencies, such as finding yourself trapped at a kick boxing match at the St. Paul Civic Center, so that leaving on your own would require fighting your way to the exits through throngs of drooling, domestic beer-poisoned men. So crying was out.

I thought about getting physical. I recall thinking that I should look in my purse to see if there was anything to cut him with. A fingernail file. A pair of cuticle scissors. Despite what many people think, as a black woman, no, I do not carry a switchblade. Just one of those hair picks with the sharpened metal tips—maybe I could ram it into the motherfucker's side. Just kidding. The only "ethnic hair care" (as they call it at K Mart) item I had was one of those pink brushes with blunt black knobs on the end. Lacking possession of anything sharp, I would have had to resort to pummeling him. I could work him over with the brush—leave for the police a body with evenly spaced grids of circles all over it. Give forensics something to puzzle out. But, no, something big and blunt would be better. My fist—or a brick maybe! I gave assault some serious thought: the pure adrenal joy of just beating the shit out of him. I know that many of you sisters share this particular fantasy. I have to confess that when I was growing up, one of my heroines was Aunt Esther on *Sanford and Son*. Girl, when LaWanda Page pummeled Redd Foxx with that big old purse of hers, it made my day. Calvin, he is one of those scrawny men (scrawny and thin everywhere, if you know what I mean. More on that later). One good swipe, I could've knocked his narrow behind through the windshield. Of course violence breeds violence, and while I had no knowledge or experience of Calvin the abuser . . . well that's the problem, you see, I didn't know. He sure didn't look like one or act like one. But, then again, he never looked or acted like the sort of man who would dump his girlfriend *on the way* to their vacation.

I thought about reaching over and twisting his ear off or yanking out a hank of his nappy hair. Or just slapping him. Hard. Having earlier ruled out killing myself, I figured it probably wasn't a good idea to start duking it out with the driver of the car in which one is a passenger. And, yeah, girls, for a minute there I did think about killing myself. But only for a minute. Pills is the only way I'd even think of doing it, and, expecting a week in paradise, I'd neglected to pack for this contingency. The best I could have done would have been to open the door while the car was moving and get out. My luck, I'd survive. My ample booty would have bounced a couple of times and all that would have happened was I'd get some nasty cinders in my knee, ruin a cute outfit, and people back in Minneapolis would point at my ragged and bruised body and say things, such as, "There's that girl who tried to kill herself over a man." They would shake their heads and make clicking noises with their tongues. Personally, I hate a public spectacle. More importantly, and as we all know, nine times out of ten, that's what they want, these men. They want you to do something crazy so they can sit around the bar and tell their friends, "See, I told you the bitch was sick."

An update: We were still going seventy-one miles per hour down I-94 in Wisconsin. There were some more trees and some more cows.

I knew I was going to have to talk my way through this. I only needed to come up with the exact right words.

I could have been rational. I could have gotten myself very quiet inside and put on my nurturing voice, full of New Age tones, sweet, the one I use when I want Mr. Waltershied, Senior Partner of Waltershied, Williams and Caruthers, to calm down before we pitch an ad campaign to a new client. (Mr. Walter-shied has the inner peace of a hyperactive seven-year-old.) "Calvin," I could have said, "Baby, can we talk?" Or, "Sugar, I'm having just a bit of trouble understanding why you're saying such a thing on our vacation. Can you share your thoughts? Sweetie? Please?"

I spent a few minutes shopping around that store, but you know how it is. The merchandise was cheesy and picked over. Nothing in there I'd be caught dead saying.

And I knew what he was going to say. He'd say: "I'm sorry. It's just the way I feel," or "Can't we be friends now," or "You see, there's this woman who. . . ." And we all know that bitch: "This Woman Who." Why do we always have to find ourselves in the middle of this same damn conversation? You can't win. It's as if every one of these dogs out there has the same damn script. I bet that in sixth grade, while the hygiene teacher was showing us girls that simple-ass *Girl to Woman* movie, the gym teachers took their ornery butts down the hall and handed out condoms and wallet-sized cards with this crap already printed up on it.

I wasn't playing that scene again.

So I figured I'd just cuss his black ass out. Call him every kind of low-down, filth-sucking, son-of-a-tree-stump-motherfucker I could come up with. That sure would feel good.

But you know what? Men like it when you call them names. They do. Especially dirty names. It gets them all excited. Also, you have to be mad to do a good cuss out. Red hot mad, and when I thought about it, I wasn't that upset. I realized that even though I had agreed to go away with this man for a week, I couldn't say that I was particularly attached to him. I couldn't find any feelings for him at all, to tell the truth. In that sense, cussing him out seemed awfully pathetic. It would be almost like begging. I'm the sort of woman who would have slapped that Diana Ross—for a lot of reasons—but especially in all them movies when she was groveling around after old slick-headed Billy Dee Williams for some attention. Please. I thought to myself, pickins would have to get pretty slim before I'd beg this nigger for shit. I ought to have dumped his ass myself.

Which was my next plan: to say, oh yeah, well, I dump you first, or I dump you back. As if this were junior high school all over again. I have to tell you that it pissed me off worse than a sticky toilet seat that Calvin got to dump me before I dumped him. Wasn't that always the way? Hadn't it always been the way? Why was that always the way? Why?

I sat there in silence and I watched the trees roll by. I remember that I felt as if I had been encased in a padded cocoon, the same way I felt the time I had taken two antihistamine tablets by mistake, as if God had adjusted the eyepiece on the scope through which I had always viewed the world, as if everything were blurred ever so slightly, every sensation muffled, every feeling numbed.

I wasn't so much upset that it was this man, or that it was this man in this particularly bizarre set of circumstances. I was thirty-seven years old. I had had my first date when I was twelve. Rather than this specific bad day, I think it was my realization that I was at the back end of about a quarter of a century of Calvins.

I reviewed all my options and chose to do nothing. I decided that this was as good a time as any to begin my nervous breakdown.

I can't say that I can pinpoint exactly the moment when my breakdown began. It's not as if I was riding along I-94 and

I thought to myself: I will have a nervous breakdown. I do, however, think that *decide* is the correct word.

I remember sort of oozing back into the bucket seat and running my fingers around the soft gray upholstery. The cushion felt like my stuffed bunny, Crinkles, and I thought to myself, I'll dissolve into this seat and disappear. Dematerialize, like when they got beamed up on *Star Trek.* I had no thought of reassembling in another place, like on a tropical island or in the arms of another lover. I thought how nice it would be to have fragments of my essence wandering the world, silently but generously dispensing loving goodwill, like the maiden aunt on a soap opera. At the same time I was aware that outside my window there were more trees and more cows. And that I had still not responded to whatever it was that had been said to me a while back.

I believe that an hour or so went by. We had come through that part of Wisconsin where the landscape looks like breasts in cone-shaped bras. I imagine it must have been awkward for Calvin, sitting in a car with someone who had not responded to something as provocative as he had put forward. Please believe me when I tell you that at the time I was about as worried about how Calvin felt as I was about the price of eggs in Taiwan. His feelings just didn't happen to cross my mind. As to his tossed-off remark, the gauntlet he'd thrown, somewhere in the interim the words had lost all meaning and presently denoted nothing. As far as I was concerned he could have said, "See Spot run."

Aha! Denial, you pop psychology fans will say, and I have certainly watched enough episodes of *Oprah* to recognize the symptoms. In fact, somewhere out there in the haze of mush that had become my brain, I had a vision of myself standing in her audience. Draped across my back was Oprah's powerful arm—I could feel it, muscular and fleshy and warm, through several layers of thick luxurious silk—both Oprah's and mine—drawing me to her, hugging me to her. I could hear her say, "Girlfriend, you're gonna have to deal with this." Mushy and hazy because at the time I had an idea—a vague one—that my brain was busy filing away my troubles in a box. This is the actual image I had: a small wooden box, the size of a three-by-five card, decoupaged, the kind one picks up at the endless craft fair at the Har Mar Mall, and on the front of the box, instead of saying "Recipes," it said "Deneen's Troubles," and I saw those troubles—career troubles, man troubles, my so-called biological clock, this on-going and nagging inability I had to find an attractive non-maternity jumper—organizing themselves on index cards and drifting into place in the box.

So it would make perfect sense, wouldn't it, that the next thing out of either of our mouths would come from me, and it would be me saying, "Shall we stop for a snack?"

Calvin took the exit at Tomah and we went into McDonald's.

When you have *your* nervous breakdown, let me know if the following happens to you. It seems that while my mind was busy packing for a long stay at the Happy Valley Convalescence Center, the rest of me—like my appetite and my taste buds—got the message that they now had free run of the joint. It's like they were the teenagers and mom and dad were out for the weekend, and they were ready to *par teee*. I kid you not: this was the best damn Big Mac I ever ate in my life. Honey, it was almost as if Jesus had discovered the recipe for secret sauce that they use up in heaven and had stirred up a big batch with His own blessed hands—can I get a witness? I was greasing on that Mac. Went up and got me another. Got me some more fries, too. Mmm, mmm, mmmp: I was making the same noise that those big gals in my mama's club used to make whenever she fed them.

Calvin picked at his food. He was never a big eater—which is why he weighed all of 150 pounds, if that. That was another reason we were doomed. How was a woman like me, who loved nothing more than a sumptuous and rich gourmet meal of many courses, supposed to make a life with a man who was perfectly satisfied heating up a can of tomato soup for supper?

"These fries are kind of greasy," he said. First thing he'd said to me. Since that other thing.

"Pass em over here. I'll eat em."

He did and I did.

Then we got back in the car and continued on our way, east, toward our dream vacation in Door County. You're probably thinking to yourself: Now wait just a damn minute. You mean to tell me you went through with this vacation? You didn't tell the nigger to turn the car around and take you home?

Well, back in the haze (remember the mushy haze, my brain?) there were a couple of different voices I heard. One was asking me what in the hell did I think I was doing. And another one was telling me to just play along with it, see how weird this shit was gonna get. But I really want you to understand that by this point I had embraced Mother Madness with both arms. She was a strong, big-hearted black sister, and she made me feel as if I didn't have a care in the world. All I had on my mind was trying to remember how Katrina said you got to that fudge shop in Wisconsin Dells. I couldn't remember whether she said to get off by the Yogi Bear Campground or to get off by the dog track. Not that it made any difference.

They have fudge shops in Wisconsin Dells the way they have pawnbrokers in Las Vegas. I bought me a pound of maple and a pound of rocky road and ate most of both boxes before we got to the inn.

We checked ourselves into a beautiful old house in Ellison Bay, or rather Calvin checked us in—I was busy feeling up the furniture and the draperies, all of which were elegant and decadent. I don't know what name he used or how he identified us. Perhaps I had just become Mrs. Calvin Colechester. We took a room overlooking the lake, and out the window through lace as delicate as moths' wings I saw shimmering water the deep blue color of a car my daddy had while I was growing up.

Enough, you say, you talk about this the same way a naive bride talks about her honeymoon. It was nothing like that. I remember thinking, this is what it's like when they hook up couples on those TV dating shows. You get sent off with a guy you hardly know to a beautiful place, and maybe it works out and maybe it doesn't. I remember looking over at Calvin every now and then and thinking, who the hell is he? Which is to say, his card had already been filed away, honey, and deep.

He, by the way, hadn't said a word since we left McDonald's.

So, there we were, and this is how we spent a week: wandering the shore, skipping stones, going from antique shop to craft boutique. I searched through the pottery in one gallery for an hour and a half, fingering a white porcelain pitcher, drooling over a rough and exquisite rakú vase. I chose a green, hand-built platter, pieced together from jagged triangles of clay. You could see the fingerprints in the work, and there was something about that that caused my American Express card to leap into the salesman's hands.

Up and down the highways there were signs announcing "Fish Boils." Calvin stopped at one our first night, but I had been unable to leave the car, unable to clear my mind of the image of Charlie the Tuna covered with infected white pimples. After that we stopped only at the finest inns. And eat we did. We ate walleye cheeks in aioli butter, roast duck sauced with fresh raspberries. Trout wrapped in pastry, coq au vin, and prime rib. And the desserts. Oh, God!

And, I know you are wondering, so, no I did not sleep with him. We slept side by side, as chastely as brother and sister. I have to confess, however trashy this sounds, that I wanted to. I really did. I thought to myself: Here I am in a lovely room, and I could hear outside the window the sounds of the lake against the rocks. Crisp linen sheets blanketed us in a bed that seemed to be made for sex. Here was a man who was not at all bad looking and had the right equipment, which I knew for a fact was in full working order. It seemed like such a waste. To be quite honest with you I fully expected to be fighting him off, or putting up a good fight and then giving in. Or something like that. I mean, you just don't think about a man not being doggish enough to take advantage of a situation like this. I've always understood, ever since sixth grade when Steven Barr had me backed up against a bookcase at his mother's house in Richmond Heights and his ding-a-ling popped right out the opening of his shorts, that basically those things have minds of their own, that there's some sort of little brain in the tip of it, and, despite what men would have you believe, that brain isn't connected to the other brain in any way, and given a circumstance such as this—a healthy young man in a romantic country inn with a lovely, Rubenesque young woman—he would have no choice but to . . . follow his instincts. (That's what they call that other little brain: their instincts.) But, we just lay there. Night after night, for a week. Somehow, within the logic of this trip, it made sense. It was as if we were two people transported to another planet where the gravity was different and you breathed something other than air: it took a few days but eventually you got used to it. I lay there some nights, and in the moon-light I could see the sharp bones of his narrow back as they moved with his breathing and the golden tones of his skin in the dark, and I would restrain myself from touching him, from running the tips of my fingers across his skin.

Yes, there was even moonlight.

Instead, I touched myself. What I began that one night there on the Door Peninsula of Wisconsin would carry me through my summer of madness the same way an eyeless stuffed toy carries a child through the terrible twos. I touched myself. I masturbated. It's too bad we women don't have a better word for this. Something with all the violent charm of jack off. A word that captures the transcendence, the spiritu-ality of it, the fact that it is a kind of worship. I'll say that, then. I worshipped.

It's not my intention for this to sound as if it were an unusual act, because, as a matter of fact, the history and fre-quency of my worshipping are entirely beside the point. The point is that inside my newly disordered head, the act had taken on a fresh and exotic quality. Whereas before my wor-ship had served as a mild tension reliever between the oppor-tunities for real sex, I now felt the same rush and shock as the very first time I stumbled into self-stimulation. Into the void left by the absence of reason flowed this previously unknown pleasure, multiplying and expanding. Each night, as I lay there, boldly, in the wake of the heat of a man for whom I felt almost nothing, alongside the joy, I also discovered a sorrow—

a cold blue sadness at the cheat, the loss of all the years of self-knowledge. Where had pleasure been? Why had I been denied? Why had I denied myself? I bit my lips and tore with my teeth at the corner of a pillow to keep myself quiet. Later in the week, remembering from somewhere in my previous life that Calvin slept as if he were drugged, I let it all out, moaning and writhing and sweating as the spasms quaked through my body.

In the morning we would greet each other cordially, Calvin and I, he in the slow morning stupor of heavy sleepers, and myself as bright and chipper as a squirrel in spring. Off we'd toddle to another day of chilled civil fun.

I don't recall a single conversation. I don't believe we talked at all. It was as if we had been sitting across the breakfast table for years and had run out of things to say to each other. Without knowing it, we had reached the hard-earned compromise of a long-married couple, worn down by decades of bickering and losses that seemed greater, really, than the matter at hand. We rarely disagreed, always accommodated, politely took turns. My "Shall we stop at the state park?" seamlessly alternating with his "Let's eat here."

On Sunday morning we got into the Camry and reversed our way through the trees and the cows. I entertained myself by inventing a game that required one player to close her eyes and count to a thousand and then open them and imagine what might have been missed in the darkness. I played the game with myself, thinking it would be better someplace more interesting, like in the city, or through the mountains. In hindsight it sounds silly, but at that point it was quite as stimulating as chess.

We stopped at the same McDonald's. I didn't ask, but, as we approached Tomah, I was thinking about how good those

Macs had been, and how I would sure like to have me another. Calvin took the exit and pulled in.

Just before dark we crested the hill coming up from the St. Croix valley, passing the Minnesota Welcome Center on the right. And Calvin said,

"The thing is, I think I'm attracted to men."

"Oh, I see," I said. My brain, which by this point I imagined resembling an abandoned shopping mall—trompe l'oeil storefronts with locked and vacant interiors—didn't even bother searching for a response. I do remember thinking, "Well, that's sort of a down note on which to end a vacation." Just then, for some reason I don't quite understand to this day, I thought of my mother. I thought of my mother's house. I wanted to be in my mother's house.

"Do you think you could drop me off at the airport?" I asked. He sighed, but it sounded like a large deflating balloon. Not long after that he pulled up in front of the Northwest Airlines entrance. Inside I would buy a ticket to St. Louis.

As I fished my bags from the trunk and handed them to a skycap, I wasted the last flash of sanity that would light my world for many a day on the following thought: Maybe this is what Katrina meant about Calvin being a chump.

# Two

"Can I get you anything?" Megan (or was it Susie) asked me, but before I could answer she was looking over at the man next to me.

The flight attendants in my section of the plane—Megan and Susie—were barely civil to the women and ever so deferential to the men. They were white girls of the kind that seem to grow on trees up here in Minnesota—blue-eyed blondes with the sort of hair you always imagined the Breck girl had, impermeable to the elements, soft-looking, but to the touch would feel like the head of one of those dolls with painted-on hair.

I told her I'd like a sparkling water with no ice, and could I please have the whole can. I was thirsty from the car trip and from the huge serving of peanuts the other Megan or Susie had passed out twenty minutes earlier. Megan or Susie poured the guy a coke and asked, "What did you want again, ma'am?" I thought of saying, "Bitch, look at me when I'm speaking to you." I didn't. I asked again for my sparkling water. She was so busy making party eyes at my seatmate that she allowed the fizz to spill over the top onto her hands. In my condition I saw this as a highly charged erotic symbol. I turned and looked at my neighbor. He was clean and scrubbed in that sales-executive sort of way, with sandy hair and tortoiseshell glasses. He was looking through those glasses at Megan or

Susie with the kind of discount lust men of his station reserve for such moments. I suddenly found him breathtakingly appealing. I wondered if that same sandy hair covered his chest. I wondered if, like the other white men I had known, his penis was red all the time, as if it were embarrassed. I even looked at his crotch, but he didn't notice. He was locked on Megan or Susie, and I thought about the fact that he hadn't noticed me at all. Was it because I was a little older, or because I was black? Was it because a man like him could not appreciate a woman who was padded for extra comfort? To hell with him. Let him satisfy himself with one of these scrawny pink peanut servers. Megan or Susie herself was still making a big production out of pouring a few ounces of pop over some ice. I reached up and took the cup from her. Wouldn't you know it: Pepsi. I sipped my drink and tried to figure out how I was going to explain this impulsive visit to my mother.

The thing is, I never went home. Since I graduated from college at the end of the seventies, I had spent maybe a total of a dozen days in St. Louis.

When I was a high school senior at Villa Duschene, I sat around with my friends, weighing this college against that one, talking with the guidance counselor to come up with our criteria for choosing: the number of students, religious affiliation, departmental strengths, cost. My main criteria: the school had to be at least a full day's drive from my mother.

I loved my mother back then, as much as any seventeen-year-old girl could say she loves her mother, but at the time she was in a serious, serious *bourgeois* phase—black bourgeois, and if you don't know what that's about, try to get a picture in your mind of a cross between Louise Jefferson, Joan Collins, and drag artist RuPaul. Imagine that the main things in your life were shopping, keeping up with the (other) Joneses, and running your daughter's life.

Reina Wilkerson Jones, those are my mother's names. Reina. Means queen, and my mother was the queen of a whole crew of women just like her; school principals, which she is, or teachers or social workers or bureaucrats. They had a club. Sometimes they'd be over at my mother's house, and when I came downstairs, they would be all over me, these enormous, overly made-up, overly dressed, loud, loud women, hugging and kissing on me, fussing with my hair and just generally getting in my face.

Which might have been okay, had it not been for the fact that at the time I was well into what you might call an anachronistic hippie phase, anachronistic because it was 1975, well past the hippie heyday, and also because, as far as I could discover, there hadn't ever been any hippies in St. Louis anyway. I would come home from school and shed my uniform and put on my scoop-neck knit blouse or my tie-dyed T-shirt, my bell-bottoms, my headband, and then lie on my bed and listen to Jimi Hendrix. (Jimi. Part of the problem in my life is that I have searched high and low and cannot discover for the life of me where it is they are keeping the brothers like Jimi— mysterious, soulful, guitar-playing brothers, with big Afros and groovy clothes.) Occasionally, me and a few of the other self-styled hippie girls I knew would go down to the Delmar Loop and hang out at the Tivoli Theater or at the record store or the head shop. Once in a while we would meet some heavy dudes from Wash U and go over to their pad and smoke a joint or whatever. This is, of course, how we talked back then, us pseudo hippie chicks. Reina, as you might imagine, threw fits.

"Mother," I'd say. "Why do we always have to have such a heavy scene? Could you just mellow out, for once."

When I chose the perfect little liberal arts college in Minnesota, I believe that deep down inside my mother was as relieved to be rid of me as I was to be going. I knew what she thought of me. I'd heard her and the women discussing the daughters of other women they knew. Chippies. Tramps. Trash. These were the sorts of names that they used, but it wasn't quite that simple. Their condemnation of these girls wasn't about chastity at all. There wasn't a one of these women who had lived a blameless life, and they didn't care who knew about it, either. They wore their old marriages like merit badges, hinted at all kinds of affairs with one another's husbands and any number of other men as well. The mistake these girls had made—these tramps and strumpets—was being "womanish." "Womanish" meant not only that you knew too much, but also that you flaunted it. That you had the nerve to parade your worldliness up and down the street like it was something to be proud of. A woman earned this kind of pride with age, and "chippies" and other such wanton wayward upstarts had a long way to go. For my mother, then, it wasn't so much the thought that her baby was out participating in a brand of wild living that she condemned. (Even if she had condemned the way I lived, she would have never let on.) For her it was the highly unlikely happenstance that one of her friends might see me living this way, the possibility that somewhere in the St. Louis area in another room full of women just like her so-called friends, my name might come up with the appropriate disparaging moniker attached. Macalester College had a good enough reputation to facilitate her name-dropping, and for me, there were enough burned-out old hippies around to make me feel right at home. Getting me out of town was as much a blessing to her as my leaving was for me.

As luck would have it, I fell in with the wrong crowd. Well, that's how my old hippie friends would have described them. Here I was, suddenly, with these relatively clean-cut, prodigiously hardworking, intelligent young people, and I turned into a model student. My grades soared, my complexion cleared up, and my wardrobe improved, if only marginally.

I would fly home at Christmas in a sharp sweater and a reasonably clean pair of jeans. I had changed (or changed back) into the ideal child I had been in grade school, and my mother began treating me as if I were some fragile porcelain doll, as if I were something precious to be kept in her curio cabinet for display. While she would parade me out for her bourgie friends and brag about me until I could feel my ears burning, at the same time, when we were alone in the house, when it was just her and my stepfather and me, she would handle me with kid gloves. I had no curfews, there were no lectures, I could do whatever I wanted. I stayed overnight one time, at the home of a girl who lived in my dorm. When I came in the next morning she asked me, "Have a good time?" As bright and as cheerful as if I'd just gotten off the roller coaster at Six Flags. I hadn't even told her where I was going the night before. Around then I recognized that, as far as she was concerned, her job had been completed. I think she was afraid that if she said anything to me or did anything at all, that that other girl—the one with the incense and the black rings drawn around her eyes—would come back. Whatever I was up to at the moment must have felt like a better risk.

It's odd: I think we have this picture of mothers steadfastly and lovingly guiding their daughters to womanhood. Or maybe I've watched too many douche spray commercials where the mama and her grown baby girl are out walking in a field. The mother ever so casually asks the daughter has she ever had that . . . you know, less than fresh feeling. Reina and I seemed to have missed the "less than fresh" phase in our relationship. I think back and try to remember a time when she and I had one of those cozy mother and daughter chats— about anything. They never happened. Maybe those scenes are totally the creation of the ad mongers, of folks like me— hey, maybe I'd swallowed my own bait.

My father was—is?—something of a dog. (Hard to get the tense correct: haven't seen him in twenty years, and it's hard to verify.) He walked out on us when I was twelve, but he had been walking for years before that. The five years before he left, mother spent trying to hold on; the five years after, casting about for his replacement. I remember a rough period in there when the mention of any man would make her rattle like a lidded pot on the boil. This during the time I was just getting ready to figure out the boy thing for myself.

I remember once she was dropping me off at a friend's place in North St. Louis. I was in this phase where I was testing the waters, making a lot of obnoxious statements to a lot of different folks. (I had recently announced to one of the nuns at Villa that I was considering joining a free-love commune. Not that I had any idea what such things were. But I had seen the movie *Woodstock*. Three times! The nun had cast her eyes to the ceiling, not in supplication, but more as if to say, "Yeah, right, Deneen. You in a commune. We'd all like to see that.")

In the car on the way to the city I had turned to my

mother and speculated how I might like to get married right out of high school.

Mother had snickered and then mumbled, almost under her breath, "Better just get yourself a nice hot water bottle."

"What?" I'd prodded, but she didn't reply.

So, I knew she was a little bitter. But, at the same time I also knew that she hadn't quite given up on the world of romance. I knew that her eyes had been open, that her circle of women were looking for a man for her, too. For women like these, it just didn't do to be alone too long.

Mother reeled in a keeper just about the time I was on the way out the door, headed to Minnesota for my freshman year in college. My stepfather, I guess he was. He was an alright kind of guy. At least for all I know he was. A bland sort of a man, I recall Mr. Jones was. He seemed to worship her, and she never said anything bad about him. I think they were happy enough. In many ways they had the blandest and most ordinary of marriages. It's a shame he died, if you want to know the truth.

Still, I think about this and I just get sad. All of that man-work took a lot of energy, I know. I mean, I know it now, at this point in my life. And, having a man meant a lot more to her than it has ever meant to me. As for me on that plane trip, I did not want to be thinking about the time I had wasted chasing one man or another. Or the time I'd spent on any of the other dead ends in my life, for that matter. Bad jobs. Faithless friends. Get-rich-quick schemes. I did not want to think about anything at all.

After college I stayed in Minnesota and began my career as an advertising maven. Which is how I am referred to by Mr. Waltershied. I would visit St. Louis for a day or two now and then and join the new family my mother had created. As the eighties began, she entered a new phase: from queen of the class wars to queen of the homemakers, from Alexis Carrington to Harriet Nelson.

I would arrive at her house—her new husband had moved her from Spanish Lake to Kirkwood (too much riffraff in North County)—and I would think I had walked into the Christmas display at Famous Barr. Every surface was wrapped or tinseled or garlanded or crèched. She kept pots of cinnamon and vanilla bean simmering on the stove in the kitchen, cedar logs burning in the fireplace. How cozy, you might think, and the whole display was certainly eye-catching and inviting. Still, her adornments left me after a while cold and rather bored. The treatment was the same as what you could see on a soap opera or in the aforementioned department store window—magnificent, but what did it have to do with our lives? There wasn't a single thing in the house with any sense of history, not one bauble that meant a thing to me.

One year—I think it was '83—I came in, and she chirped, "Look, we're having an old-fashioned Christmas this year, just like in the old days." Her theme that year was drummer boys and nutcrackers, and I thought, old days? I don't remember any such old days. I remember that my daddy would show up sometimes when I was little, and he and mama would make a pretense of opening gifts. I remember that we went to Jamaica for the holidays a few times when I was in high school. That was about it. Mama's old days must have been in some life other than the one I had lived.

About twelve years ago I stopped going home for good.

Home. I don't even call it that anymore. I had no friends back there. My girls from high school—hippie and otherwise— had moved on after college, just as I had. I'd hear from them,

26

on the East Coast or out in California. I got tired of spending my money to fly down to St. Louis and sit on my mother's sofas.

So, I called, once a month or so. I talked to my mother and my baby sister.

Baby sister. That was another thing I couldn't get past. Forty-seven years old, with a grown daughter—me—and the woman goes and has another baby. That was the other reason I stopped visiting her.

I begged her not to have that child. I said every hateful thing I could think of. I told her she would die in childbirth, or that the baby would be a mongoloid retard. I told her she had better arrange to have the child put in a home right away, cause I wasn't raising it. Mother hung up on me. Over and over again.

She had the baby. Ciara. (Chee-AH-rah.) They were both fine. I really didn't know the child, but she had always sounded like a sweet thing on the phone.

My stepfather died five years ago. So now it is mama and Ciara, and I could never imagine what it was they did with themselves down there, this slightly past-middle-age woman and her child, their dream house in the suburbs. I received snapshots in the mail of Ciara posed in front of a well-known monument, and of mother and Ciara posed together in front of another one. They looked rather innocent and mannered.

Let me tell you: I had no idea. None.

I get dumped on a trip to Door County. At the *beginning* of the trip. (That's my favorite detail.) I have my boyfriend, Calvin, the chump, drop me off at the airport and I get on a plane to St. Louis to visit a family I have avoided for years. I would trace the logic of that, but, as I am trying to explain, I was in a happy land beyond reason.

Yet, there I was, flying back toward my so-called roots. I guess it was sort of a cyclical thing: You drive east on a dream vacation to Door County. You spend a week. You turn around, you come home. Or:

You go away to college.

You make a life for yourself.

Twenty years later you fall apart.

You come home.

I was acting—insofar as I was doing anything conscious at all—in a script that seemed already to have been written. And as I casually drank my Pepsi and munched on yet another linebacker-sized serving of peanuts I had filched from Megan and Susie's trays while they struggled past me with the drink cart, I felt no anxiety at all. The most rational awareness I had was knowing I was going to have to come up with a plausible excuse as to why I, who hadn't set foot in St. Louis since disco was king, would be making an unannounced visit to my mother's house.

I considered the alternatives.

*1.* I would claim that it was my mother who had invited me in the first place, that she had insisted I come. I would remind her of a nonexistent telephone conversation we had had in which she made the invitation and I accepted. I would offer other examples of her senility that might explain how she could have forgotten such a call.

*2a.* I would tell her that I had ratted on my boyfriend, Vinnie, and his mob brothers. I needed a place to hide out until I was placed in the Federal Witness Protection Program.

*2b.* Or that I was the one on the lam, that Vinnie and I

had pulled off a heist at the Commercial State Bank, and that I was lying low until the heat was off.

3. I was job hunting. Things at Waltershied, Williams and Caruthers had gotten ugly. I was checking out the game in St. Louis.

4. I would just show up, as if it were nothing out of the ordinary. No explanations, no story, no nothing.

Can you guess which I chose? Have you picked up the pattern yet? Good for you. Yes, it is door number 4.

At the airport, I chose a taxi and gave him my mother's address. Thirty minutes later he pulled up in front of her house in Kirkwood and set my bags on the porch. I rang the bell.

Ciara answered the door. "Who are you?"

"I'm your sister. Deneen."

"Mother!" she called out.

I heard familiar footsteps coming from back where her kitchen was.

"Mother! This . . . person says . . ."

"Oh, hi, Deneen." My mother waved at me cheerily, pointed to the portable phone in her hand, and went back to the sentence she had been in the middle of.

Ciara stood in my way giving me the kind of look that makes your teeth itch.

# Three

What is your picture of depression? Is it a color? Is
it a place? This is a personal as well as a professional
question. One of our largest accounts at Waltershied, Williams
and Caruthers is pharmaceutical company that produces anti-
depressant medications. That's what I do, you see. Sell folks
pills and hair spray, promises of beauty, freedom from despair,
a hope for a better tomorrow. That sort of cliché crap. The
classic pill spread crosses the centerfold of the magazine and
features on the left, depression, and on the right—health, I
guess you would call it. The bridge across the chasm between
them is emblazoned with the name of our client's product.
"Health" looks like an illustration from a Disney cartoon.
"Depression" is charcoaled, tornadic. I met the artist who
drew that picture. He thought the campaign was a piece of
shit. Before he began working on it, the manufacturer had
sent him to talk to psychiatrists, who then referred him to
their patients. He said that each one had different ideas about
how to picture depression, but that what struck him most was
their eyes. He described what he saw there as a black hollow-
ness. He knew that if he could see what those eyes were seeing, he could draw the picture. He chickened out. He had
been afraid to look, said he knew that the hollow horror
would freeze in his own eyes as well, and went with the
schlock instead. And sold a whole bunch of pills to boot.

I bring this up because after I described to a therapist that I see from time to time how I spent the first week or so at my mother's, she told me that I had been deeply depressed, a classic case. But I have to tell you, what I felt was nothing like those pictures, no windblown black clouds, no oppressive low sky, no mazes or tunnels. And my eyes, at least from my perspective, were quite pleasant, vivid even, in a deer-caught-in-the-headlights sort of way. Considering the circumstances, I thought I was doing quite well.

After we stood there in the door for what seemed like an hour and a half, my mother ordered Ciara to show me to "my room" in the basement. She led me to a dark-paneled enclosure off what my mother referred to as a "rumpus" room. There was one small rectangle of a window, high up a dark-paneled wall. During the day the light was strangled and blocked by tall grasses and the guttering mother had had built around a catch basin.

My room. I'd never in my life been in the basement of this house. I guess it was "my room," though, because the few things that decorated it were mine from when I was a child— some high school pennants, a poster of Jimi, a jewelry tree painted in psychedelic patterns, things that had been mine long before my mother bought this house—and they had been arranged in a haphazard, if marginally tasteful, fashion, the way a farmer might display the last few choice tomatoes at the end of a good day at the market. My mother had had these things enshrined in a room on the second floor of this house, but I figured that that room must belong to Ciara now. My life had been consigned to the basement. I could imagine my mother boxing the trinkets and whatnots carefully and carrying them down and organizing them. I was aware at some level that a few things were missing, and that bothered me slightly. I had the same kind of feeling as when the low-budget touring company of a Broadway show hit town: the feeling that they couldn't fit everything in the truck, but they'd brought just enough to give you an idea of how it looked in New York. I bet myself that Ciara had been down here, helping herself to whatever might be useful to her little life: some jewelry that had cycled back into style, an old record . . . no, they didn't play records anymore. If I cared, I didn't care much. I'd removed whatever I wanted while it was still at the other house. How touching that my mother kept a room for me, even if it was a dark cell in the corner of the basement. Even so, I arrived at what could have been a room at the local Holiday Inn. The posters and doodads were just quirky coincidentals left by someone with the same unfortunate taste. Mine.

I balled myself up on the bed that first night, and I went to sleep.

The next morning—it was a Monday morning—I had the presence of mind to call in sick to work in Minneapolis.

"Waltershied, Williams and Caruthers," said Katrina, who answers the phone and opens the mail and makes coffee, and fixes her so-called friends up with chumps like Calvin.

"It's me," I said.

"Hey, girlfriend. How was that trip?"

"Different."

"Started to call you last night, then I said, naw, the sister's gonna need her sleep after all that good loving."

I needed sleep all right. "Listen, I need a favor. I'm sick."

"You catch a bug up there?"

"Yeah, that's it. Tell everybody I caught a bug up there. Tell them I'll be out for a while."

"How long's a while?"

"I don't know? How long is a while?"

"Deneen? Are you . . . you know."

"Am I what?"

"P. R. E. G.—"

"Hell, no. I'm in St. Louis."

"Oh. Well. So."

"I can't stay on this phone. Look, if Mr. Waltershied is looking for me, you call me at this number. But don't give the number to him. Okay?"

"Got it. Are you sure you're—"

"I got to go." I hung up on her.

Those few minutes on the phone wore me out. I got the blanket off the bed, picked up the remote control, and made myself a nest in front of the TV on the couch in the "rumpus" room. I napped and I channel cruised, and napped and cruised some more.

Upstairs I found a box of cereal. Something with raisins in it. I brought it back to my nest and fed it into my mouth by the handful. There were crinkly crisp flakes of some kind, and soon I had so much of it in my mouth that I had to stop and chew for a while. I looked at the flakes. Each one was fairly uniform, amazingly so, as if they had been stamped out of a mold or something. I examined piece after piece, and I wondered if at the crinkly crisp factory someone had the job of standing over the assembly line and rejecting the flakes that were malformed or damaged. And then I got horribly sad. I thought about those poor rejected crinkles, plucked from the line by some callous Inspector 12. I wondered what happened to the flakes on that floor. Did they wash them down the drain? Did they feed them to pigs? And, yes, I know, there is something really trashy about anthropomorphism. I, for one, have always been deeply offended by raisins that sing and

talking gorillas, have inveighed strongly against them at my
own place of employment for years. My mind, it seems, had
turned a corner and entered a different place. I was comfortable here, but the atmosphere was a little on the dull side.
Like reading a scientific abstract or listening to a slow-witted
politician, stimulating things may have been happening somewhere, but they weren't happening here. Every now and then,
something like a piece of cereal, for instance, would wander
through, and suddenly cereal was the most remarkable thing
on the earth.

I became aware that another of those mind doors was
cracked open a tad, and a sparkle from the room beyond that
door caught my eye. The door was marked "work," and
I would peek in there now and then and experience a thrill
of hope.

I liked my work. I was good at my job. Waltershied,
Williams and Caruthers is a good shop in what can be a nasty
business. I remembered the top file on my desk. Before my
ill-fated vacation, Mr. Waltershied and I had bid our way into
an account with a maker of feminine hygiene products. They
wanted us to do some "American-looking" ads for use in the
emerging economies of the East. Mr. Waltershied saw mini-
skirts and diners and hot dogs with lurid yellow snakes of
mustard and a large revolving donut. Rhythm and blues playing on the jukebox. I saw something else entirely, even if
I didn't know what it was yet. Whatever. We would slam
dunk this account, win awards, make big money. Thinking
about the account was a lot like being a little girl imagining
her wedding. I could have been inventing the future out of
what I'd seen on TV. Still, I knew the campaign would be a
success. I knew at least that this one thing in my life would
be okay.

I knew that that very door would in some way be my entry back to the world. I stuck a mental Post-it note in the center of that door for future reference.

Of course, as most of us know, there are no shortcuts to sanity. There *were* bran flakes and rococo patterns on an embroidered afghan. And there was TV, and on TV there was nothing but sex. Perhaps it was my delicate emotional condition, but as I cruised through my mornings and afternoons I could find nothing on television but sex. Talk shows about sex. Soap operas about sex. News reports about sex. I cruised, five seconds max per channel, and I would catch words and phrases: *clitoris, implant, nipple, ejaculating, penetration, dysfunction,* and then I would catch a scene on a soap opera which seemed to be illustrating what had just been named. And then I would catch someone on the news talking about what had just been talked about, showing scenes of them talking about it. And then there would be a feminine hygiene commercial. Next came a show about why all these programs spent so much time talking about sex. Plip! Plip! Plip!

Everyone considers channel cruising a male thing. I myself had always thought so. I didn't know any women who cruised: We enjoyed watching the shows from start to finish, didn't we? But there I was: Plip! Plip! Plip! In my condition it was the perfect activity. You may draw your own conclusions.

In my previous life I had always thought a person would get bored watching TV after a while. No way. I found it exhilarating. The raw power! I was Spike Lee and the Hudlin Brothers and Mario Van Peebles rolled into one. Plip! Plip! Plip! Who says we don't have interactive TV? I was creating the world's finest home video, and best of all, one that never ended.

Eventually, over the course of that week, I began to realize that as a person who was truly open and available to the media (i.e., crazy) I was privileged to insights about the programming I viewed that others were not receiving. I realized, for example, that the shows had disingenuous names, meant only to disguise their real purposes and content. As a truly savvy and informed viewer I felt cheated and condescended to. I felt it would have made my viewing experience much more honest had they chosen to give the shows names such as *Talking about Sex with Jerry*, or *Talking about Sex with Ricki*, or *Sex News*, or *The Sex of Our Lives*. I also became expert in picking out which members of the studio audience the talk show hosts would have delivered to their dressing rooms to have sex with. I often disagreed with their choices. We'll come back to this subject.

Where were my mother and sister while I was getting my advanced degree in teleliteracy and sleeping? I know it seems odd and unbelievable, but I can't say that I saw or heard from them much that first week. The fact that I could be in a house with two women for five days and not interact with them in any way seemed, frankly, almost normal after being dumped an hour into a one-week vacation.

Every now and then my mother would come to the top of the stairs and yell something, such as, "Deneen! We're going to the mall," or "Deneen! I'm taking your sister to practice," or "Deneen! Turn it down, please."

I would go up to the pantry every so often to get a box of food to eat. I ate boxes of food that week, not meaning box loads, but meaning that I ate only foods that came in boxes and only one box at a time. A box of crackers. A box of dried fruit. A box of candy. Putting together a meal that consisted of a variety of items from different food groups was an impossible chore—I couldn't imagine how people did such things.

Besides, preparing food would cut into my precious viewing time. I also loved the fact that, for the most part, in a box of food there were no surprises: you could be pretty sure that the last Ritz cracker would taste the same as the others before it. I craved comfort of just this kind.

I would go upstairs to see what other boxed items we had, and my mother would smile at me, and I would wave and smile back. There wasn't much discourse to speak of, and I don't have much awareness of either of them being there. For her part, I remember that mother made me dizzy those first few days. She was running a summer school up in U City and always rushing from one activity to the next. While I was in the rumpus room watching TV, from above me would come this hustle and bustle, sometimes rhythmic, but often just chaotic and incessant. As to Ciara, I couldn't get a fix at first on what she was up to, but I had a sensation sometimes that someone was looking at me. I would turn around, and usually no one was there, but once or twice I caught her, perched on the stairs, checking me out. I would smile at her shyly, signal her to come and sit with me, but she would rise and disappear, like a piece of bait on a hook, dangling, just out of my reach. Once, during a particularly steamy scene on *General Hospital*, I found myself reaching into my panties to begin a session of worship. I stopped because I heard a noise, but by the time I wheeled myself around to see, she was gone. If she had been there at all.

Mostly I stayed in my nest. The patterns of the house were such that there was no reason for me ever to be disturbed. The washers were upstairs, as well as several other TVs, and lush exquisite bathrooms. No one came into that basement for anything.

When I think about it now, my isolation makes me sad, but it didn't then. Isolation was what I wanted. I'd like to think that they knew what I needed, but I'm not sure. Perhaps they were just a woman and a little girl who didn't know what to make of an adult person who showed up on their doorstep unannounced and with no explanations. I probably could have sat there forever. I could still be there now.

Which brings us back to sex. You may have identified sex as one of our themes.

Into the empty space where once there had been friends, colleagues, self-esteem, and often at least somewhat intelligent activities, I invited a whole bunch of new folks: bigamists; lesbian strippers; women who sell erotic products in their home; Brooke, who is having an affair with her brother-in-law, Kane; Dr. Ruth; Montel Williams; various studs and blind dates. Do you see the general direction I had headed? Let's just say that while once our heroine's sense of the world had been informed by a liberally educated and eclectic core of well-reasoned and sophisticated ideas, suddenly she was operating from a critical mass of funky and overripe sleaze. I'm not talking about getting turned on, though I did, particularly during Montel sometimes, and I would "worship" discreetly, taking extra precautions in case my sister happened to be lurking about. What I'm talking about here is . . . convergence. I'm talking about how a quorum of interrelated ideas can come together and sometimes even help a girl to make sense of her world.

After days and days with Sally and Jerry and Jenny and the rest of them, it occurred to me that at the heart of almost every problem in life there was sex. The fact was as clear to me as the industrially woven pattern on each cracker in a box of Wheat Thins I'd scarfed, and I felt a deep indebtedness to my TV mentors, though I knew, as they themselves often said, that for them, assisting the feeble and dysfunctional was all in a day's work. Just the same, friends, for me a dim lamp had begun to burn in the darkness, and in that little bit of light I recognized that perhaps I myself was in trouble as well—just like the woman who liked fat men only, and the midget who married an exotic dancer—and that maybe, just maybe, if I could get to the bottom of this sex thing, I would be okay.

Which is why I started my sex book. A journal would be a better name for it. I found an old notebook in my bedroom, and I thought the first thing I should do was to give the book a name. I called it Deneen Wilkerson's Handbook of Men Who Have Literally Fucked Her Up. Lurid, I know, but remember at the time I had had a fairly heavy dose of sensationalism. I was used to seeing people on the television with captions under their faces that said things such as "Hates her husband's penis."

In deciding what to include, I thought it would be useful to have on file sex resumes of the various men I had known. All of it. The good, the bad and the ugly, as they say. If my story was to change lives—as had the stories of countless others who had drifted through my day, courtesy of Ricki/ Rolonda/Montel—then it must more than anything be instructive to those considering a similar path. Resumes would give my readers a pretty good idea of what they were getting into.

I started at the beginning, which—in the words of one of them singing or flying nun gals—is a pretty good place to start.

|                  |                                                                 |
|-----------------:|-----------------------------------------------------------------|
|        *Name:*   | Kelvin "Kelvy" McIntyre                                         |
| *Date of birth:* | One or two years either side of mine. (I was 15)               |
|      *Height:*   | At the time, about an inch shorter than me, about 5'           |
|      *Weight:*   | All in his feet                                                 |
|  *Occupation:*   | Teenager                                                        |
|     *Cologne:*   | Aramis                                                          |
|       *Organ:*   | Still growing, I hope                                           |
| *Performance:*   | He was happy                                                    |
|    *Comments:*   |                                                                 |

Well, what is there to be said about being felt up in the back of a car in Creve Coeur park with the son of one of your mother's club members. Kelvin was a sticks-and-bones lanky old thing, with glasses and, at the time, a mustache that didn't quite know if it wanted to be there—you know, a vague shadow on his upper lip, like a chocolate milk stain, only blacker. Mother thought that Kelvy—with his nerdy good looks and cheese breath from those casseroles his mama was forever making—was just the kind of upright young man that a wild hippie girl like me needed to bring her back to the safe world of the middle class, so she fixed us up and arranged to have him come take me someplace once a month or so. Little did she know that the only thing usually upright on that Negro was his wee-wee, and from somewhere he had gotten the notion that girls liked to spend a lot of the evening being encouraged to touch the damn thing. Touch it, I wanted to say, I can hardly see it. But, I was a fast one, and all the other groovy chicks I knew claimed that they were out every night getting down with their old men. So, I figured what could it hurt. One night, as instructed, I grabbed a hold of the little fella and shook it good once or twice. Kelvy let out a gasp and his teeth chattered and his glasses went crooked on his head. "Oh, Thenie," he said. (I was going by Thenie back then. I hated the name Athena more than anything in the world.) "Thenie, baby. That was the best. Thanks." That was it? I was sitting there with what felt like baby snot on my fingers, and that was it? I told the nigger to drive me home and never spoke to his yellow ass again. Except for when my mother made him take me to my prom and made me go with him. Even then I didn't so much speak to him as I spent the night shooting him dirty looks and telling him he made me sick.

*Recommendation:*

When I got to the recommendation line I made my first decision as a writer of confessional, self-help prose. I decided to give the old boy a break. On the top of the first page, where I had drawn my ratings code—my happy face scale, with one reserved for the ho-hum and four set aside for "rocked my world" (and with the option of the occasional frown, if need be)—I added another category. It was a drawing of me with a gag around my mouth. I drew it in behind Kelvin's name and felt quite virtuous in my restraint. The poor little guy—both of them, actually—well, what could one expect against my even-then formidable womanly wiles.

Even before Door County I had often been lying down and having the sort of sleep where you feel neither fully awake nor fully subsumed. The experience was not so much sleep as lying in a dark quiet place and patiently waiting for something to happen. I finished that first entry, and that night I slept the sleep of the angels. I dreamed, I remember, that I was walking down the road with a camera. It was a cheap camera, a very cheap camera, one of the kind you buy at the souvenir stand at an amusement park, use once, and then is destroyed when the film is processed, and in the dream the fact that the camera was so inexpensive was very important. My job was to take pictures. I was in a place, a very blank place, and first I was outside of myself, watching while I looked around for something to shoot. I saw myself aiming and shooting, and then I was me looking back through the lens.

I woke up before the pictures were developed, but I felt very refreshed.

# Four

I don't mean to overemphasize the redemptive qualities of sex. I think if you were to put all the harm done by sex and all the good done by sex on the balances, removing the dead weight such as children and tantric practices, my guess is that the scales would tip heavily toward the bad side. Which is not to say that sex is bad, or that too much sex is bad; more that, considering that there are more women than men in the world, and that, judging from the women I know, we have a lot of bad experiences with sex—many more bad than good—I'm inclined to lean in that direction. And it's not as if I'm the sort of person who seeks comfort in sex in times of trouble. What can I tell you? I was in need of fixing, and the talk shows and *The Young and the Restless* were there for me. On Saturday morning, I arose from the basement like Venus from the sea.

Go ahead: slap me for the literary allusion. I went to good schools. I majored in English. I work with language. Anyway, I really did sort of see myself as Venus, a particularly juicy, soft, and padded one. Luscious and ripe, I felt, like a peach— soft, pink, and sweet. I think I had the same look on my face Vivian Leigh had after she had been ravished by Clark Gable.

"Good morning," I said.

Mama and Ciara were sitting at the kitchen table, and I rather floated into the room, swept in with my robe splayed out behind me like Loretta Young's gowns had done in flickery old black-and-white memories I have of some old TV show.

"It's afternoon," Mother said.

They were having lunch. Mother picked through a plate of salad greens while Ciara munched crudités.

Undaunted by my chilly reception, I bent and gave each of them a kiss on the tops of their heads. Which seemed to annoy them.

Finished with boxed foods, I rummaged through the cupboards looking for something to eat.

"Anything in here?" I directed that toward my sister, but it was Mother who answered.

"Plenty to eat. Serve yourself."

"I'm looking for something good."

"There's tuna fish, and there's some Lean Cuisines, and there's plenty of soup. There's leftover baked chicken."

Personally I was hoping more for something along the lines of salsa and chips or a pint of frozen custard. Just because I had moved on from boxes didn't mean I had developed any nutritional sense. I wanted something tasty and crisp, or chewy and sweet. I wanted a gooey butter cake. You can only get a gooey butter cake in St. Louis. When you ask for gooey butter cake in Minnesota, people just look at you funny.

I got out the peanut butter and a box of raisins. I scooped out a spoonful of brown goo and mashed in a bunch of raisins. I scraped off the spoon on the roof of my mouth.

My mother and my sister were giving me dirty looks.

"So," I said to Ciara. "You and I haven't had a chance to get to know each other." I didn't say it too clearly because my mouth was glommed with the butter and the fruit. She heard me, though.

"All you do is sleep and watch TV," she said, and I thought I saw my mother shoot her some sort of look across the table.

"Well, I'm on vacation," I told her. "How's school?"

"It's summer. Only retards go to summer school."

"Ciara!" mother warned.

"Summer camp?" I asked. She was a surly one, I could tell. And apparently I was failing the big-sister test.

"Ciara is busy with a lot of her little activities, aren't you, precious?" Mother reached over and patted her on the hand, giving her a look that was both condescending and at the same time mixed with fear. "You finish up your lunch, sweetie. Come on. Join the clean plate club."

"Gotta get ready for skating," Ciara said. She grabbed a handful of carrots and celery and left the room. Mama looked at her watch and started clearing plates.

"So you're up and about," she said to me.

"Yeah. I thought I'd pick up some groceries."

"We don't keep a lot of junk in the house."

From what I could see, they didn't keep any junk in the house. I'd already eaten everything that might reasonably pass for junky, and personally I always consider snack crackers more of a staple item.

"I was hoping to borrow your car," I said, feeling the need to go driving around, to maybe go look at the old neighborhood.

"You can ride with me when I drop Ciara," Mama said, and then, as she bent over to place the last dish in the dishwasher, she added. "You'll be taking a shower, of course." It was a question, really.

My mother can be as bitchy as the next woman, even with her loved ones, she can, but the way that she said this to me betrayed something other than bitchiness. Rather than sniping or admonishment, I heard reluctance, a kind of frightened embarrassment. She spoke to me the way a person might offer to help a homeless person who had fallen in the park. There was a crude mixture of sympathy and reticence in her voice that stung me and started a ripple of shame.

"Of course," I said, and for some reason I felt worse for her than I did for myself. "How much time?" I turned up my wrist to look at a watch that wasn't there. I hadn't consulted a clock since Wisconsin. Another sign, perhaps, of my improving health.

"Hurry," was all she would say.

There was a small bathroom with a shower in the basement. I went in there and took off my robe and jumped in the stall. I put the water on hot. There was one of those loofah scrubbers hanging from the showerhead, and I took it down and loaded it up with the liquid soap my mother keeps in all of her bathrooms. I went to work. I had never before used a loofah brush. I am more the kind for a washcloth and a bar of Ivory. But it was there, and there wasn't a washcloth, so I thought, what the hell. I held the hot pink handle and pulled the brush across my stomach. It was rough, like a cat's tongue, but, lubricated with soap, it crossed my skin in a wake of bubbles, leaving a trail of prickles and heat beneath the surface. I twisted my arm behind me and dragged the brush across my back. I squeezed on another layer of soap and ran it up and down my legs and my arms. I was panting and my breath was coming hard and fast. I gripped tighter, urging the brush deeper into my skin. I ran it between my legs. I collapsed back against the wall of the shower, sank down, rinsing and breathing deep, the pulse of the water drumming against my torso. Does this sound vaguely pornographic to you? Like one of those tapes another old boyfriend

of mine, Ron, made us watch, where one of those women
with the plastic bodies writhes around in the shower to bad
disco music? I rather felt that way, partially because I hadn't
bathed in a week and partially because this was my first
loofah experience. Looking back I recognize this shower as
the opening ceremony for a time of my life that I like to refer
to as Deneen's Voluptuariana. What had happened, I believe,
was the confluence of the sensuality that had accosted me in
Wisconsin and the permission I had been given by Oprah and
Sally and Maury to enjoy it. That's the real charm of those TV
people, you see, or the danger, depending on your perspective. They present some practice or some opinion that may be
entirely perverted or completely reprehensible. They show
things sometimes that are slightly beyond the pale, but somehow make them sound so innocent, to the point that the
people that appear on the shows are as ordinary as white
bread. I would say they look just like you and me, but often
they are a lot plainer, more banal. Many of them are downright homely. And so these people come on and they talk
about things such as men having sex with teenage boys and
women who like to whip men with a cat-o'-nine-tails, and
Oprah and Ricki nod and shake their heads, and a disgusted
look may cross their faces, but that look—their approbation or
condemnation—is really beside the point. The point is, you,
the viewer, watch whatever is going on and you think, particularly if you are a person like me with an open mind
(crazy), hey, if *they're* doing it, maybe it's not so bad. Maybe
I should try it. As for my open mind, try to picture something
like the opposite of Pandora's Box where instead of releasing
all the evil in the world, someone had packed away all of my
id. For someone like that, someone like me, imagine that if
you are able to follow the logic of a man who claims to be

married to his five daughters, there certainly wasn't much of a problem with getting off in the shower with a loofah brush.

So, I was lying there, my skin looking as if I had been cleaned with a Brillo Pad, patches and strips of peeled-looking skin, glowing and pink against my creamed-tea coloring. At this point I had the vague expectation that one of those porno movie men with the enormous penises would be tearing back the shower curtain, and the disco music would start playing again, and I would be another hour and a half getting dressed. Instead I heard my mother outside the door.

"Deneen! I said hurry!"

If you imagine I was jolted back to my senses, I was not. I was rather more like a puppy who had been playing with a ball and had then been thrown a stick. I thought, "Oh, well, I guess I'll do this for a while."

I got out of the shower and wiped the steam from the mirror. I looked at my hair. And although it was in the sort of condition that could get me summarily dismissed from MABLE (Minneapolis Association of Black Ladies of Enterprise), I was delighted. My hair sprang from my head in coils and snakes and wires and whorls. Here and there dreadlocks had formed. I thought of fountains and, for some reason, cruciferous vegetables, such as cauliflower and broccoli.

"Deneen!"

I wrapped a towel around my hair and ran and threw on some clothes.

My mother and my sister were waiting for me in the living room. Mother was spinning her keys and tapping her foot. Ciara had her hands on her hips and was shooting me daggers.

"I'm late," my sister said.

"Sorry," I replied. "I'm ready now."

She gave my mother the look I always give my boss,

Mr. Waltershied, when he asks me should he buy his wife
a birthday present or just take her out to a nice dinner: the
is-you-crazy? look. Ciara stomped over to the closet, took out
a Cardinals baseball cap, and handed it to me. I took off the
towel I was wearing—a festive towel with pale pink roses on
a field of yellow—and stuffed my hair into that. As much of it
as I could.

They looked at each other and we got into the car.

In this way I was initiated into the routines that made up
the lives of my mother and my sister. Most days were just like
this one. At some point we would drive Ciara to a studio or
a classroom building or a recreation center. A covey of other
young women of various complexions, though all of them the
well-heeled type, would be waiting for her on the parking lot.
A few would break off and come and greet her in that breathy
and shrill-sounding way of twelve-year-old girls. That first
day when we stopped at the skating rink, there were only a
few girls waiting. One of them looked Korean. "Where were
you?" I heard her shout, and as they scurried away to their
lessons I saw Ciara turn around and point in my direction.

How did I respond? I waved of course. Ciara and me, it
was still early in our relationship. We'd get used to each other.
Also, I was too fascinated by what these girls were wearing
to sense any ill will. They wore these little jumpers and shorts
sets in what I, at their ages, would have thought were juvenile colors—bright primaries and secondaries—combined in
stripes and primitive patterning, like bad or imitation Keith
Haring. The designers had figured out, since I outgrew the
junior department, some way of making short shorts look
almost chaste. The girls showed plenty of thigh, but it didn't
look the least bit provocative. Or at least not to me. (Perhaps at
the time I was not the best judge.) I did feel for just the tiniest

of moments a tinge of trashy melancholic nostalgia. Ah, to be able to shop in the junior department. Or in petites, for that matter.

"To the store," I said cheerily.

Reina put the car in gear and peeled away from the curb like a gangster.

Though in my craziness I had a vague sense that the woman I was with was my mother, it would be more true to say that I knew that she was *a* mother. She exuded those motherly vibes, the ones that our built-in mother detectors were designed to pick up. You know how back in the days before optical scanners you would be walking through the Target store, and you would find two identical pieces of merchandise—say, two sweaters—except that one was marked two dollars higher than the other, and the expensive one didn't have any flaws, and the cheaper one had a great big string hanging off it, and you said to yourself, I'm gonna just switch these tickets, and you started to do it, but you stopped because a mother walked by. Those are the motherly vibes I'm talking about, and though at the time—having locked away any sense of shame or guilt or propriety—I was fairly immune to my mother's voodoo, I still found myself trying to please her. I tried to behave for the same reason you try to be patient with the elderly man beside you on the airplane: you don't know him and you don't care about his grandkids, but, like your mother said, a little courtesy never hurt anyone. That the particular mother who might have taught me that was sitting right next to me wasn't important.

She took me to the Schnucks Superstore on Manchester. Going into that store I had the reaction that the lions had when the Romans lifted the gate and they saw those Christians standing there. Food! I grabbed me one of those talking shopping carts and I took off.

I remember everything I put in that cart, because I remember how hard it had been to figure out where even to begin. Anything I had ever wanted to eat was in that store. How to decide? I tooled my cart up and down the aisles.

"Delicious Del Monte green beans on sale, while they last, two for eighty-nine cents. Limit four."

My shopping cart said that. I didn't want green beans. My shopping cart also told me about specials on flour and toilet paper and cake mix and Malt-O-Meal. Apparently I had selected a cart that was only interested in staple items, and I was headed back to the front of the store to exchange it for a companion with more exotic tastes, when I got an idea. What if this were my last meal? If I were on death row, what would I ask the guards to bring me just before they pulled the switch and I fried like a big fat piece of bacon? What did I enjoy most? I thought about egg rolls and shrimp toast and those rumaki things that Felicia had at her wedding. Oh, and those miniature wieners soaked in barbecue sauce. Hors d'oeuvres. My favorite food was hors d'oeuvres. I headed for the hors d'oeuvres department, but its location was not readily apparent. I typed h-o-r-s onto the keyboard that was attached to the part of the shopping cart that had been doing the talking, but it only told me that horseradish was on aisle two. I should have known that this particular cart wouldn't know or care. Through the haze I could hear this voice saying to me, "Deneen, Deneen. Get real. You have to make hors d'oeuvres. You buy all the stuff and you make them yourself." Occasionally I would hear what I believed was a voice of reason, pushing me along, helping me with the tough decisions.

At the time I was comforted to believe that I had some sort of foothold in the rational world, but in looking back I recognize that every time I heard those voices they were advising me about matters involving food or sex or some marginally ethical behavior. Following the voice's recommendation I headed to the deli department, and to my amazement and delight they did, in fact, have hors d'oeuvres, in many forms, some already prepared and cut up into tempting bite-sized pieces. I selected spinach dip and King's Hawaiian bread; a half-dozen egg rolls; little links and a bottle of Open Pit barbecue sauce; a pound of chopped liver; half a pound of smoked salmon; a two-inch slice of paté; and something called crab deluxe. To be on the safe side I stopped and got a couple of cups of that Kaukauna cheese spread and a box of Ritz crackers.

I found my mother waiting by the greeting cards, riffling through them, but not really looking. I saw her before I recognized her. I saw this short, carefully dressed woman with medium brown skin, and I noticed that she had had her hair done in the elegant way that many older African-American women with a certain amount of money did. Styled up off the crown of her head, it cascaded in a graceful flip above each of her ears. Rinsed into it were shiny silver highlights. She wore the kind of simple jewelry that wasn't meant to catch your eye but was designed to blend into her outfit—a mannish, tailored pantsuit. (Although one could tell that those bracelets and rings and necklaces were anything but cheap.) I saw this woman standing there, and I was admiring how well she had applied her makeup—the deep purple and warm gold treatments above her eyes—when she spoke to me.

"Deneen?" she said.

I had been standing there admiring her. In my one-activity-at-a-time-only-please mode, the acts of admiring her, recognizing her, and greeting her had only progressed as far as activity number one.

"Shall we go?" I said.

Wheeling along behind her on the way to the check-out stations I realized that I had no money. Not one cent. The last monetary transaction I had made was when I boarded the plane to fly to St. Louis. I had used a credit card. I could sort of see a purse, sitting on the floor by the bed back in the paneled room in mother's basement. I remembered it as if it were an old friend someone brought up in conversation. "Oh, yeah. The purse. I haven't thought about her in years. How's she doing? Does she still have that nasty scratch across her butt?"

I placed my purchases on the conveyor belt next to my mother's. The voice told me to do it. "Deneen, Deneen," it said. (I can't tell if the voice is a he or a she because it speaks in a husky androgynous whisper.) "Put your stuff up there with your mother's stuff. Go ahead. She won't mind." I tossed my treats up there and then I gave my mother a big smile. She hadn't noticed my goodies yet. She dug through her own purse, looking for her billfold.

"Ninety-seven dollars and seventy-nine cents," the cashier said.

Mother looked at the cashier, then she looked at the food. A boy was tossing our groceries into thin plastic sacks. Then she looked at me, over the rims of her half glasses. What a lovely beaded chain, I thought. She removed a card from her wallet, swiped it through a machine, and pressed some buttons. She was shaking her head the whole time.

I grabbed two of the sacks, and left the other one for her. The automatic door blasted open in front of me and a wave of shimmering heat and humidity battered me in the face.

I gasped. Rays of sun burned through my baseball cap, and a wet ribbon of sweat rolled from the nape of my neck and into the shelter of the back of my top. My mother arrived behind me at the car and punched the buttons that unlocked the door.

"I told you we don't eat a lot of junk," she said. Her voice had assumed the edge that she used with recalcitrant sixth graders when their teachers sent them to her office. She had dropped it about a half register; done that trick where it sounds as if she's talking louder but really she's talking more softly; had emphasized, if only minimally, the words "told" and "eat" and "junk."

Well, you've got your nerve, I thought. In my world, when someone in the audience spoke this way, they could expect a scolding from Ricki and Jenny and Richard. They had a way of picking out people like her. If you notice, her kind rarely ever gets to speak. Rolonda certainly never allows them to hold the microphone. I mustered up my best, nonjudgmental, nonshaming Maury/Geraldo/Sally voice.

"Well. You don't have to eat it," I said.

Mother made one of those noises that people make when their panties ride up on them or when they're trying to pass a large bowel movement.

"Deneen, what on earth is the matter with you?" she asked.

Me? I started to ask. Me! I don't believe my voice reaches the required octave to register the indignation I felt. Me?

But I didn't say that. Instead I forgave her. I remembered that what she was, after all, was one of those mothers. Doling out unsolicited nutritional advice was more or less a requirement for her job.

# Five

My first foray back into the world was less than a complete success. Like testing a nine-inch all-butter pound cake, I had stuck a toothpick into myself and discovered I was not quite done. I returned to my lair. Over the next several days I would emerge now and then, up from the blue light of the television set into the brightness of my mother's world, squinting and covering my eyes against the glare. I'd arrange another tray of canapés and return to the cellar to continue the educational growth and development that was facilitating my recovery and was being so graciously provided by the soap operas and talk show hosts of America.

My trip to the grocery store was not entirely without benefits. Before, when I had some sort of half-realization that there were two other people in this house, and that one of them was my mother and the other was my sister, when I thought about the mother part, I would hear the quiet tinkling of an alarm bell. I would get the same kind of tingling along my skin they say you're supposed to feel just before lightning strikes, and I knew that it was probably a good idea to stay out of her way, even if I didn't quite know why. After I had forgiven her for snapping at me in the car, and after we had come home and put away the groceries—she supplying a full repertoire of nonverbal noises and gestures to signal her disapproval (as if a person dared reasonably disapprove of such foods as chopped liver)—and after I had arranged myself a platter of egg rolls and cheese crackers, I went back to the rumpus room, where immediately the equivalent of the cliché lightbulb went off above my head.

I thought, "Oh. That lady."

I had help from my friends Oprah/Maury/Sally. One of the most important services they provide is to help those of us who are seeking answers to our problems (crazy) to find the right language to categorize the things that are bothering us. They helped me, finally, to classify this woman, my mother, as a "toxic person." From that moment on it was easy for me to take the right precautions, and for a while there I thought of her as if she were a big coiled rattlesnake or a bottle of cyanide tablets. I would look at her sometimes and see a giant skull and crossbones.

They (Jerry, Maury, Montel), in a series of episodes, featured persons, who, according to the resident expert psychologist, are like many of us and contain the essence of as many as a half dozen or more individuals in one body. This helped me to develop the understanding that there were in fact two people to be dealt with upstairs: one of them was my mother, who raised a girl named Athena in a house in Spanish Lake; the other one was a woman named Reina, who lives in a house in Kirkwood with a girl named Ciara.

As I developed this understanding and was thereby enabled to spend more and more time out of the basement observing her activities, I could see quite clearly that just as I am not nearly the same person who grew up in St. Louis, this woman, Reina, was nothing at all like the mother who raised me. Or her. Or whichever person this sentence refers to. (I plead with the gods of syntax to grant special dispensations for the emotionally challenged. The crazy.)

There was, for example, the jumping that I heard in the mornings—really a blessing, because it woke me up in time for Rosie, and when I stuck my head up there to see what it was that my mother was allowing Ciara to do, I discovered Reina, in her family room, hopping up and down along with Jane Fonda. Jane was telling my mother to "take it to the side" and to "grapevine." That same porno music was playing in the background.

"Come on, Deneen," Reina said. "Get in here." She was hardly out of breath, and she seemed to be right on the moves just as Jane was doing them.

"Work it, girl," Reina encouraged.

I flapped my arms up and down two times, but I looked more like I was waving for the lifeguard than doing jumping jacks. I went to the kitchen and spooned down some crab deluxe. I took the container to the basement.

*My* mother was fifty pounds overweight. She used to cook foods such as pot roast, and chicken and dumplings, and skillet spaghetti smothered with cheese.

My sister and Reina eat foods that are green and crunchy. They broil fish and chicken. With the skin off. They consider lemon juice to be a sauce.

Ricki/Sally/Jenny keep us regularly informed on the latest in nutritional information, and though I am new to the fold, we have each of us struggled alongside sister Oprah in her battles with the calorie, so I am not unaware that Reina and Ciara have taken to heart the admonitions of regular guests, such as Dr. Covert Bailey, and modified their diets accordingly. But as those of us in the audience know, and are ready and willing to comment on when Jerry/Montel/Richard sticks the microphone in our faces, people can take such dietary proscriptions to the extreme. Furthermore, we know that they adjust the recommended daily calorie charts to account for the occasional Twinkie or handful of Doritos. Those people are scientists. Understanding human nature is their job.

If I am honest and if I look at the two women objectively, I can see that Reina is a vast improvement over the woman I grew up with. She has stopped smoking, there is a snap in her step, and I can even see that her skin has a brighter tone to it. There wasn't much to recommend the lumbering and the huffing and blowing that took place when my mother went shopping back in the old days. But I wasn't into comparisons this visit. As I said, those women were two separate entities, and my real concern was with the hustle and bustle that went on up there on a regular basis. For a woman and a girl on what they claimed was a summer schedule, there didn't seem to be a whole lot of summering going on. No lying on the patio in the sun or dawdling over a cup of coffee. They were either going somewhere or coming back from somewhere or walking around up there getting ready to do something else. My mother had found herself one of these big old frame houses with the wooden floors, and all day long it was creak, creak, creak, creak, creak, creak, creak. Until I wanted to blow somebody's brains out.

Right about the time I got tired of their creaking, another terrible thing happened. I was watching Oprah/Ricki/Sally and was overcome suddenly by a nagging uneasiness of the kind which only television engenders. They were talking about adultery. Or incest. Or gay and lesbian senior citizens. Or strippers. It doesn't matter. What matters is that I knew that I had seen this show before, which was impossible, since I had only been watching daytime television for less than two weeks. I cruised around from channel to channel and the shows seemed extremely familiar. At first I believed that between

*60*

them the television networks had cooked up a diabolical con-
spiracy designed to force me deeper into madness, but as I
calmed down and as I continued to look at the programs more
carefully, and as I really listened to Jenny/Geraldo/Rolonda
and to their guests and to the audience members, and really
thought about the dynamics of the programs and what it was
they were trying to teach me, I understood that what had happened to me was that I had become ... enlightened, as it were.
I had become one of the few fortunate viewers who had completely absorbed the lessons of daytime television and was
ready to move on.

Those lessons are:

> *1.* that we each of us have within us the resources to
> make the world a better place;
> *2.* that there are good things and bad things in
> everyone;
> *3.* that a little loving criticism never hurt anyone;
> *4.* that you should hug people—they will get used to it;
> *5.* that people have a right to their opinions, and that
> mine is just as valid as yours;
> *6.* that things will get better.

Suffice it to say, I could go on.

I had become a graduate of daytime television. I felt the
tears rolling down my cheeks. I understood in my newfound
state of illumination (craziness) that it was my calling to rise
up from that basement and make to my mother and my sister
a beautiful gift of my knowledge and power as a healer.

I showered with the loofah and got right to work.

It was a Thursday, I think, when I became saved. I dressed
myself and stuck my hair up in the Cardinals cap. I knew that
in order for my mother and my sister to be able to open up

their hearts fully and receive my gifts, it was necessary for me to remove as many obstacles from their path as I could, and though we have been taught that it is bad and evil to judge others by their appearance, it was clear to me that to my mother and sister—wallowing in heathendom—a person's appearance said more about her than almost anything else.

I found a clean sweatshirt.

"Mama!" I threw my arms around her.

"And Ciara!" I threw my arms around her.

They were once more sitting at the table, eating more of their green foods.

"She's up again," Ciara said.

Reina took a long sip of coffee.

I could see I had my work cut out for me. I got out the container of garlic and herbed cheese spread and a package of salami. I peeled off four or five slices and spread them with the cheese. Ciara was looking at me with her mouth hanging open. Strings of celery connected her teeth like retainers. I smiled back at her. I was stronger (crazier) than she was and had been trained to smile in the face of ridicule. I rolled the salami slices into thin tubes. I leaned close to my food items and kept my head facing in her direction and continued smiling. I picked up a salami roll and, biting into it, sucked at the cheese.

"You are so gross," she said.

"Ciara," Reina said. She raised her eyebrows at her.

"She is," Ciara said.

I was unfazed. Were Oprah herself here, she would wrap her arms around Ciara and pull her close and stick the microphone in her face and tell her that she really didn't mean to say such a thing about her sister, did she, and then she would keep on hugging her and prompting her until she relented.

I, too, knew she didn't mean it. I remembered how hard it was to be twelve. I also hated everyone at her age.

"That's okay," I said, and I smiled.

I chewed on my lunch and I considered the young woman who was my sister. She had such lovely lovely hair. With her almond-colored skin and her hazel eyes and her straight white teeth, it took me a few minutes to find anything wrong with her, but I knew there was, because she was making me nervous the way game show contestants did. The contestant coordinators always try to find attractive people, but often there is just a little something wrong with them. They do that on purpose, because Alex/Bob/Pat have it in their contracts that there can't be anyone on the show better looking than they are. At first I thought it was her lovely lovely hair, which was wound up in those pink plastic sponge rollers that I used to use. Those probably *were* my pink plastic sponge rollers—they don't even make them anymore, as far as I know—and I thought, hey, she never asked me permission to borrow those, and for just a moment my smile went a little sour as I resisted the urge to reach over there and snatch my rollers out of the witch's hair. That impulse passed, and I knew it wasn't her lovely lovely hair that bothered me, and she was pretty enough, in that Janet Jackson isn't-my-face-round sort of way. Then I saw what the problem was: she was too skinny. Much, much too skinny. Much, much, much, much, much. Speaking as a woman who once entertained, though only briefly, the idea that living through certain kinds of unspeakable horror (such as a famine in Africa) wouldn't be so bad, because at least for once I'd be able to choose from a wider selection of outfits in the better dresses department, I surprised myself in thinking this. She didn't look unhealthy, and she had plenty of energy, and her arms and her legs were well-shaped. Maybe she was fine. God knows, I'm not the best judge. I think all the women in *Vogue* are too skinny. My realization was that there didn't seem to be anything to grow on, no margin for error. Not one drab of baby fat on this one. Should a growth spurt occur—as has been known to happen at her age—she would become as stretched and stringy-looking as a rubber band at its absolute limit. What did I know: maybe she was finished growing up, had reached her peach-perfect peak.

So I acted on instinct. I extended to her my tray of salami tubes.

"Iiiiiiiiick," she cringed, as if I'd offered her a plate of vomit.

"Hawkins will be here soon," Reina said.

My sister gathered a collection of orange and green sticks and left the room.

"She is so sweet," I said to Reina. Reina took an extended sip of her coffee.

"So," I said. "What's on the agenda for today? What needs doing?"

"I'm to assume you've rejoined the living?"

Ignoring my mother's sarcasm, I said, "I'm making a fresh start today."

(One of our foundational beliefs.)

Reina's widened eyes wandered her kitchen. "Actually, there is something you can do for me."

"It would be my pleasure," I said.

"I have to attend a principal's meeting. Drop me off and then pick up Ciara for me. I'll get a ride home. Can you handle that?"

You'd think she was talking to a crazy person or something. "No problem. I'm here to help."

"Is *that* why you're here?"

Why are people so threatened by giving?

The doorbell rang while my microwave popcorn was popping. I answered it. There was a middle-aged man waiting there, a light brownskin man with freckles and a white sports coat. The long collars of his shirt were rounded on the end and stuck out above the lapels of the jacket: it was one of those fifties' shirts, made out of that obscene-looking material they used back then, with a pattern of black and white poodles on a red background.

"Oh. Hello," he said. He looked at me over his tiny rectangular wire-rimmed glasses. He had a greasy bouffant like a soul singer on *Shindig* back in the olden days.

"Hi," I said. "I'm Deneen."

"Well, all right then," he said, and he gave me the double-O: up and down with his eyes, then up and down again. I stood there in the door. Smiling. This was new. Evidently Reina had various sorts of men coming to her door at all hours of the day.

"I'm looking for Miss Ci . . . Ah! A vision from heaven."

My sister came up behind me and yelled. "Mother! Hawkins is here! We're leaving!" She shoved me out of my way with her sports bag, took his arm, and they headed down the walk.

I went back to the kitchen and emptied the popcorn into a bowl. "Want some?" I asked. Reina shook her head. She was unloading the dishwasher, so I set the bowl on the counter and helped.

"Can I ask a question?" I asked. (We are taught to be mindful of boundaries issues.) "Who exactly is Hawkins?"

"Hawkins DeAngeles," my mother said. "He's the cousin of Roxanne, one of my club ladies." Then Reina, plucking out the silverware by categories, added, casually, "He's Ciara's pageant coach."

Because I was at the time fully absorbed in my newfound selfless devotion to family (out of my mind nuts), those words didn't sink in. I picked at the popcorn and helped put the plates and bowls where instructed.

After we stowed the kitchen, I followed my mother down the short hallway. Then I followed her up the steps. Then I followed her to her bedroom. She turned and looked at me. I smiled at her.

"What are you doing, Deneen?" she asked.

What was I doing? I didn't know. I looked at her in case an answer might become apparent. One did not. Looking back, I think I had probably been magnetized by her energy and her activity. Very busy people have a way of making you want to be very busy yourself—or they exhaust you, depending upon your mood—and I think that the part of me that was not in flux had been drawn to her the way a vacuum draws idle and loose dirt.

"What are we doing next?" I asked.

"I'm getting ready for my meeting," she said. She emphasized the "I," and I had a seat on her bed. I said okay, and I smiled some more. She sighed and rolled her eyes and came and sat next to me.

"Look, Deneen," she said. "I've been very patient. I've given you lots of room." She put her arm around me. "I don't know what's wrong. I don't know what you need from me."

I kept smiling. I thought how much nicer this room was than the one in her other house. She had finally gotten some of that Ethan Allen furniture, all rich-looking and dark brown. I heard alarm bells, and then there was this other voice: the voices of Oprah and Sally and Ricki and Jenny and Rolonda and Jerry all combined together, saying, "Give your mother a hug. Go on. Hug her." And I did, and the audience applauded, and then the voice said, "We'll be right back," and we went to a commercial.

"I know what," she said. She reached over and wiped something wet off my face. She had it on her face, too. "While I get ready, why don't you go down to the office and straighten it up a little bit. Would you do that?"

"Sure," I said. She was rather blurry looking. She patted me on the back.

"Just run a rag around and straighten up the books and pick up a little. Okay?"

I gave her another hug. My lessons had not been in vain.

I am not being trivial. Had it not been for Oprah/Montel/ Maury there was a good chance that to this day I would still be down in the rumpus room, balled up on that sofa. They had talked me out of that cellar. And my mother had touched me. And, though I have always turned up my nose at those vile and fraudulent religious faith healers, I think perhaps now I should give that kind of therapy another thought. My mother hugged me. I don't want you to believe that there was some instant miracle and that suddenly everything was clear and I was whole, but as I was down there dusting in the room off the left side of her foyer—the room she calls her study— I was again aware that something else inside me had changed. No, there weren't any more doors opened or doors closed or lightbulbs or bells, but I did know, finally, why I had come here. My mama. Not my mother or Reina, but another person I once knew, the one who washed out my cuts with Bactine— and it didn't sting—and put Band-Aids on top; the one who read me a story at night and let me get up into her bed if there was a thunderstorm and it got scary. The one who wouldn't let the mean boys down the street pull my hair. I don't know what I expected her to do for me. I don't think I thought about it at all. I do know that the mean boys had been pulling on my hair again lately, and doing other bad things, too, and that as long as my mommy was nearby I wouldn't have to be bothered with them.

I put down the dust rag and I called work.

"Waltershied, Williams and Caruthers."

"Katrina. It's Deneen. Tell Mr. Waltershied I quit."

"Calvin called," she said.

"I'm serious. I'm moving back home. To St. Louis."

"He said he tried to call you. Asked me if I knew where you were. I told him, her and me used to be tight, but she don't seem to have time for her friends no more."

"Katrina."

"You could give a person a call now and then. See how she's doing. See if she's still alive. It wouldn't kill you."

"Katrina, I need for you to listen to me."

"What do you want me to tell Calvin when I see him?"

"Calvin who? Look, Katrina, tell Mr. Waltershied I quit."

"Tell him yourself."

There was a click.

"Walt here."

"Mr. Waltershied?"

"Deneen. Where in the hell are you? Listen to this: Two gals, blondes. Mother/daughter. Sisters. They're at the amusement park. Merry-go-rounds. Ferris wheels. Lots of energy. Hip hop beat. Blonde says, 'I never knew I could feel this fresh.' Blah, blah, blah. Show the product. What do you think?"

"Derivative."

"Okay. Same sort of thing. School carnival. Same blonde. She's the teacher. Dunk tank—"

"Mr. Waltershied, I don't know . . ."

"Come on. Work with me here, Deneen."

"Mr. Waltershied, I'm thinking of moving to St. Louis."

"The hell you are. What they offer you? A car? Partnership?"

"It's not that, it's—"

"Screw it. You try and leave me, I'm coming down there and dragging your ass back personally. I got to go. I got another call. Think blondes."

He hung up on me.

I didn't want to think about blondes or douche sprays, or Waltershied, Williams and Caruthers. I wanted to stay here with my mama. Mr. Waltershied—he is one of those brilliant insane people with whom the media industries are chock-full. Mike Williams makes the sales. I'm the writer. That leaves poor Mr. Waltershied to stir up the accounts and run the office. Actually it leaves me. And Katrina. If it wasn't for us, the place would fall apart. Poor Mr. Waltershied. I had been gone for better than two weeks, and he hadn't even noticed yet.

It's the tension in our lives that keeps us alive, I guess, and the foot that I had kept in the door of my work life was becoming a whole leg, even as the rest of me was being pulled back to my mama's house. I couldn't help it: as much as I wanted to not give a damn, I found that it was very impor-tant to me what went into this ad campaign, and I had told Mr. Waltershied before I left for Door County that I wasn't sitting still for any douche spray commercials with a covey of blondes running around on the beach, and he said Deneen, please don't say douche spray, and I said douche spray, douche spray, douche spray, just to annoy him, the same way I always call him Mr. Waltershied to annoy him. He wants me to call him Walt. He says the company's profits are up

200 percent since they hired me, and that he wants to make me a partner and add my name to the door. I tell him that there's not enough room on the door for Waltershied, Williams, Caruthers, and Wilkerson. He says that since Caruthers is dead they can just erase him. We can even become the three Ws or W cubed or something cute and won't we have a great logo?

They may want me, but the question is, how bad do they want me? Let's say that instead of some blondes we just had some ordinary women and one of the women says to the other one, "You spray this on your vagina so that the animals don't follow you home from the park." Okay, that's gross, but the point is, I want Waltershied, Williams and Caruthers to break some new ground. We should be able to say in simple English (maybe a bit more *tasteful* English) what the product is for and why someone might consider using it. I mean they have those ads for jock itch. As a woman I would much rather hear about a simple odor problem than to have to listen to a discussion of jock itch. Give me a break. Men grabbing their balls: that's not even a medical condition, it's a bad habit. They don't need a spray for that. They need behavior modification. I realized I had placed almost half of my body in that door. They were doing this commercial my way.

I dialed the agency.

"Waltershied, Williams and Caruthers."

"Katrina."

"I'm not talking to you."

"Tell Mr. Waltershied: No blondes. Tell him I said: Or else."

I got the drop on her: I hung up first.

I gathered my mother's papers from her desk and dropped them into a bottom drawer. I found a legal pad and sat down in her chair. I know what you're thinking: Boy, she sure got better quick. Put that out of your mind. I was crazy as a jaybird. But what a lot of you normal (less crazy) people don't realize is that many industrious people are absolutely out of their minds. I offer as proof of my fragile condition that it made perfect sense to me that from my mother's desk I would be able to control events taking place in an office five hundred air miles away, including managing and developing a major advertising campaign. I didn't see any problem with it. I'd throw together some ideas and give them a call. No sweat.

I picked up the pen.

All I could think of was Calvin.

*He* called me. He *called* me. He called *me*.

If he called me, that must mean he wanted something, so I tried to think of what that could possibly be: to say hello? To apologize? To go on another vacation? I tried to imagine anything that he might possibly want and was there anything on that list that I might want as well? No. So, the only reason he was really calling me was that he thought I might want something from him. Which I didn't. And the only reason he might think so was because I hadn't told him otherwise.

My talk show lessons had helped me to work through that logical slime pit quickly and also provided me with a solution. I had to write him a letter. Our psychologist/panelists regularly recommend the writing of such letters.

> *Dear Chump:* I began.
>
> *You bastard. I ought to cut your balls off. You are worse than human filth.*
>
> *Call my house again and see don't I slap a restraining order on your ass.*
>
> *I hope you get AIDS and die.*
>
> *Love,*
>
> *Deneen*

It was a little intemperate, but I seriously thought about sending it. I'm glad I didn't, and I couldn't anyway, because I had stabbed through the paper with my pen in many places, including removing some of the best words. I would have had to write it again, and I couldn't just then. From one of the locked rooms an enormous sadness had escaped, and it had gotten to my chest and my eyes before the attendants could grab it. I was heaving and crying and my heart was twisting in my chest.

"Deneen." My mother called me from the hall. I dabbed at my face with the tail of my sweatshirt.

"Coming," I said.

She drove us to her school in University City and then asked me if I was okay to drive. She gave me directions to Hawkins's place.

I pulled up in front of this new townhouse just off Hanley Road, part of a complex. The other houses on the street were different, but the same: like the clothes in the Gap. I rang the bell. No answer. I buzzed again. I tried the door. It was open, so I went in.

I found my sister in a room downstairs, prancing back and forth across the room in tempo with what sounded like the Lawrence Welk Orchestra's version of "Tie a Yellow Ribbon Round the Old Oak Tree."

"Brighter!" Hawkins yelled. "Brighter!"

She was walking between two strips of duct tape on the floor.

"Smile! Lots of teeth!"

Ciara was spinning this pink umbrella as she walked, and, as she pivoted on her heels, she turned and flashed a smile back over her shoulder.

"More shoulder! Less butt! No, no, no!" Hawkins snatched

the umbrella from her, took the runway himself and demonstrated. "See, we dip the shoulder, and we put just a little hitch in the hiney." He walked toward me, grinning broadly, spun, strutted back, smiling over his shoulder, umbrella twirling. He handed the umbrella back to Ciara who mimicked him to the T.

"May I ask what's going on?" I asked. Still in my nonconfrontational mode.

"We're practicing," Ciara said to me through her shiny and clenched and perfect teeth.

"Practicing for what?" I smiled back.

"Girlfriend," Hawkins said, dropping his arm chummily across my shoulder. "You are looking at Missouri's next Miss All American Dream Doll."

The music plinked and tinkled away in the background.

"Huh?" I said.

He backed away from me a bit, peering at me through his tiny glasses. He reached up and started feeling around the hair coming out of my cap. "What you wash this hair with, girl?"

I batted his hand away.

"Let's go," Ciara said to me. "I got a stop to make on the way home."

"Make sure you got your bag, Miss Thing," Hawkins said. "You work on that song, you hear me. I want to hear that catch in your voice next time, just like I showed you."

They bobbed back and forth by each other's heads, smacking their lips in the air.

"Love ya," Hawkins said.

"It was very interesting meeting you," I said. I led the way up the stairs.

In the car Ciara turned the radio on. Loud. One of the local pop stations. I turned it back down.

"I need to stop at Venture," she said. "There's one up here."

I pulled into the lot and stopped by the door.

"I need ten dollars," she said.

I looked in my wallet. I'd have to hit the machine soon. I had six and some change. I offered it to her.

She gave me a look. "Forget it."

We sat there for a minute. Then I started for home.

I could feel her eyes on me the whole time we drove out Manchester Road. "Something wrong?" I asked her.

"Yeah. Why do you have such a fat butt?"

"I beg your pardon?"

"Your ass. It's so big."

The shrew.

"I just hope that doesn't run in the family or something."

At the rate she was going the little bitch wouldn't live long enough to grow a behind or nothing else neither.

# Six

I had appropriated my mother's desk and was sitting
there euphemizing. I had decided that the only way
I could convince Mr. Waltershied to lose the blondes was to
develop a scenario and write the script myself. I was trying to
come up with a list of words which would stand in for the
words that we would probably not be allowed to use. I was
desperate. I got out the thesaurus. There didn't seem to be
any vaginas in it. Just for fun I checked, and I couldn't find
any penises either. This lack had often been a theme in my
life. I wrote down the following words:

> *lady parts*
> *down there*
> *the land between the legs*
> *the happy place*
> *Jennifer*
> *my regions*
> *personal area*

I thought "personal area" had some possibilities. I tried to
use it in a scenario. Two women are having a civilized lunch
in a nice restaurant. Diane says, "Debbie, there seems to be
a problem in my 'personal area.'"

I realized that a big part of the problem with this scenario
was that in my entire life I can't recall ever sitting with

another woman in any kind of restaurant and discussing the problems I was having with my "personal area," that is with the possible exception of the problems that had been caused for my "personal area" by men.

And then I wondered why there weren't any commercials for men who had that "less than fresh feeling." As a person with no direct personal experience in this area, I could only go on conjecture. Maybe men didn't know when they were less than fresh. I'd certainly known men who were. Ron, the one with the porno tapes, would often fall asleep with his "man juice" smeared all over himself, and then in the morning our bed would smell like the Monsanto chemical factory. That's the truth, and I know worse stories than that one, which I know you'll thank me for sparing you.

Then I said to myself, maybe that's what "jock itch" is a euphemism for. Maybe back in sixth grade, when we were in one room learning about "that less than fresh feeling," the boys were in the other room learning about "jock itch." And there lies the problem: we should be able to be direct and open about these things, men and women both. Shouldn't we? When we, those who happen to need such products, can feel free to go into the store and ask for them without a whole lot of the snickering and carrying on that a person sometimes gets, I will have been successful.

So I'm busy working away at my mother's desk when along comes Ciara.

She came into the room and made a pretense of browsing through the bookcases. Between you and me, there wasn't one book on those shelves that a twelve-year-old would be interested in reading, not a 1990s teenager, for sure, and particularly not this one. I doubt that any of those books had ever been opened. Reina had invested in sets of leather-bound "classics," and her decorator had arranged them around assorted bric-a-brac. Some of those "books" weren't books at all. Some of them were paintings of books that masked cubbyholes and storage space. But there was Ciara, transparently singing a little nonsense song and running her fingers along the spines of the fake and forlorn-looking library.

"Good afternoon," I said.

"La de da de da. Hi."

We had been very cool with each other ever since she told me I had a fat butt. I'd avoided her for days. She strolled around behind my desk and tried to get a peek at what I was writing on the legal pad. I turned it over.

"Looking for a particular book?" I asked.

"Well," she said. She sidled her narrow hips up to the front of the desk and leaned across it toward me. "If you want to know the truth, Reina keeps all the good books up in her room."

"Reina?"

"That's her name, isn't it?"

I was careful to not respond to that one way or the other. I glanced down at the pad in my lap, rocking the chair back and forth.

"Whatcha working on?"

"Just something for my job. I'm in advertising."

"Yeah. That's what Reina said. Can I see?"

"Maybe later."

"Sure. Later," she said. She did some more of her nonsense singing as she slithered out of the room.

The way she said "later" should have been some sort of a sign to me.

When she cleared the door I took a big inhale and a big exhale. I turned the page and started another letter to Calvin.

*My dearest Calvin:*

 *Why did you do this to me? Why? Why? Why?*
*I thought we had a good thing going. I had already*
*picked out names for our children. LeRoy, Antwan,*
*and LaTabishette. Maybe it's not too late. You know*
*that little problem you mentioned, about men? I can*
*fix that. I've cured other men. I'm on the payroll of a*
*number of right-wing Christian organizations. Call me.*
 *Your love goddess,*
 *Deneen*

I tore that letter up right away. It didn't sound anything like
me. Yes, I liked Calvin, and yes, I thought we had a nice
relationship, but he certainly wasn't the sort of man a woman
wrote a desperate letter for. Something had possessed me.
Someone else's hand had been controlling the pen, making
me say those bizarre and pathetic things. Maybe this room
was haunted. Maybe some horrible evil had taken place not
far from where I sat. And then, as I entertained this new form
of madness, I knew the truth.

It was Ciara. It was my baby sister. She was the human
equivalent of the Love Canal.

I was rapidly losing faith with Oprah et al. Where were the
warning bells this time? I tried to remember the ten common
warning signs of "toxic people."

1. They make you feel bad about yourself.
2. They make you feel bad for them.
3. They cause your teeth to itch.
4. They steal your belongings.
5. They make you act like a four-year-old.
6. They are responsible for your killing them.
7. They cause you to tear out your hair.

8. They are usually members of your family.
9. They cause you to do desperate, pathetic things.
10. If you think they are toxic, they in fact are.

And I tried to apply that list to Ciara. Any three symptoms are enough (according to the experts/psychologists/panelists), and she fit a lot more of them than that. And, of course, why would I suspect her? She is a child. Who wants to believe that a little girl, especially a cute little girl, is evil? All the same, I decided that in order to maintain whatever equilibrium I had, I had better be careful.

I doodled on my pad, trying to stir up some more euphemisms. I was blocked, and I was bored.

Ciara had disappeared with Mr. Hawkins, and my mother was puttering around the house, as usual, on some important project or the other. Her particular summer school program ran in the afternoon—a bad idea for the St. Louis summer, but she had some seemingly logical bureaucratic explanation for this happenstance. Whatever. Most days, like today, she was around until well after lunch.

It was midmorning. Around this time at work in Minnesota, everyone would be settled in for the day, and Mr. Waltershied, fueled by a gallon or so of coffee, would be in his creative mode. He would call me into his office and say, "Deneen! Let's make some magic!" and we would start shooting the ideas back and forth. He is a genius with the colors and the pictures and the flashy stuff like that. I do the words and the big concepts. Together we knock their socks off. We spark together, he and I, and out cascades brilliance and light. Sometimes we go on all day, and Katrina brings in pizza or Chinese from the Leeann Chin carryout. The crew in the art department drops in and out, and Mr. Waltershied hugs them or tears up their work and throws it in the trash. I am much nicer to the writing staff. Usually. Occasionally I get into my high-school-English-teacher mood and stroll through the department, leaning over shoulders with a red pencil.

At that moment, bored, in St. Louis, in my mother's den, I wanted to be back in that office more than anything in the world. But it was only one of the many doors in my head. Those others were barred with dead bolts. No way was I ready to go home yet.

I picked up the phone.

"Waltershied, Williams and Caruthers."

"Katrina."

She hung up on me. I dialed again.

"Waltershied, Williams and Caruthers."

"Hang up on me again, bitch, and you're fired."

"You can't fire me. You're in St. Louis. And who are you calling a bitch, ho?"

"Look, Katrina, I'm sorry I hurt your feelings. Things are kind of rough, you know?"

"A little apology is supposed to make up for bad treatment, huh? Didn't even bring me no present from Wisconsin."

"I'll bring you something from here."

"Better be nice, is all I can say. Ooh, you know what I'd like: I'd like me one of them—"

"Katrina! Katrina! Put Mr. Waltershied on."

"He's not here."

"Where is he?"

"Over at your house."

"I told him I was out of town."

"I did, too. He got all huffy. I told him if he didn't believe me, he could go over there and check for his own ornery self. So he did."

"I'll call you back." I hung up the phone.

I'd call him after lunch and fix it. Feed him another story of some kind. When he found out I really wasn't home he'd stomp around for a while. Have himself a couple of Scotches at lunch. By about two he'd be wound down—enough for me to work him around to seeing things my way.

I was back to doodling and making lists. I found myself still blocked. And bored. Until this point, when I was done with TV and done with napping and done with snacking, I had amused myself by rummaging around the house, discovering bits and pieces of things here and there that I remembered from when I was growing up, things from the other house out in Spanish Lake. There wasn't much of it left. When she began her new life here with my late stepfather, my mother got rid of everything from her previous life, every stick of furniture, every figurine, every vase, even her china and all of the linens I remember: the white terrycloth towels with a bold color band across the base, the dinner plates with the fleur-de-lis and the band of silver on the rim. All of those things were gone. The only things from the old house were mine—or me. Pictures of me, here and there, in a cap and gown, and with pressed hair down to the shoulders or with a gigantic blown-out Afro. A prom picture of me with Kelvy. And the things in the guest room. Pitiful scatterings, the leavings of a life I can't even remember leading.

I had already explored all the rooms but my mother's.

So I wandered in there.

I had always hated those department store display rooms of furniture where everything was color-coordinated and where in every corner there was the perfect small detail: the tiniest of photos in an antique frame, the cut glass bowl with a rainbow of scarves blooming from its center. I had always found those rooms precious and unlivable, and I had always leaned toward hard-core post-college eclectic. My friends and I have houses where, for the most part, whatever it is, you can't break it because it's most certainly already broken or chipped or nicked or scratched. Guests are lucky if their salad bowl matches their plate, or anything else on the table, for that matter. Here I was, in Reina's magazine-perfect bedroom, and I felt completely at home. I sprawled myself across the bed and smeared my body around on the comforter, a tropical floral pattern, purples and reds, jewel-toned. It was silky and soft, smooth as enamel. She had those accessory pieces, too, back by the headboard: piles of frilled pillows and bolsters and what have you, covered in that same material, the kind of stuff I always see in the Sunday ads and never quite know who it's for. For people like Reina, of course. No, I wasn't re-pelled a bit. I was soothed, in fact. Perhaps because the tableau had become so familiar over the past days. There was a room just like this one on *The Young and the Restless,* and it occurred to me that if I lay there long enough, perhaps someone would happen by with a script that would solve all of my problems. But that was unlikely. I would not be one of the blessed char-acters. I would be like poor Jill—always in trouble. Decades later, she was still in hot water, and I wondered if in all that time, since I had stopped watching the show to go away to college, she had caught any breaks at all, ever. Somehow, though, it would be easier to go through that misery if you were able to do so from the shelter of a lovely room such as this one. I drank it in.

I slid off the bed to examine the bookcase. Here were sup-posed to be the hot titles Ciara referred to. Toni Morrison. Bebe Moore Campbell. Tina Ansa. I was expecting a lot of those Sidney Sheldon and *Story of O* type books; here instead was a collection of quality fiction by African-American women, and though I'd read only a few of them, I knew there wasn't anything here too titillating. That told me something about Ciara's development. Reina had become a reader, evidently, in the last few years. When I was young she was content to scan the paper, and I remember her studying for her administrative license. And she read *Essence*, of course. But she was never one to spend time on a serious book.

I read the titles on the spines while I resisted the urge to rifle through her chest of drawers. I hadn't done that in twenty-five years, and my fingers were itching to get in there. I remembered running my hands beneath layers of nylon and silk and lace, and inhaling the heady mixture of sachet and wood. I remember finding her S & H Green Stamp books, and a drawer containing old pictures, including one of her and my father. Somewhere in there I knew that I would find something thrilling and naughty—with photographs in it, I hoped— but I never did. She caught me once. For punishment she pulled open all the drawers and showed me the nothing that was there. "Feel free to straighten up for me anytime," she said, tossing me a dust rag, inviting me to wipe away at the scratched-up old furniture she had had in Spanish Lake.

As I stood there, I found myself smiling at that memory of my mother, of how hard it was to do things to make her angry, and how she had learned, perhaps through her job, to deal with children who were bad or wrong without hitting them or shaming them. At the agency we had done pro bono campaigns against child abuse, and so I knew that I was lucky to have had such an upbringing. And when I spotted my mother's purse that day, gaping open with the wallet on top, I believe it was these happy memories—combined with my vacationing id—that convinced me to open her wallet and remove a twenty-dollar bill. I didn't need twenty dollars. I could have gone to any cash machine in the country and accessed my account. But I told myself that going to the cash machine would mean going into *my* wallet, and going into my wallet would remind me of the last time I spent money, which would remind me of Calvin, etc. etc. Wouldn't it be easier, I thought, to get twenty dollars from my mother, who certainly had it to spare? Of course, I couldn't come right out and ask her for the money, because then she'd want to know why, and even if she didn't ask, I would feel as if she deserved an explanation and I didn't think I could give her one. Even if she didn't care, there is something sort of pathetic about having to ask your mother for twenty dollars when you are in your late thirties. So I took it. And the voices that told me to take it also told me to be sure to keep careful records and to pay her back.

"Hello. Is someone there? Is that you, Deneen?"

I jumped just like a dumb coed in one of those babysitter/slasher movies. Once again the story of my life: Commit a little trespass and there's a mother within calling distance.

"Yes, mama." I stuffed the money into my jeans. I opened the door to her bathroom. She had been so quiet I hadn't known she was there.

"Were you looking for me?" she asked. She was in her huge bathtub, one of those whirlpool kinds into which you can submerge yourself completely. She was steeping in some kind of soup. There were cut-up pieces of greenery floating around in the water. Mother peeled some vegetables from her eyes and asked me to have a seat.

"Do you know what time it is?" she asked.

"Near eleven, last time I looked."

She sighed. "A few minutes of peace and quiet."

"What is this?" I asked her.

"My aromatherapy bath. Here, hand me that towel." She pointed to what I believed to be a stack of towels on a recessed shelf. It turned out to be one towel, a plush, sheet-sized thing. She rose from the water, green leaves sticking to her here and there, almost as if she had been bathing in a lake.

Her body showed her age. I had not seen it for as long as I could remember. Though she was toned from exercise, there was loose skin: it draped at her thighs and on her arms like bunting, puckered. It wattled across her sagging breasts. I held up the towel and she folded herself into it.

"Thank you, darling."

She sat on her bed, freeing her hair from some sort of headdress which had been protecting it. I sat on a chair that was upholstered to complement the bedding and the drapes.

"You live a cushy life, mama," I said.

"Think so?"

"This lovely old house. Long sensuous baths."

She shrugged it off. "We do the best we can, when we can," she said. She dried herself, and I sat there, awkward, searching for a conversation maker.

"You have a lot of good books over there," I said.

"You're welcome to read them."

"I don't know. Ciara told me there was some pretty racy stuff."

"That girl. Twelve going on thirty. I tell you; her and her antics. It wears me out some days." She patted and prodded her hair, treating it as if it were made out of crystal. "How's it look? Got to last me till I get in to Hawkins on Wednesday."

"It's fine," I said.

"How bout you?"

I felt at the fringes around the baseball cap. "I kind of like to let my hair rest sometimes," I said.

"No, not your hair. You. How are you doing?"

I looked down at the rug. It was a rich turquoise. There were traces of its color in the draperies and the bedspread and the upholstery. I could hear the little alarm bell, but it was very faint this time, and I could hear the voices telling me, "Go on. Say something to the woman. Go on." My mother saved us from my silence.

"I should run and get your sister now," she said.

"I'll do it," I said, the words popping out like hot toast, sudden and with a snap. "You just relax. Enjoy the quiet a bit longer."

"Okay," she said. She lay back into her mound of decoration, extended her legs as straight and stiff as a mummy. A beatific smile settled across her face.

Probably remorse made me volunteer the errand, I thought. As I reached into her purse to retrieve the car keys, my hand once again brushed past her wallet. She wouldn't miss a few dollars. There was plenty of money in there. At that moment I probably couldn't have told you the meaning of the word guilt.

Yet, when I saw her there, her body and the record of all the years upon it, I felt sorry for her. Not as my mother, but as a woman, near sixty years old, who, when she should be spending her summers cruising the Caribbean with her club members, was chauffeuring around and picking up after her child and hundreds of other people's children as well. Her life couldn't be easy. I knew that she had brought these problems on herself, that she had made the choice and taken the risk of late childbearing of her own free will, and that the consequences she now reaped ought to have been weighed into the original equation.

I told myself to find some compassion. She was a woman,

alone, bearing a load that would exhaust a woman half her age. I was proud of her, really. As I drove to get my sister, I reviewed my mother's performance in my head, the same way I would play my Jimi Hendrix albums full blast at her old house, drowning out her hectoring and her bold and brassy friends. The other thoughts in my head, usually deeply buried and securely locked away, thoughts as red hot and burning as an ember, were about how I myself was childless, rapidly approaching the age when my mother made her choice to start a second family. I played her life louder and louder to drown out mine. I examined the way she was raising her daughter as if it were some kind of sociological case study. I began to prepare my critique.

Ciara and Hawkins were upstairs in his living room at the piano.

"Let's take it from the top," Hawkins said. He played a short, tinkly introduction on the piano.

"I-in-separable," sang Ciara, and I was seized with an involuntary gasping cringe. Not only was this the Natalie Cole song that the worst contestants on *Star Search* sang, Ciara was just . . . wrong. She was fingernails-on-the-chalkboard wrong. I looked around for my gong. This sister was out of here.

"Excuse me," I said, tapping Hawkins on the shoulder. "Excuse me."

He stopped playing and gave me a look that would rot cheese, up and down with his eyes, and with his lips all pouted out.

"She's really off," I said. "I own this record," I added, figuring it didn't hurt to call upon the authority of Natalie herself. Ciara cut her eyes at me.

"Again. From the top," Hawkins said, ignoring me.

This time she was closer, almost on that first note, and by

the time she had quavered her way through the first word, she was there. Almost. Hawkins flourished away on the piano, and she hacked her way through the song.

I was like those women in the audience on amateur night at the Apollo Theater—where this song was also an old war-horse for the tone deaf. They sort of encourage these gals along with their hands, trying to keep their eyes from getting real big when they hit the clinkers. Ciara reached the bridge, where there is a soaring note on the word "love." I bit my lip and felt my fingernails digging into my palms.

"Bring it on home, girl," Hawkins yelled. "Remember that catch."

She wove her way to the conclusion. On the word "wonderful" she did this little thing where she sort of inhaled through her nose and her mouth at the same time. I guessed that was the catch.

Hawkins grabbed at his chest. "Chills. Chills," he said. Then he asked me didn't I think it was the most beautiful thing I'd ever heard.

Was he kidding?

"I'm not a very good judge," I said. Ciara, who had been radiating in the light of his praise, dimmed a bit at my lack of endorsement.

"Although," I added. "I was really impressed with that little thing you did with your voice." She brightened up again. She didn't need to know that I was impressed with the fact that it was the most transparent, cheesy bit of theatrics I'd seen in a long time.

Hawkins came over and started feeling at my hair again. He was wearing what was either a dashiki or a maternity blouse.

"Don't touch my hair," I said.

He splayed his bottom lip, wandered his eyes all around

me as if I were on display in the wax museum or something. "I could give you a hot oil treatment just like that," he said, snapping his fingers.

"No thanks. We have to go. Are you ready?"

Ciara sneered at me. "Where's mother?"

"Having a little rest. You know how hard she works."

"She said she'd take me to the Galleria. Are you taking me to the Galleria?"

"We could stop, I guess."

"Fine." She grabbed her bag and headed toward the car.

"Five days and counting," Hawkins said.

"I can't wait," Ciara simpered. She rubbed up next to him and shimmied.

"Five days till what?" I asked.

"The pageant, stupid," Ciara said.

"I can just about smell that trophy," Hawkins said, sucking the words in through his teeth and rubbing his hands together. They both did some more of that shimmying.

"Are you sure she's ready for the pageant?" I asked.

Ciara shoved past me and went on out to the car. I'm sure she thought she was.

"Think about that hot oil treatment," he yelled behind me. "You'll be the cutest thing at the pageant."

"I'll think about it," I said, smiling and waving. I'd shave my head before that man touched my hair.

The lunch hour rush was in full throttle when I pulled into the lot at the Galleria. While I was cruising for a space and stopped in front of the Dillard's store, Ciara threw open the door and jumped out of the car.

"I'll meet you by the fountain in a half hour," she said. She slammed the door and took off at a run.

The little witch.

At first I got really hot. She didn't know who she was messing with. Even I didn't know who she was messing with. People who are like I was back then (criminally insane) are not to be trifled with. There were about ten minutes there when, for her sake, it was a good thing I couldn't catch her, because if I had, I would most certainly now be spending time in a squalid women's prison for perpetrating unspeakable evil on my sister's person.

And, I thought, God knows what mother will think of my losing her other daughter. Hey, maybe she wouldn't have minded one bit. Maybe she dropped Ciara off at shopping malls all over town and let her go in and wander around by herself. Who was I kidding? Here I had thought I was giving the woman a leisurely respite. She trusted me with a simple task. Now her precious baby angel would be kidnapped by white slavers and forced to go to New York, change her name to Candi, and live a life of degradation. And though it would be her own fault for jumping out of the car, I would be blamed. People would point to me and say, "There's that Deneen. You know: the one who lost her baby sister at the shopping mall."

By the time I had parked the car I was a little calmer, and I thought back to what it was like to be twelve and to be around adults every waking moment. I thought about my mother and the houseful of club members she always had, and how sometimes I used to close my eyes and pray that when I opened them they would have magically disappeared. And they never had.

She was fine in there. I knew it. Just being a normal naughty teenage girl. Mama would deal with her when we got home.

What she and I needed was a fresh start. I was the adult—

albeit a disordered adult—and I needed to reach out to her in some way. I decided to buy her a gift.

There were fifteen minutes left until she said she would meet me by the fountain. I had noticed that she had pierced ears, so I went into a store, one of those that has racks and racks of cheap costume jewelry. Young girls like to have a lot of different things to match up with their outfits. I know I did. With the help of a salesgirl who was not that much older than my sister I picked out three pairs and paid for them with the twenty. I knew that money had found its way to me for a reason.

I walked the length of the mall, searching for the fountain or something else with water in it. I wasn't having much luck.

"Deneen!" It was her, calling my name. She pranced up a stairwell from the level where the movie theaters were.

"I was looking for you," I said. "I was looking for a fountain."

"Well, you found me. Let's go." She didn't seem to have bought a thing.

I said "fine" and walked her in the direction of the exit. I could tell she was cruising for a confrontation, but I was determined not to have one. We didn't say a word all the way to the car.

"I suppose you're wondering where I was?" she said to me. We were heading south on Brentwood Boulevard.

"That's between you and mother," I said.

"Ooh, you would be a big fat tattletale, wouldn't you?" She sort of waved her head around and sneered when she said that. I ignored her.

"I'll just tell her you threw me out of the car," she said. "Then we'll see who gets in trouble."

Though I probably should have slapped her, I felt a rush of tenderness for her just then. Such a big, bold little woman, all gangly and tall and sure of herself. "I don't want to get you in trouble," I said. "I want for us to be friends."

"Really," she said.

"Really."

"Then you won't tell her I went off by myself?"

"I don't know. Maybe not. What I hope is that you tell her yourself."

"Then you don't know me very well."

"No. But I'd like to. See, there: that bag on the seat. When I went into the mall, at first I was very angry. And then I thought: I remember when I was her age."

She was giving me an indignant look.

"And I said to myself: I sure wished that I had had a big sister to look after me. So the first thing I did before I came and found you was, I stopped and picked you up a present. That's it. In the bag right there."

She looked at the bag as if were made out of turds.

"Go ahead. You can open it."

She picked up the bag with just her thumb and forefinger. I wanted to tell her it wasn't going to bite. She peeked inside with her lips puckered out and her nostrils flared.

"What are these?" she asked.

"They're earrings, silly. I thought they'd look cute on you."

"Oh, yeah, right. Thanks." She crumpled down the top of the bag again and tossed it into the back seat.

The war was on.

# Seven

Ciara was right about one thing: I was a big fat tattle-tale. A big fat giant four-year-old brat of a tattletale baby, and it was her fault—for being a "toxic person." As you recall, one of the traits of being a toxic person is to drive other people toward juvenile behavior. She glared at me the rest of the way home. I ignored her. I was the big girl, after all. As soon as I put the car into park, though, I made a beeline for the door. She wasn't getting to Mommy before I did. But when we got into the house, she was as cool as spray-on deodorant. She glided up the steps to her room, eyeing me with one of those looks that said that as far as she was concerned I'd better watch my step.

I found my mother in the kitchen chopping up some more green foods for their lunch.

"Did you have a nice rest?" I asked her, wanting to sound cool, not wanting to seem, like National Public Radio, a little too eager to be bearing bad news.

"Yes, thank you, darling." She leaned over and pecked me on the cheek. "I expected you girls sooner. Lunch is ready. I called school and told them I was running late."

"We had to make a stop," I said. I was trying to stretch it out. I was going for the drama. I wanted the little witch to sweat for a while before the boom got lowered.

"Problems?"

"You could say that. You see—"

She interrupted me. "Oh, before I forget it, a man called for you."

A man? For me? "A man? For me?"

For just a moment I thought one of my major fantasies had been realized. I like to think that there are men out there checking me out when I go to the shopping mall, and that one of these days, one of those men will see me and recognize me as the woman of his dreams. He will be perfect for me, as well. He will trace me through my license tags and find me and call me. We will meet and fall in love and live happily ever after in a resort community with reliable pizza delivery and good cable service. Since we had been at the mall less than a half hour earlier—and since the car I was driving was registered in my mother's name—it had been a long shot, at best.

"Somebody named Walters or Welter-something."

"My boss. Mr. Waltershied. Did he say anything?"

"No. Sort of a rude fellow. I told him you were out, and he hung up on me."

"I'll call him back," I said.

It was lunch time in Minneapolis. I went on with my story.

"So anyway, Ciara said that you told her that it was all right with you if—"

She interrupted me again. "You know what, Deneen? I was just thinking about something. Do you remember your Aunt Ernestine, my club member, the one who had a nephew named Anthony?"

My mother made me call every one of her club members "aunt." Aunt Jean and Aunt Claudia and Aunt Naomi.

"Of course," I lied. Except for a few old grudges, the ability to do my job well, and the names of my favorite foods, the rest of the closets containing memories had been shipped to another address for storage.

"He's in town, Ernestine tells me. He's very successful. So they say. A lawyer, up your way—in Milwaukee."

I skipped the geography lesson. An educated woman, my mother had this notion that the cities north of St. Louis were huddled together, sort of suburbs of each other—that somewhere north of the Missouri border there was a megalopolis called Des Moines/Minneapolis/Milwaukee/St. Paul/Duluth, and that the people who lived in this megacity knew one another, assuring me from time to time that there is no way I could not have run into Mrs. Johnson's son or her dentist's cousin.

She continued: "I think he was kind of sweet on you back then. Remember? At our club picnics?"

Oh, yes, the club picnics. At once I was express-delivered a whole batch of memories, not of some Anthony, but of how these woman and their husbands would stake out a picnic ground in Forest Park, and how they would line up six or seven tables together, wrap them in oilcloth and then cover them with food: barbecued chicken and ribs and burgers and hot dogs; and fried catfish; and potato salads and coleslaw; and baked beans; and macaroni and cheese; and collard greens and mustard greens; and ten different kinds of cakes and pies and cobblers. I held onto the counter to keep from fainting. Suddenly my plates of pizza rolls and guacamole seemed woefully inadequate.

"I remember those picnics," I said.

"Anyway, he's in town, and I was thinking of asking him over. What do you think?"

"Sure," I said, though I wasn't really paying attention.

I, along with my tongue, was remembering how one of my mother's club member's husband, Uncle Benny, used to make a barbecue sauce that was sweet and pungent, with a heat that started at your tongue and burned down to your toes.

"Sure, invite him," I said.

Mother was saying things such as "as long as you're here," and "since you're not settled down with anyone."

Me, I was swooning. I have this thing about barbecue sauce. Give me some slices of dried-out pork, a burnt black hot dog, a piece of rancid chicken—it doesn't matter: as long as you slather it with a great sauce. A lot of people, they think barbecue sauce is just ketchup with hot pepper in it. They are living in darkness and ignorance. It is not a one-note thing at all. Like a symphony, it is the expert blending of many great talents, the biting trill of vinegar, the percussive snap of a pepper flake, the honeyed tones of sweet molasses. Uncle Benny was the maestro, God rest his soul. Like all great masters, the secrets of his sauce went with him to his grave.

"Sure," I said. "Invite him. Can we have a barbecue?" At that moment I would have done anything for a rib tip sandwich.

"You leave the menu to me," she said. She patted me on the arm and went to the hallway. "Ciara! Lunch!" she called.

Damn. I'd forgotten. "I have to finish telling you, . . ." I started, but before I could, the little witch traipsed into the kitchen.

There we sat, they with their plates of green foods and no-fat dressing, me with my sensible platter of succulent tidbits.

"It's nice being here with my two girls," my mother said. She smiled. I was entering my third week in her house. It was as if she had just realized I was there.

"Deneen," my mother said, "did you know that Ciara had 'outstanding' checked on every category on her report card for two years running. Fifth and sixth grade."

"That's great." I smiled over at my sister. She was eyeing me through narrow slits, chewing her celery and carrots on one side of her mouth like a cow. I figured that for my mother's sake I ought to make nice with her.

"Pizza roll?" I offered. I lifted the goodies in my sister's direction.

"Be careful, Deneen." My mother placed her hand on the plate I had proffered, returning it to the table. "She'll eat every last one those if you let her."

"Mother!" Ciara protested.

"Sorry." I popped a savory nugget in my mouth.

"Ciara has also been selected for her junior high cheer-leading squad. Haven't you, baby?"

"Yes," the wench said, between crunches.

I felt awfully strange having this chummy small talk, but it didn't make me nervous in the least. It seemed almost natural. For the first time the alarm bells were inaudible, if not completely still: much of the tension between my mother and me had eased. The tiny, sane part of me had resented her uneasiness with me since I had arrived, until I understood that the feeling had nothing to do with my problems. It wasn't about me, Deneen, her crazy daughter, as much as it was about, me, Deneen, a woman living in her house. When I had been here before, even in my twenties, she still saw me as that rebellious proto-hippie with the beads and the peace symbols. Now, out of nowhere, she had a woman on her hands: one she didn't really know. I can't say I'd be too thrilled myself to have some woman show up on my doorstep and move in, though evidently mother had reached her accommodation

with it. I was to be Deneen, her big girl, the one she could
send on errands and fix up with the children of her friends.
I was a woman who could really appreciate just how proud she
was of her baby. Hell, I was even supposed to share that pride.
I was going to be something like a big old trustworthy pet.
*I* was to be the maiden aunt.

"It sounds like you're just having a wonderful year," I said
to my sister. I almost choked on those words.

"And this pageant coming up already," my mother continued. "The state finals! Can you believe that, Deneen?" Her
voice was somewhere between excited and weary—I couldn't
tell. "Did you get to see her practice?"

"As a matter of fact I did."

"We're thrilled. Hawkins is doing a wonderful job with
her. She may even make the top ten."

"I'm winning that pageant," Ciara said. She said it cold and
plain, the way she might announce that the paper had arrived
or the name of her favorite soft drink.

"Of course you are, dear," mother said.

Ciara rolled her eyes and bit off a large chunk of carrot
stick. "I gotta get ready for tennis," she said.

My sister had a way of announcing her afternoon appointments that made them sound as if they were some sort of
great burden to her. She gathered her usual changing-outfits
snack and flounced out of the room.

"My angel," mother said, picking in her salad with a fork.

I couldn't hold it in any longer. "Your angel was a little
devil this afternoon." A surge of electric satisfaction ran
through me.

"Oh?" mother said.

"She ran away from me at the shopping mall." I looked
her right in the face just then to see her reaction.

"She did, huh?" she said. What I saw was a sort of resigned smirk. "Well, that's my Ciara, too."

I persisted. I said, "I was worried. You know the things kids get into. And these creeps out there, preying on young girls." I threw all that in, hoping to sway the jury in my direction.

Mother chuckled. "Our Ciara handles herself pretty well."

I flushed the guacamole from my plate and stuck it in the dishwasher. What was this anyway? If I'd run off at the shopping mall, she'd have been outside cutting a switch off the willow tree to tear up my behind with.

"You don't seem very upset," I said.

She puttered around behind me, briskly, filing away the lunch items. "Most of the year, I spend my days with an office full of naughty girls and boys. You learn not to get too upset."

"Well, I don't spend my days with children, and I was the one responsible for her."

"Drop it, Deneen," she said. Her face was open and patient and friendly.

"And another thing," I said. I wasn't dropping shit. "About this beauty pageant. I don't much like the idea of little girls parading around while a bunch of judges grade them like sides of beef."

"You're working yourself up, sweetheart. Set this in that cabinet for me." She handed me a platter she had been using for crudités.

"I am not getting worked up." But I was. "Mother, this is the nineties. Progressive people everywhere turn their noses up at such crap."

"It's not your concern, Deneen."

"I beg your pardon?"

"*I* will worry about Ciara. Okay?" She came over to me, put an arm around my waist and patted my side. "You leave her to me. You, I want you to think about fixing yourself up nice for our little dinner party."

There was a gasping inhaled sob. From me I guess.

"Please don't be upset."

"I'm not," I cried. I slung the dish towel across one of the chairs, went to the den and slid the doors closed.

I believe I was in the middle of the adult version of the three-year-old's lying on the floor, kicking her feet and yelling, "It's not fair." Other adults do this by burning down their places of work, throwing their spouses through windows, and cutting off innocent people in traffic. Some of us don't grow up very much.

I have no idea what I was so angry about. A child had been impulsive, a mother had been patient, no one had been hurt. But in my own quixotic world some enormous injustice had been committed, and, somehow, I had been the victim of it.

My mother wasn't evil. I knew that. It was that girl. Ciara. She was the problem. Mama was as much a victim as I was, and now I was going to have to look out for us both. I could do that. I was the big girl. It was my job. I started breathing easier, relaxing into the plush leather of the swivel chair behind the desk.

And believe it or not, it was only at that moment that it registered that I had agreed to go along with my mother's dinner plans. I had allowed myself to be fixed up. I was going on a blind date. Somewhere deep in my head a quiet scream began. It got louder and louder until it filled my brain and caused me to throw my head back against the seat.

What had I done? A blind date? I remembered how I got my last blind date: Mr. Calvin Colechester himself.

Katrina had flounced into my office. She was wearing one of her outfits that really oughtn't to have been allowed in the workplace—in this case, a leather miniskirt and a black tank top with lots of jewelry at the neck, black boots and stockings, and her hair all ratted out like Tina Turner. No one says anything to her about these outfits because, if you knew Katrina you'd know that they fit her personality, as well as her beautiful body. And furthermore, since it is always cold in the office, she wore this virginal-looking sweater over her shoulders, clasped at the neck with a cameo. She flopped herself into a chair and said, "Have I got a dude for you."

"Sure," I said. I'd met some of Katrina's dudes before. Duds was more like it.

"I'm telling you, girl. This one's hot. He's a big, long, hot steamy hunk of a man."

"I pass."

"Suit yourself. Lots of other women out there in line. A lot of em be happy to catch a man like Calvin."

"Calvin. You want to fix me up with a 'dude' named Calvin."

"Honey, I been working with y'all long enough around here to have learned it don't matter what you call it as long as it smells good."

Katrina had been with us a long time, but apparently, as that last statement reveals, she was confused about one of the fundamentals of advertising.

"I don't think so," I said.

Thinking that was that, I found myself over at her apartment on the pretext of helping her pick out some things from a catalog. Who should show up?

"What a surprise," Katrina'd said. "Look who stopped by." The simple, manipulative, lying ho couldn't even keep a straight face.

We actually had a pleasant evening. One thing about Calvin, he could charm you out of your drawers when he wanted to. He did me for almost a whole year. Just look what happened.

I got out my pad.

> Dear Calvin:
>
> Haven't you caused me enough trouble? Why don't you leave me the hell alone? I was good. I went away and I didn't say a word. What do you want from me, anyway? Let me get on with my life. I beg you.
>
> Sincerely,
>
> Deneen

As much as I liked that letter, I realized it was misdirected. It was Reina who'd gotten me into this . . . whatever it was gonna be. Calvin was long gone.

I knew I had better start focusing in on what was going on around me. The reason it is so easy to victimize crazy people is because we are often too busy trying to deal with the immediate issues at hand—such as breathing and trying to get food from the plate to our mouths—to keep our minds on the subtle nuances of living. I had been lulled by her comforts and attention into the, in retrospect, ludicrous idea that my mother was benign. Once again I had confused the lack of malicious intent with innocence. She was my mother, for heaven's sake: she was issued ulterior motives in the delivery room the day I was born.

I ought to just go in there, I thought, and tell her what she could do with her stupid dinner party and whoever-it-was's stupid nephew. I would have, too. I started up from my chair to do just that. Then I remembered how patient she had been, and how careful of me. It seemed unfair to be petulant. And she had done the whole thing above board (as much as it is possible to be above board with someone who is listening from another frequency): no traps, no rabbits (or men) pulled out of hats—her dirtiest trick of all, maybe, being straight-forward for once. A person knew to be on the lookout for the usual maternal manipulations, but which of us had been trained by her parents to be treated as an adult? Especially by them. Finally, I thought of the little witch—the one who just skipped out the house in the darlingest of tennis dresses. It was more like her to tell Reina that she wasn't going through with some plan mother had put her heart and soul into. I couldn't do it. It didn't fit into my new role. I was going to be the "good" daughter.

But a blind date. I couldn't deal with this. I picked up the phone.

"Waltershied, Williams and Caruthers."

"You've got a nasty streak in you, Katrina."

"Who's calling, please?"

"You know damn well who this is. What you want to go give that man this phone number for?"

"He made me." She did a whole bunch of fake sniffling and boo-hooing. "He said if I didn't tell him where you were, I was fired. And if he was going to fire me, who was going to protect me from you firing me."

"You're fired, Katrina."

"I ain't studying you, Deneen. Walt'll protect me."

"You lucky I'm five hundred miles away. I'd knock them hoops out your ears."

"How'd you know I had my hoops on."

Katrina always wears hoops on Monday, but like most of us she didn't even know her own patterns. I figured I'd mess with her head.

"I know what goes on in that office," I said. "Think I don't see you, sitting there with your purple nail polish on?"

She'd spend the rest of the day looking around for a hidden camera.

"Put Mr. Waltershied on," I said.

"Okay. But if you tell him I'm fired, I'm telling him it was you gave him that box of Midol at the Christmas party."

"Transfer the phone, bitch."

"When I feels like it, ho."

There was a click.

"Walt." He sounded tired and run-down, his voice almost like a record on the wrong speed.

"What's the matter with you?"

"Deneen! Where in the hell are you?"

Be smart, Deneen, a voice told me. It was a different voice, a familiar one. It was that woman, Deneen, the one who talked her way into a good agency and worked her way almost to the top, to Vice President of Creative Services. Be smart, she said. Hold on to this damn job.

"I'm on to something," I whispered.

"What are you saying? Why are we whispering?"

"A big account. I'm not where I can talk."

"How big?"

"Look, I don't want to jinx this. I've got to court these people and lay low. It may take a while."

"How long is a while? I'm going out of my mind up here. I need you up here. Today."

"Come on. It's summer. Things are slow. All the clients are up at the lake."

"What about the commercial for . . . our . . . our product?"

I was going to make him say it. "What product is that, Mr. Waltershied?"

"You know, Deneen. The stuff."

"Douche spray, Mr. Waltershied?"

"Shshsh. Don't say that. This is a public conveyance."

"Would you prefer I said pussy perfume?"

"Oh, Jesus, Deneen. I'm turning red here. Okay, look, try this: Two sisters, one's in a wedding gown and the other's helping her—"

"'Less than fresh' on her honeymoon, Mr. Waltershied? I don't think so. Never."

"Oh. Didn't think about that."

"And you know what else, Mr. Waltershied? No blondes. And no mother/daughter or sisterly chats."

"Deneen—"

"No. We talked about this."

This is the point where he stands up and does sort of a war dance around wherever I'm sitting. He flaps his arms and makes his speech about how ridiculous I'm being and about how nobody except some damn radical feminist, prima donna, prude, dyed-in-the-wool conservative (the chosen description fitting the circumstances or his ugly mood at the moment) would hold the line on this issue. I would get up and stand behind him and grab his shoulders and guide him to his chair. I'd pet his arm and tell him to sit down before he gave himself a heart attack. Then we'd call a truce and take a time out and take a few spins around the Monopoly board we have set up in the bull pen. We play for real money, beginning a new game as soon as all the property is developed. Last count, I was up $5,475.

"I need you here. I'm floundering. We all are."

I swallowed. I needed to be there. But I also needed to be here, too. For a while.

"Give me a month," I said.

"Are you out of your mind?"

Yes.

"We can work on the phone," I said. "I'll call every day."

"I don't think I can—"

"Please, Walt." It was the tiniest voice I had.

"You called me Walt. There isn't any account, is there?"

"No."

"You okay?"

"I will be. I hope."

"I'll talk to Williams. I'll work it out."

"I appreciate that. I understand if you can't. But I need to be here for a while."

"You just come back to us. And you call me every day, or else. And you figure out a way to help me keep Katrina in line. She's nuts. She's sitting out at that desk dressed up in her biker girl outfits giving people orders like she was you or something."

"I'll straighten her out."

"And I want blondes. Or those brunettes with the red highlights."

"Gotta go." I hung up on him.

I closed my eyes and thanked God for the things He had given me: the rare privilege of working with people who needed and appreciated me, the inner strength to be able to walk away when I needed to, the blessing of having some-place to go when I did.

I am burdened by this knowledge—the recognition that I am a relatively well-off woman of a certain class and that there are many others with no such blessings or resources. I guess I was like all of us here in the more developed parts of our planet—people like you and me, who have time to read novels, and who sit in our comfortable homes, bellies full, watching news footage of emaciated children in East Africa scraping in the dust for the leavings from a ripped bag of grain. We have a way, don't we, of being able to turn away from our televisions, and, without a trace of irony, complain to our partners because there is pepperoni on the double-topping pizza instead of sausage as the package suggests. Suffering, after all, is not relative. Pain is pain. My misery was as real and as valid to me as that of any madwoman in any state hospital in America. Looking back, any sense of shame I feel is less related to my self-indulgence than it is to the fact that it seems now like such a pointless waste of a summer. It takes a good long time to be crazy.

# Eight

"I have a suggestion," my mother said. We were out on her ivied brick patio, setting things up for the dinner party. We were to eat outside that evening. It was shaded back there and, as summer in St. Louis goes, not a particularly hot day. Having gotten myself into this fix in the first place—that of having a blind date in the middle of a nervous breakdown—I proceeded cautiously with the discussion.

"You wanted a different centerpiece?" I asked. I hoped she would recognize in my simple-minded diversion a general lack of suggestibility on my part.

"These irises are perfect. No, my idea is: on the way home from picking up Ciara, why don't you girls stop off someplace and pick out a nice new dress. For you. For tonight."

"I brought some things with me," I said.

My vacation outfits were abandoned and crumpled, still packed from the fiasco in Door County. They probably didn't fit anymore anyway, seeing as how I had in the past few weeks moved from Rubenesque to well on the road to just plain sloppy on a diet of Doritos, Hawaiian Punch, and Little Debbie snack cakes.

She came and dropped an arm across my shoulder. We faced her white wrought iron table with its glass top, admiring her work on the table arrangement. "You know, Deneen," she said. "Sometimes when a woman gets to feeling down in the dumps, there's nothing like a brand new dress to make her feel like a whole new person."

Leave it to my mother to summarize my problem as having been "down in the dumps." Poor woman. She didn't have a clue as to what was wrong with me. All she knew was that her daughter had shown up late one Sunday evening and had parked herself in the basement, that she hadn't combed her hair, was sleeping a lot, and seemed to act as if this were normal behavior. In that sense it was perfectly logical to prescribe the miracle elixir that Western society assumes will fix any woman's troubles: a trip to the shopping mall.

"Fine," I said. As a lot of students at Marvin School knew, many times it was better to shrug and get on with your punishment than it was even to attempt to discuss or explain anything to Principal Reina Wilkerson Jones, EdD.

I went and got her keys from her purse. While I was there, I borrowed another twenty.

Hawkins was in serious dress-rehearsal mode. He was wearing a floor-length caftan and doing final fittings for Ciara's pageant costumes. He shouted "play wear," and she pranced into the room wearing a set of sailor-inspired togs: a white bare-midriff blouse with a V neck collar and a blue straight-collar tunic under that. Across her back was a huge, blue-trimmed yoke, embroidered with a gold anchor. Ciara spun in front of us, splaying her short pleated skirt and revealing some frilly blue bloomers underneath. She had the regulation saccharine smile plastered across her face.

"Go on down to the end of that runway and show your sister here how you work it," Hawkins ordered.

She strutted past me and stopped, where, evidently facing the judges, she did a kind of a half-squat, butt-shake deal. She turned around and strutted back.

The light from her teeth was giving me an Excedrin headache.

"Okay, party wear. Fast change."

She scissored out of the room like a majorette.

"Maybe I shouldn't say anything," I said, having every intention of saying something, "but isn't that outfit a little young for her?"

Hawkins looked at me over his glasses again. His eye-balling always made me feel like I had a booger on my face. "How many pageants have *you* attended?" he asked. Before I could answer he put his hands up in front of my face and said, "Spare me. None." He blew out his breath and added, "These people." He rolled his eyes, and went over to fuss with the sheet music on his piano. I would apparently be treated to another version of "Insufferable" before we left.

In my normal life I carried around a whole suitcase full of anxiety caused specifically by the Hawkinses of the world. Let's start, shall we, with the fact that as a woman who has spent a large part of her life viewing television and maga-zines and feeling sometimes woefully inadequate, I had always had a problem with a certain kind of gay man, par-ticularly drag queens and types such as Hawkins. I had got-ten over it. I had learned, with the help of a therapist and a few memorable gentleman friends, to appreciate the full magnificence of being a large and lovely black woman. Still, it was an extra bitter pill to swallow to have to deal with a man who was more comfortable with his femininity than I was. I know what you're thinking: Calvin had stirred to the surface my deep and simmering homophobia. Well, maybe. Even so, long before Calvin, I always had this nagging sus-picion that men like Hawkins were in some way taunting me by becoming, through some miracle of cosmetics and performance art, a better woman than I'd ever be. It just wasn't fair.

Even worse, what I want to know is, when am I going to reach the point in my life when I'm old enough so that people like Hawkins—men and women alike—feel it is no longer their prerogative to talk to me as if I was some sort of mentally deficient teenager? I had asked a simple question. One that certainly did not deserve a bitchy answer such as that. Didn't he know who I was? Hadn't mother told him that I was a high ranking and highly regarded employee of one of the finest advertising agencies in the Twin Cities? Firing faggots like him was my hobby. Okay, so maybe Calvin had gotten to me more than I admitted. It wasn't just people like him, either. What about that woman in the candy department at Dayton's who acted like it was a big inconvenience for her to bag up some cashew clusters, and that hussy at the Post Office who knows I want a receipt? She's seen me come in there every day for the past two years. You think these people talk to everybody that way? No way. There was no way around it: My fate was to go straight from disrespected youth to patronized old age.

Which didn't mean I had to let this one off the hook.

"All I was saying was, for a girl as tall and as—"

He pounded out five majestic chords on the piano. "Looka here, Miss Thing: I have coached five out of the last seven St. Louis Junior Misses. Five out of six Teenage North Counties. Before I finish listing all my credits, you be more worn out and haggard looking than you already are. I suggest you leave me to do my job."

He blew a whistle. "Time, sugar," he yelled toward the changing room.

He touched my hair and said, "Mmmph, mmmph, mmmph."

Ciara toddled out in a dress made of what appeared to be lace lamé. Its bodice stretched past her narrow hips and flat butt, and at the bottom of the creation was a flare made out of rows and rows of some sort of sheer netting. Through the thin material of the dress I could see the tiny beginnings of her future breasts rounded up ever so slightly like a flaw in the fabric. Mosquito bites, my mother called them.

Toddled is exactly the word for the way she walked. She took these phony hesitant steps and had her shoulders hunched up almost imperceptibly as if there were a slight draft in the room. She had shifted her smile to a pained-looking simper that was probably supposed to pass as demure, but instead looked as if she were wincing from a toothache.

"That's it, that's it, pretty," Hawkins encouraged. "Now when you get to the end of that runway, what?"

She turned her hands out to the side and very tentatively touched each foot behind the other, two of the slightest and sweetest dips you could imagine.

"The curtsy, that's right, my lovely. Perfectly executed, as well." He looked over at me as if daring me to comment.

I was speechless.

"Now, quickly, your performing dress. Hurry." And then he said to me, "Come in here for a second."

He opened a door off his pageant room and revealed a complete, one-station-and-sink beauty parlor. "Hot oil treatment: twenty minutes. What do you say?"

Among the things I'd sworn I would do before letting this man anywhere near my scalp were: eating lye, wearing a see-through blouse to a Cardinals game, having sex with various animals, calling a talk radio show, eating a whole array of putrefied foods.

But, I had this blind date coming.

The worst part was having my head back in the sink while Hawkins snagged his fingers through my hair with the shampoo and said things about rat's nests and the Bride of Frankenstein. He was stronger than I would have suspected. I was ow-ing and crying and struggling against him. Sister DeAngeles had me pinned down so tight I could barely catch a breath.

"I'll comb this nappy mess out after the oil has a chance to tame its ass," he said. He slathered a tube of goo into my hair and set me under a drier to cook.

Being under the drier wasn't so bad, particularly since it kept me from having to listen to today's renditions of "Interminable." I found I was actually quite comforted, sitting there with the warm air swirling around my ears. The goo had melted, and I had the same sort of feeling you get when you put a cake in the oven: that there was some sort of magical chemistry going on, except that in this case the magic was happening on top of my head.

The experience was more than nice, really. I felt wonderful. I thought about how I had never had time to do this in my life; to sit back and let someone massage things into my scalp. I went to one of those salons—up on Broadway—where they ran you in and out like cattle. That's what I liked, it was quick. Frankly, I'd never had much done to my hair. I usually just had the scraggly ends trimmed up and a hot comb run through.

I had always envied Katrina. Sister liked to spend money at the day spa, and she'd tell me how she would lie there and let someone do her nails and do her feet and put six or seven different kinds of treatments on her face. Later, another attendant would come and massage her to a sound sleep. The process always sounded good, but where was there time in my life for something like that? There were always things to do: meetings to run, pitches to make, problems to ignore. I decided to let myself enjoy this pampering while I had it. I drifted away for just a moment, feeling a warm greasy trickle down my neck. Then Hawkins came and unwrapped me from the drier.

"Weeeeell," he said, lifting up a hank of hair. He ran an electric pressing comb quickly through each section. Once.

"That will have to do for today," he pronounced. He spun me around to the mirror.

I was festooned with shiny black banana curls. The ribbons cascaded around my head like party decorations.

"Fool," I hit at him. "You gave me LaToya Jackson hair!"

"Hands! Hands!" he said, batting mine away. "What you need now is a brush out and a style."

I reached for some utensils. "Start brushing and start styling," I said.

"Ain't got time for you today. Got my Miss St. Louis/ America coming. She make that fish Vanessa Williams look like dog doo-doo."

"You expect me to go out there looking like this?"

"Girlfriend, it's a hell of a lot better than what you looked like coming in. When you let the cat suck on your head as long as you did, can't even someone like me fix it overnight." He gathered my hair up in an off-center ponytail at the top of the back of my head. "Cute," he said. "Now, brush it out tonight. Don't wash it. Tell your mama I said to comb some VO5 through it Friday morning, and I want your ass in this chair Saturday morning, 9:15. I won't wait, neither."

He stuck his hand out. "Fifteen will be fine."

Once again, there had been a reason for my mother's (unknown to her) generosity.

I stuffed the ponytail and all its flashy tendrils back up in the baseball cap. I just wasn't sure the hair suited me—or anyone else, for that matter, save the members of a certain extraordinarily wealthy California clan. I wanted it covered, and also, I had fallen in love with my new lid. It was jaunty, and riding around St. Louis with a Cardinals cap gave you a certain caché in some circles. I signaled my sister and headed for the door.

Ciara was in some sort of benign seething mode where every couple of minutes she would look over at me and ex-hale harshly through her teeth. I had stopped trying to make conversation with her. Some days when we rode in the car she would put a hand up by her face to hide from me, and we always had battles over the volume and station on the radio. I would end those by rolling down the windows so the music could not be heard anyway. She liked her air conditioning so much that she usually relented, on the volume at least.

A little advice for free: Always go with your first instincts. But it felt unnatural to me to be riding around in the car every afternoon with my sister and not to be at least making small talk with her. What was the harm in that? I would catch her out of the corner of my eye, sitting over there, glowering, and doing everything in her power to get under my skin. What an awful lot of energy she must have been using to maintain that level of anger and to radiate such bad vibes. Once again I felt sorry for her.

I'll extend another hand, I thought. I'll be the adult. I could meet her on common ground. I would ask her about a subject no teenager could resist.

"I need to pick out a dress. Any suggestions where?" I asked her. I did it casually, a neutral smile on my face.

"They have one of those fat girl shops at the Galleria. They might have something that fit you."

An act of sheer will kept me from steering the car into oncoming traffic. That, and the realization that, being on the side closest to the car that would hit us, I would be the one dead or maimed. She would live to waltz her way down some runway, waving at her adoring fans.

"Well. I guess we'll go to Crestwood, then."

"I guess we'll go to Crestwood, then," she mocked me.

She hopped out of the car while it was still rolling. I didn't even bother to arrange a place for us to meet. If I was lucky she would be sucked up by space aliens and never be heard from again. Then I thought about my poor mother and how heartbroken she'd be. I tried to imagine a fate that might befall my sister that wouldn't cause my mother too much pain. The best I could come up with was that she would be spotted by talent scouts for a touring company of *The Wiz* and become one of those children who live on the road with tutors and guardians. She'd be happily out of our hair for years.

Then I remembered her singing voice. We were stuck with her forever. Not even gypsies would steal this wench.

At Famous Barr I found a flowing and colorful sundress with a high waist and a round neckline that showed off a bit of my cleavage. Though it was a little precious, it fit and had been marked down for summer clearance. I went out and explored the mall.

When I was growing up, Crestwood was a mismatched suburban shopping district with a collection of stores gathered around the Famous on one side of the street and the Stix on the other side. Now Stix was Dillard's, and the whole mess had been gathered together under one long narrow roof. And while it was now shut away from the heat and the rain, the whole thing, even with its updated facades and neon brightness, had a faded and tattered feeling about it. Crestwood was filled that day with herds of wandering teenagers, idle and eager-looking, wearing those same sharp-colored outfits Ciara and her little friends wore. I, too, wandered down the mall, scanning the crowd for her familiar, round, and hateful face.

I felt a troubling uneasiness that I quickly recognized as being caused by false familiarity; the sensation of having been here before, though I knew that it couldn't be true. There was the Gap and Casual Corner and Nine West. I could have been in Rosedale or Brookdale or the Mall of America, or probably any other mall in the country. The feeling was both disturbing and comforting. Crazy people, we're not too big on surprises. We don't like it if you change the routine or throw in too much information. We like game shows. (It took many of us a long time to recover from the day when they would no longer let you buy prizes on *Wheel of Fortune*. I'd like the lawn furniture for $650, please. And this business about giving you the R, S, T, L, N, and E for free, well, that was the end of civilization as we have known it.) I imagined being able to stroll into the Limited and walk right to the fall jackets without having to deal with a toxic sales clerk. I enjoyed knowing that you could go anywhere in the world and still feel right at home.

I wandered down a stairwell into the food pit. I love a shopping mall food pit: the yellow sharp smell of greasy fried foods, the sounds of guilty pleasure as families huddle together at tables shiny with spills, enjoying foods that even the children know probably shouldn't be eaten. There was the hot dog stand and the stir-fry stand and the taco stand and the pizza stand.

There was Ciara stuffing a giant cheeseburger into her mouth. I hid behind a support column, mesmerized.

She tore at the sandwich, removing enormous jagged hunks of meat and bread and toppings with each bite. The bun was glassy with grease. She picked up whole fistfuls of French fries and stuffed them in her mouth and then washed a wave of Coke into it to flush the mess down. I was thrilled and repelled, and I didn't have the foggiest idea of what I was supposed to do. Should I go over there and make some comment? And, if so, what kind? Sarcastic? Supportive? Should I threaten to turn her in? *Should* I turn her in?

She made quick work of the burger and the rest of her meal. I chose to stay hidden behind the post. She dumped her garbage and stacked her tray and I followed her as she headed up an escalator. She got off at the top and waited for me there with her arms crossed. Rising toward her I had the illusion that she was huge and ready to throw me back down into the pit. I stepped back into an older woman behind me.

"Spying on me," Ciara said, her face set with rigid threat.

"I was looking for you," I said. I waited until I had crested the top and had regained the head's advantage in height I had on her.

"We should start home," I said.

"Why? So you can run in there and tell your mommy what I did? You can't wait to get me in trouble."

"It's getting late, Ciara."

I turned and started walking toward the car, not caring if she followed. When I peered back she was just over my left shoulder, huffing with rage.

"You should mind your own business," she panted. "Just leave me alone." She choked on the last words, tears brimming from her eyes.

I turned around, too abruptly, I guess. She stopped just short of me, backing up as if she thought I was going to hit her. "Look," I said. "I don't know why you're upset. I haven't done anything to hurt you. Let's just go home and try to have a nice evening. For mother's sake."

"I hate you," she sobbed. I turned and continued to the car. She was making a horrible scene, and she had dragged me right into the middle of it.

She sobbed all the way home, that bruised-sounding, desperate kind of crying, almost as if something inside was being torn open. We pulled into the driveway and I reached over and grabbed her arm and squeezed it tight.

"That's enough. Do you hear me? Enough."

She snatched her arm away but gave up on the crocodile tears.

"You need a Kleenex," I said. I reached in my purse and dug out a tissue. "Wipe some of that grease from around your mouth while you're at it."

Our dinner guests arrived at 6:30, Anthony along with Aunt Ernestine. Since she was my play aunt, I guessed that made us play cousins or some other kind of make-believe relatives. He shook my hand eagerly and called me by my name.

"I remember you when you were just a little thing," he said, and I wondered which dimension of little he was talking about. There was nothing the slightest bit familiar about him to me.

We repaired to the patio like the elegant people my mother imagined we were. She had entered a new phase of entertaining, going from the sort of woman who, when I was in high school, threw potluck buffets for her boisterous club ladies, wading around the house barefoot and casual, to having embraced the quiet elegance of a candlelit supper in the garden. Mother wore a white blouse with a frilly bib and a pair of crisp pleated gray slacks that must have belonged to one of her suits.

Ciara had called up a friend and disappeared for the evening. I was glad she was gone. With the hustle and bustle of getting the food prepared, there hadn't been time to talk about what I had seen. I had used the time to reflect, and in that time I knew that what I had seen was sadder and more sinister than my first take on it. I wondered if maybe Ciara was as upset as she was because in my finding her when I did, I had prevented her from going into the bathroom and vomiting her secret lunch out of her system. She had eaten in that greedy, pleasureless way of other bulimics I know. I wouldn't be surprised if she were a bulimic, but even if that were not the case, the episode spoke to me of some deep hurt inside the child, and I knew that I would have to find a way to talk about it with our mother.

Reina removed the marinated chicken from the barbecue and invited her guests to the table. Her timing was perfect. We had been standing around the patio, as if posed for one of those slick cigarette ads in *Ebony,* and we had about run out of small talk. Under the best of circumstances I find it trying to stand around with a glass of wine and make nice with people I don't really know. I always expect that there is going to be a test at the end of the evening—that I'm going to be expected to remember the names and quirky bad habits of children I've never seen, or the punch line to someone's wry anecdote about a trip to Door County. I myself had no anecdotes about Door County that I wished to tell these people, and had found it immensely difficult to explain my presence in St. Louis to strangers when I'd never even explained it to my mother.

"I just popped into town for a little visit," I said, sounding as optimistic and confident as a woman with LaToya Jackson hair could sound. My mother had insisted that my Cardinals cap did not match my new dress. She had replotted the pony-tail so that it was even more rakishly off center and had fixed it tight with a silver band of some kind that she must have borrowed from Ciara.

"Pathetic," had been Ciara's comment about me as she left for her friend's house.

Although I might have looked silly, I felt myself loosening up. Perhaps it was the wine, or maybe it was all the coerced goodwill we are forced to put out at social occasions. I was probably like a sorority sister during rush week, basking in bonhomie and the fervent desire to like everyone and to have everyone like me right back. I sat back, relishing my meal, and grinning at Aunt Ernestine, who was shamelessly bragging to my mother about her nephew's accomplishments. Apparently he had won a Nobel Prize, been appointed to the Supreme Court, and single-handedly landed a crippled 747.

In my good mood I only mildly dreaded Reina's recipro-cating with stories of my own good fortunes, whatever those were. A creeping annoyance began when she was not forth-coming. I told myself that she had grown out of this phase, but I remembered how shamelessly she bragged about Ciara to me. Perhaps she was protecting me, respecting my privacy, and for the most part I didn't care. I was busy out of one corner of my eye, looking at this Anthony.

Anthony was on my right. He had an "aw-shucks-folks-it-was-nothing" grin on his face as his auntie sang his praises.

He'd tell her to stop, protesting a little too much for my taste. He was one of those large men, tall, and round in the middle but tapered toward the ends, like Roosevelt Greer, a football player my father used to like; or like the comedian Sinbad. He resembled Sinbad, too, in a way, but he wasn't a redhead. He had widow's peaks on both sides of his big square head, fair skin with a big mustache, and the shy reticence of a lot of large men.

"Deneen works in advertising," said my mother, finally. I seethed. Mother's usual infomercial for family members had been edited with a meat ax and all that was left was that nugget of gristle.

"Advertising, yes," Anthony said and grinned. "She mentioned that." He stabbed another chicken breast off the platter. He'd eaten two already—not that I was counting. I was sort of hoping there'd be enough left for a sandwich, or six. The chicken was really good. All the food was. Reina had prepared one of those delicious healthy meals that the nutrition experts on the talk shows were always telling you about, ones that were succulent and also low in fat and calories. "The way we should eat everyday."

What those quacks didn't tell you was fixing this chow would take, as it had taken my mother, all day and some of the previous evening. Even so, she was sitting over there as coolly as if the dinner had been a mere flick of the wrist, beaming at the way we were shoveling down the wonderful cold couscous with currants and mushrooms she had prepared.

Somebody's beeper went off. Since I had for the most part been disconnected from the world of urgent matters, I was pretty sure it wasn't mine.

"Damn that hospital," Aunt Ernestine said. "Let me use

your phone." She was a psychiatric social worker. Apparently this was her night to be on call.

Reina escorted her into the house, leaving Anthony and me to sit there chewing and giggling nervously. You know those obnoxious TV situation comedy episodes—like on *The Love Boat*—where the couple keeps gazing at each other and then looking away, embarrassed. Well, we did that. Until I got tired of it. It's hard to know what to do with your eyes when you are crazy, because you don't want people to know there's anything wrong with you. Staring out into space is a dead giveaway, as is shifting your eyes around recklessly from one object to the next. Staring fixedly at someone is as much an invitation to have them call the men with the coats with the wraparound Velcro sleeves.

So I looked down at my plate.

"Good food," he said.

"My mother was always a good cook."

"Yeah, she sure is that."

The thing is, I was so incredibly turned on, my panties were wet. It had been almost three weeks since I had seen a man. A good-looking black man. The closest I'd come had been Montel or a few brothers they'd had on the talk shows, but those men mostly had captions under their faces that said things such as "Thinks All Black Women are Sluts" and "Traded His Baby for a Down Payment on a Car." Here was a real man. From what I heard, a very successful and world-famous one. I took another chicken leg, and prayed that the Lord would give me strength.

"We have to run, Anthony," Aunt Ernestine said. "They've got an emergency on the ward, and they can't find anyone else."

"Let him finish his dinner," I said. "I'll drive him home."

I insisted, and I prevailed, and we finished our meal, and then I did what I said I would. I drove him home.

And then—in a manner of speaking—he drove me home.

Thinking back to that evening, I hope I was subtle. I think I was.

I don't recall saying anything too vulgar. Anything like, "Let's go big boy. Show Mama your meat." I didn't say anything about jelly rolls or stirring my pot. Nothing like that. There is the possibility, however, that I was marginally trashy, in a Mary Poppins-on-her-honeymoon sort of way.

I remember asking where he was staying, and Anthony saying he had borrowed a place for a few weeks from a friend who was out of town. "How convenient," a voice inside my head said, in the tone of voice used by the Church Lady on *Saturday Night Live* reruns. The apartment was down near Washington U. I pulled up by the building and I believe— I'd have to double-check this—that I got out of the car and walked to the apartment without being asked.

To make a long story short, I found myself inside the apartment and then I found myself inside the bedroom of the apartment, and then I found myself with my legs wrapped around his back with him inside of me, screaming out various things that might have been mistaken for directions to a road crew. Here is the report I wrote for my journal:

| | |
|---|---|
| *Name:* | Anthony K. Jardine, Jr. |
| *Date of birth:* | Mid-twentieth century |
| *Height:* | 6′ 3″ |
| *Weight:* | 235 lbs. |
| *Occupation:* | Legend in his own time |
| *Cologne:* | Paco Rabanne |
| *Organ:* | All beef and plenty of it |

*Performance:* Well-above-average

*Comments:* Not bad. Not bad at all. I'd like to line me up about six or seven of these Tonys, maybe one for every night of the week. Or maybe just two of them. Alternate nights. Yeah, that's the plan.

*Recommendation:*

Under which I drew a whole page of happy faces with big toothy grins.

I wandered away about midnight. He was sound asleep.

I figured if I got home before one, I'd stand a pretty good chance of being able to give a credible explanation to my mother. I told her we had stopped at a club and run into some old friends of his, and one of mine as well. She was pleased that we had had such a lovely evening. The best laid plans, I guess.

He called me once before he went back to Des Moines or Milwaukee or one of those other places there on the top of the weather map, but I didn't talk to him.

That night I put away my journal and fell into a sound sleep. I dreamed I was Katrina, but instead of sitting at a desk with a modern phone module, I was seated behind one of those old-fashioned switchboards with the fat wires you punch into holes to connect the calls. I was wearing Katrina's favorite nightclubbing outfit: a raspberry, butter-soft leather jumpsuit with a zipper that starts at the crotch. I had a giant Afro and the phones were all ringing at the same time. I plugged away until everyone was connected, and then, just like Katrina, I leaned back in the chair and filed my nails.

# Nine

Hawkins had a hank of my hair wrapped around his fist. I was pulling away from him as hard as I could.

"Ow! Stop!"

"You better sit still, heifer, fore I snatch this hair out your head."

He wrestled me around and ran a comb through the handful of hair he held. I heard popping and ripping. I slapped at him and twisted in the chair.

"Yeah, you gonna be beautiful if it kills you," he said.

It was Saturday morning and this sort of thing had been going on for about forty minutes. I can't even begin to tell you why I kept the appointment, but I'm sure you can imagine. Good old Deneen, rising out of bed and driving herself halfway across the county like some sort of zombie.

At least I didn't have Ciara with me. Hawkins believed it was bad luck to see his girls on the day of the competition. He would meet her backstage at the pageant site, carrying a kit the size of a steamer trunk.

When I left the house, Ciara and my mother were at the beginning of what I could see was going to be a long and difficult day. Ciara was cranky with nerves, and my mother, in trying to be calming and helpful, had instead become officious and annoying. She had been following my sister around

the house making suggestions about what she should do
with her morning and about which outfit she should wear to
arrive at the theater where the pageant would be held. I remembered my mother on prom nights and on other such
occasions when there was extra energy in the air. She would
drive me crazy, sticking her head in the door every fifteen
minutes, looking over my shoulder in the mirror, generally
being a pest. I thought about dear, sweet Ciara getting
a whole day full of that familiar obnoxious treatment and
experienced a rush of delicious glee.

"Don't even tell me," Hawkins says to me. "You get your
hair cut at one of them price-chopper places."

"I have never been in one of those places in my life," I said.
He yanked me back around to face the mirror and I swatted at
his fat thigh. "I'll have you know I patronize one of the finest
salons in the city of Minneapolis."

"And probably the cheapest-ass stylist up in there. What
you want me to do with this rat's nest anyway?"

"I don't know. Do . . . something. Give me a . . . a look, or
something." I was feeling reckless. And I had something on
my mind. It was my mother's fault.

"You want I should give you a Patti LaBelle? A Jasmine
Guy? You'd look good in a Diana Ross, but I'd have to weave
some hair into this short shit."

"How about a Naomi Campbell, you know, the model?"
I asked.

"That skinny old thing? You can't go there." And then he
said, "You leave it to me." He started pressing and trimming
my hair into the tailored-looking style they sometimes gave
her in the magazines.

It was my mother's fault that this fever had been planted
in my brain and that I was having these unhealthy thoughts

and having my hair done by a crazy man in a townhouse in Clayton.

"Easy with that hot comb," I said. Hawkins stood back from me with his hands on his hips and shook the appliance at me in a threatening way.

"Keep messing, see don't I hurt you with it."

An idea had been simmering since the dinner party. What would be the harm in meeting some more men? Like that Anthony. My mother had thought it a good idea, although she probably hadn't counted on the after-dinner refreshments that he and I had shared. Surely the city of St. Louis was bursting at the seams with more adorable black men who were just waiting for a fine sister to pass a little time with. It was just a matter of going out and finding them. I figured I'd start at the damn beauty pageant. Hell, I had to get some enjoyment out of it. And I figured if I was going to pursue this new hobby, a beauty treatment from Hawkins wouldn't hurt as a first step. So there I was getting the shit yanked out of my hair.

"Stop that!" I screamed. He was pulling through my hair fast with his fingers.

"For a person with good-quality hair there is no excuse for this mess. None at all."

"I'm a busy professional woman."

"How long do it take to run a comb through your hair?"

"I've been sick," I said, abruptly, not wishing to continue this discussion. But he was stuck on it. Maybe that's what he did all day: sit in this townhouse and fuss at women about their hair.

"Look at your sister. She has beautiful hair." He made the first syllable of the word beautiful into a three-measure opera.

"It should be green to match her attitude," I mumbled.

"Say what?"

"Nothing." I diverted the topic. "Tell me how you got into the pageant business."

"Humph," he said. "A person don't get into the beauty pageant business. The beauty pageant business comes to you."

"So people just started showing up over here to let you make them into queens?"

And where better?

He looked at me over his glasses again. One of these days I was gonna snatch those glasses right off his face.

"Don't look at me like that," I said.

"Bend your head forward," he said, pushing it down as if it were some kind of cabbage. "Let me work on this nappy mess back in the kitchen. You won't have to see me looking at you at all."

He started telling me about how he worked at a salon over on Clayton Road that was *the* place to get your hair done back in the seventies. He started out as a "shampoo girl"—his words, not mine—and worked his way up until he had as much business as the owner. Eventually he bought into the business, bought half of it. He said that he and Michael, his partner, also had "a thing," "if you know what I mean," and for about five years they'd prospered, had a wonderful business and a terrific life together.

"These rich things you see out here, these black lawyers and so forth, all them football players' and baseball players' wives, I did all them bitches."

Things went okay until Michael got "it." "You know." Hawkins wouldn't say the word. I don't think I ever heard him say it.

"I have lost so many," he said. He stroked at my hair more gently for a few moments.

"I didn't care about no stanky old business no more," he said. "I found some buyers and took the money and bought this townhouse. I kept a lot of my old customers. I do them right here in the basement.

"You know how hard it is for a black woman find some-body knows something about her hair," he said, and then added, "Or maybe you wouldn't know."

Bitch.

He never did tell me how he got into the business of grooming girls for beauty contests, but if you think about it, it's sort of a natural spin-off. A desperate mother with some ugly duckling of a daughter signs her up in order to build up her self-esteem. She brings her to Hawkins for a makeover. Word spreads.

Eventually I would learn that Hawkins was competing to control the Missouri franchise for the All American Dream Dolls Pageant, and that a winning contestant was a big plus in the competition. He had selected Ciara to be his ticket to the big time. Hawkins flipped and snipped the last bit of hair, and spun me around in front of the mirror so I could see myself. The do was cute. The man sure could work a pair of scissors.

"Next time we gonna try some Phylicia Rashad on this hair," he said.

"And what makes you think there's gonna be a next time?"

"Your ass is in this chair next Saturday morning, or I come out there and snatch it out of bed." He held his hand out.

I handed him the new twenty I had "borrowed" from my mother that morning. That made either forty or sixty. I would have to update my records one of these times.

In the car I was momentarily diverted from my plans for the evening because I was thinking about what had happened to poor Hawkins's lover, and then I was obsessing about it, and I couldn't get it out of my head. I had to go home and write a letter.

> *Dear Calvin:*
>
> *As a woman who was more intimately involved with you than I myself would even like to consider, and in light of the honest but doggish confession you made on our trip to Door County, Wisconsin, I think I have the right to ask for a full accounting as to where your dick has been for the past fifteen years. Please respond to this letter with a full list of names, dates, and specific sexual acts, and the complete medical history of all those concerned. (Photocopies acceptable.) Fail to comply with this request at your own risk of life and limb.*
>
> *Litigiously,*
> *Deneen*

I saved that letter but I didn't send it. I probably should have. Or called him. Perhaps it was that he had just come up with this notion that he liked men. And then again maybe he dropped me off from our dates and went and had anonymous sex in Loring Park. We did it, I would say, somewhere between eighty and ninety times. And what about all that kissing and other junk? I kicked myself for not having paid attention to the 800 numbers that they give out on television for the Center for Disease Control.

I calmed down a bit when I remembered that Calvin had told me I was his second and that it had been a long time between number one and me. And as much as I hated him at the moment, I knew it was true. It wasn't exactly the sort of thing a man would brag about, considering that if you asked most black men where you were in the queue, they gave you a number somewhere in the low ten thousands.

Which made me think about Anthony. Just a few minutes ago our encounter had seemed so easy and harmless. Not until that very moment did I recognize the potential dangers of my combination of restricted id and an unquenchable desire for sensual satisfaction. Despite the fact that—and my superrationalizing mind kept emphasizing this—my mother had practically forced him down my throat (metaphorically speaking, to be sure), I could have been at real risk. Good thing Anthony had been a true gentleman. He had a whole cache of those cute little foil packets. (At first I thought we were going to be taking a time out to share an Alka-Seltzer. We had both overeaten at my mother's house.)

I know what you're thinking: how irresponsible and casual you are, Deneen. But I'm not, really. Not always.

Back there at the beginning of the crisis when nobody believed straight people could get it, I was more worried about figuring out which day of the month it was, and pretending that a cursory examination of a man's fire-fighting equipment was enough to tell me whether he had herpes. Then I got scared and I stopped doing it at all for about two years, and then I would only do it with somebody I had known for at least a couple of months, and then came Calvin.

I sat there and another tiny alarm had been fully installed, a sign of health maybe: to know enough to worry about something and to actually spend time doing so. I sat there in my mother's study with the latest letter to Calvin, and I thought, if I've got it, that's terrible, but there's nothing I can do to un-get it, and if I don't have it I don't want it, so the best thing that I as an individual can do is everything in my power to stop this monster right in its tracks.

With resolute good cheer and an optimistic eye toward my plans for the evening—and many evenings beyond this one if I had anything to do with it—I grabbed my mother's car keys and another twenty-dollar bill. I put on a pair of dark glasses and drove to a Walgreen's in Overland where nobody knows us and I invested in condoms. I got an assortment. Could it hurt to give a fella a choice or two over the course of an evening?

When I came in from the store I passed Ciara walking toward the stairs. Her face looked like a caricature of her face. Her eyes were wide open and her nose was pinched and her mouth was drawn back into a hideous grimace.

"What's the matter with her?" I asked my mother. Mother was sitting at the kitchen table, sipping at her mug and massaging a temple.

"I upset her. She's trying not to cry. She doesn't want to be puffy or red-eyed tonight."

"I can tell that this whole pageant mess has both you and her—"

"Deneen. Don't. Don't start. I cannot abide today one more disagreeable word from any of the women in this house."

"Sorry," I said.

She looked me over, her eyes droopy and flat with tension. "Hawkins did a good job on your hair," she said.

"I guess so. Thanks. He's a character, though."

"He is that," she said, disgorging the tiniest of laughs.

"Is he all right?" I asked.

"How do you mean?"

"You know? Is he sick? You know?"

Like Hawkins, I also didn't appear to be able to say the word.

"Oh." She looked down at her mug and then back up at me. "Lord, I hope he's okay, bless his heart. People say things. A couple of the girls quit going to him." She swirled the dregs around the bottom of her cup. "We have got to pray for folks, Deneen. For our folks, in particular." She rinsed out her mug and went to get dressed for the evening.

Ciara started smiling even before we loaded her into the car. I thought at the time that she was like an athlete, psyching herself up before the big game, but I now know that she had smeared Vaseline on her teeth to facilitate a big juicy grin. She was, in fact, unable to keep her lips together.

We dropped her off backstage with Hawkins and I went out front to get to work on my new hobby. The auditorium was filled with what was surely the most motley collection of grandmas and grandpas and parents and siblings you'd ever want to see. That's what they had to be. Who would plunk down five dollars of hard earned cash to watch some ugly children you didn't know prance around on stage for a couple of hours? There must have been quite a few Catholics there— it seemed to be the kind of activity that attracted families who had at least a half-dozen children, and apparently they had all been fed sugar and amphetamine sandwiches before coming out for a pleasant evening in the theater. And rarely did a person see in the same place gathered together so much discount-store couture. All the women were dressed in what the psychotic buyers at the various Marts decide American women want to wear—badly constructed separates made from cheap material. Prints that one wouldn't choose for a dish towel, let alone a blouse. There were any number of haggard-looking dads who didn't seem too pleased to be trying to keep the rest of the brats in line while mom was backstage teasing out the princess's hair. For my purposes, the pickings were pretty slim.

I caught a look at one promising candidate. He was tall and black (neither of which are a prerequisite, but don't hurt none either), and he had hanging on his fine frame the sharpest suit I had seen since Blair Underwood's on *LA Law*. There didn't seem to be anyone around him, either, no crumb-snatchers and no woman hooked on his arm. I thought to myself, maybe I'll just stroll up that way and check out the lobby or something. And so I did.

He was every bit as delicious up close, let me tell you.

Having gotten myself to the lobby, I was going to have to figure out a way to get back to my seat without seeming trashy. I hung around the atrium for a few minutes, reading the posters on the kiosks. Ciara had had to be there an hour before curtain to get ready, so there was plenty of time. We had come in a stage entrance, so I had not seen this area. Mobs of girls—wannabees, I figured—thundered through the lobby. They clustered at tables under a banner announcing "The All American Dream Dolls Boutique." They were cooing and calling out to each other and flashing money around. There were so many of them that I couldn't get close enough to the table to see what all the commotion was about. I couldn't imagine they were buying programs, and I honestly didn't care that much what they were doing. I wanted to get another look at that man!

I popped my head back inside the door. He wasn't there anymore. I stuck it in further, and when there was no sign of him I started down the aisle.

"Hi." Over my left shoulder. I jumped.

"Didn't mean to startle you," he said. "Mark Layton." He extended his hand.

When I could remember what it was, I told him mine.

"Aren't you contestants supposed to be backstage?" he asked.

I slapped at his arm and called him silly. I asked, "So, do you have a daughter in the pageant. Or what?"

"I'm an 'or what,'" he said. He had one of those deep musical voices that sounded like honey and butter melting into warm bread.

"Oh. So your wife is in the pageant," I said.

He laughed. "You're funny. I like a funny woman. I'm here on business."

What kind of business, I wondered, would a good-looking forty-year-old man be doing at a preteen beauty pageant on a Saturday night? Two chances to one it would be something I didn't want to know about. The lights in the auditorium blinked three times.

"Can I show you to your seat?" he asked.

"Sure." I said. I said it the way one of those bimbos in a gangster movie would.

I have to tell you that this was a new experience for me. Back in Minnesota I was not exactly what you would call a man magnet. I don't want you to have the impression that I didn't have dates and that men didn't approach me, but it usually took a ton of work and days of planning and preparation, and it didn't hurt to have Katrina around, priming the pump, as it were. She knew all the tricks and had a half a dozen dudes dangling on the line at any given moment. Even so, some nights we'd sit at these clubs, me and Katrina with her beautiful self, and it would be like we were invisible, men crawling all over each other to get to these tables of Minnesota blondes. I could bat my eyes and flirt and walk past a man six or seven times and he wouldn't even see me. Here in Missouri, I look at a man once, and I got him.

Katrina says it's about vibrations. She says that there is

a reason why we call men dogs, because—like dogs—men can sniff out and tell when a woman's ready to party. She always accuses me of sending out the wrong signals. Very few men in clubs have put on a suit and their best aftershave because they want to have intelligent conversation, she says, and I had best switch off the smart-girl vibes and turn on the wild woman ones. Apparently the new folks who have taken over the apartments upstairs have flipped the switches on their own. I'd just caught me the finest nigger in the house, and didn't have to show him no thigh or nothing.

We squeezed in past my mother and he took the seat on the other side of me. I introduced her and she gave me her just-how-trashy-are-you? look. I'd remind her later whose idea this had been in the first place.

The lights dimmed. There was a drumroll.

"Here we go," he said, rubbing his hands together, and I thought, for a businessman he sure was eager about this.

An unusually brassy version of "Everything's Coming Up Roses" started playing, and after a loud and unnecessarily enthusiastic announcement telling those of us who might have wandered in there by mistake that this was the "Missouri State All American Dream Dolls Pageant," the curtain went up, and there on the stage were three dozen or so girls. They were all standing straight and tall and flashing their thousand-watt smiles. Mother pointed at Ciara and beamed.

The master of ceremonies was a local TV weatherman, of the type who has so much good cheer that you never believe the tornado is coming until your trailer is ripped from its concrete slab and deposited in a ravine. The music changed to a Muzak medley of such chirpy songs as "Thank Heaven for Little Girls," and "A Pretty Girl Is Like a Melody." One by one he called the girls' names and they stepped down the runway in their playsuits. There were some cute ones, but many had a serious problem of some kind, and more than a few were just pitiful. One girl had buck teeth that looked perpendicular to her mouth, and another girl had a charming face but the legs of a famine victim, absolutely lean and straight and not one hint of muscle.

My heart broke for these girls. The early teens are often not an attractive time in a young woman's life. Poor things: displayed up there like so many half-finished oil paintings, this one only partially sketched in, and the next one mostly all there but missing one critical element.

"Miss Amber LaVonne Clifton!" the announcer called.

"That's one of my girls," Mark said, as a mostly complete-looking blonde sashayed toward us wearing a denim jumper with a red and white blouse underneath. He applauded her with gusto.

Aha! A wolf in lamb's clothing. "I thought you said you didn't have any kids," I whispered, my careful preparations for the evening dissolving like so much hair spray.

He kept smiling and applauding. He leaned toward me. "They're not *mine*," he whispered. "I sponsor them. My business does."

"Oh," I said, as if something were clearer. It wasn't.

As the weatherman announced each girl's name a portion of the audience would erupt in wild cheers. The family contingent. The rest of us sat there, drumming our hands together lethargically. I realized that for my mother's sake I would have to help cheer on Ciara. There were only the two of us there for her.

A girl who had garnered a layer of pre-growth-spurt body fat waddled down the runway. The audience ooohed and aaahed as if they thought there were something particularly special about her. She smiled back at them, giving them a big, jiggly arm wave.

"She'll be in the top ten," Mark whispered. "The judges love spunk. This next one's mine, too."

"Misty Dawne Jackson!"

This girl was tall and beautiful, with long black hair, and she took that runway as if it were made for her. She'd put Tyra Banks to shame.

Mark was clearly less enthusiastic about her. "She was gonna be my winner," he whispered. "The damn gal went and grew tits on me."

I touched his arm sympathetically. "They'll do that," I said. He shook his head sadly.

"This next one's Hawkins DeAngeles's girl," he said. He sat up as if he were going to take notes.

"Ciara Renee Jones!"

"Damn! Check that girl out," Mark said through his clenched teeth. On the other side of me my mother beat her hands together harshly and screamed the words, "Go on, baby!"

I clapped.

"What's wrong with her?" I asked Mark.

"Look at her. She's a thoroughbred, a goddamn ringer."

"That girl?" I asked. That wench? My sister? Ciara was up there in her sailor suit strutting it just the way I'd watched her in Hawkins's basement, only, if possible, more cutely and seductively.

"She's a pro," Mark said. "If she's twelve, I'm thirteen."

"I'm fairly sure that girl is only twelve," I said, remembering her mosquito bites.

"She's the one to beat," he said, making a note in his program. "Damn that Hawkins."

Mark had three girls in the pageant. One of his, an unusual-looking olive-skinned girl with green eyes, made the top ten, as did, to my horror, you-know-who. He wrote something down about each girl as they paraded by in another outfit, or to deliver their "Why I Should Be the All American Dream Doll" speech. I had forgotten how easy it is to sound dumb when you are twelve. All the contestants spoke with that vacant-sounding brogue that was first associated with certain young women from the San Fernando Valley in California; the one that sounds as if the words are like stuck in the back of your throat. And every sentence is a question? and, please, please, please, English teachers of America: tell these girls that *really* is really not a very interesting adjective, and that it doesn't really prove your convictions to use it three times in the same sentence.

Mother kept excusing herself to go to the bathroom. She would come back and sit next to me wringing her hands and squirming in her chair.

"She's doing fine," I whispered to her.

"You think so? She's prettier than those other girls, isn't she?"

"Even if the judges don't agree."

She clutched my hand all through the performance of "Insoluble." Ciara actually got past the opening riff and wailed her way through the song. She had added these gestures I had never seen, including a waving, pleading hand during the bridge, and a shrug of the shoulders during the fake catch-in-the-throat deal. The wench even squeezed out a tear.

"Damn, damn, damn," Mark clapped.

The scary thing was, Ciara was far from the worst. Far from it. One of the competitors did one of those tap dance routines with batons, one that was all flailing arms and jumping up and down. Less a dance, it looked more like someone had set her on fire. Another young lady performed a really bizarre psychotic skit in which she played all the characters. She kept throwing on wigs and trying to assume different accents, French and British, I think. From what I could gather, some man in this play was trying to persuade some woman to go to a hotel with him. I thought it was great, though I believe I was the only one laughing at her jokes. She didn't win the pageant—her skit was entirely too sophisticated for this crowd. I was buoyed by the knowledge that I had just witnessed the birth of a great performance artist, and that someday quite soon I would read that she had won a grant from the National Endowment for the Arts.

The heavyset girl did a great job. She belted out a soulful rendition of the song, "Saving All My Love for You." She put me in mind of Janis Joplin, and I wondered where it was these chubby little white girls learned to sing the blues. The dress would do her in, though: blue chiffon. Chubby little white girls are not built for blue chiffon.

And Mark's girl knocked me out, ripping through one of those showy Tchaikovsky or Rachmaninoff numbers on the piano. This was a girl with real talent. I liked her smile, too. She was smiling from somewhere inside herself, I could tell, her lips parted slightly and a glow about her eyes. None of the face-peeling cringes of the rest of this crowd.

"The tenth runner-up," the emcee announced, starting down the list. The children were standing across the stage holding hands the same way the big girls did in Atlantic City.

How cruel, I thought, making those poor young women stand there and listen for their names. They should just shoot nine of them in the head and put the crown on the one left standing.

"The eighth runner-up:"

Despite myself, I clutched with excitement. Call her name, I kept wishing. Call her name. Get her out of there.

"Crystal Willow Finnagen."

It was the performance artist. I gave her a big hand.

"The fourth runner-up, and the winner of the complete set of 'All American Dream Dolls' storybooks:"

Come on, God, smite the wench. Do it for me.

It was the fat girl. We gave her a standing ovation. That left Ciara, Mark's girl, and a blonde who had done one of those spastic dance routines.

"Oh, Deneen. I can't take this," my mother said. "I think I'm having a heart attack. I didn't imagine." She grabbed my hand and held it up by her chest. I could feel her breathing deep and hard.

"It's almost over for her," I said. Come on, God. Nuke her.

And then it was down to Ciara and the spastic blonde. Mark had crumpled with disappointment. His girl had been pretty and bright, but someone—her Hawkins, maybe—had failed to notice that this was not a classical music crowd.

The weatherman made the compulsory "if for any reason speech" informing anyone who'd been in a cave that the first runner-up got to take over when the dirty pictures of the winner got published, and then he said, "The first runner-up, and the winner of the complete 'All American Dream Dolls doll collection' is," and while I was trying to imagine what on earth dream dolls were, he called the blonde's name, Ciara and my mother started screaming, and once again I had called out to heaven only to get the answering machine.

"You know her?" Mark asked. I gave him my annoyed look. Here, a woman I had introduced him to quite clearly as my mother had spent the past two hours whooping with joy every time Ciara walked on stage. Did he think we were like gamblers, come in to plop our hopes down on the best-looking horse? Did I know her?

"It's my sister," I said. The witch. We were all standing there applauding her as she strolled down the runway, holding her scepter and wearing her crown, tears dripping from her jawbone. Crocodile tears.

"Then you know Hawkins DeAngeles," he said, and I thought his expression was awfully angry and suspicious.

"We've met," I said, "recently. I just dropped into town a few weeks ago. I'm headed home soon." I raised my eyebrows the way Groucho Marx does. Shameless, I know, but I wasn't letting this little incident on the runway ruin my chances for a fun evening; limited prospects being a serious concern in this audience.

"That man," he said, blowing air through his teeth. We kept applauding and smiling, all of us in the audience, and Miss Ciara was waving and smiling back. Get her off already, I thought.

She strolled back to the emcee who signaled the other girls to come down and congratulate her. If that wasn't the most phony moment. Name a grudge nastier than a twelve-year-old-girl grudge. As if any of those others wanted to do anything but kill my sister. If we were lucky one of them would.

I followed Mother down to the stage. Mark followed me.

"But I've only met Hawkins a couple of times," I said. Not too desperate, was I? "Oh, and he did my hair."

He stopped and gave my new do the once over. "That's his work, all right. Where did you say you were from?"

"Minneapolis, actually. Me and Mary Richards," and I gave him my goofiest Mary Tyler Moore simper.

The losers—which is what I believe they are called—were wandering away quickly. One of the dads had one of the girls by the arm and was warning her sternly that she had better do better next time. Across the stage another loser smiled bravely as her parents congratulated her on her performance. A boy who appeared to be her younger brother had been saddled with the makeup kit. He ran around the stage hyper-actively, buzzing the other contestants and strafing his sister with the words, "You're ugly!"

My mother caught Ciara just before four men in suits surrounded her and pronounced her "perfect." Mother gave her a big hug and the men placed her on a throne, which I think was really just a wicker chair covered in aluminum foil. Before the pictures started, Hawkins rushed over with a brush.

"There he is," Mark said. He strode over to Ciara, now being touched up by her mentor. "So, you got yourself a winner," he said.

"Hallelujah. Shame about them spindly little things you had up there. Have to throw them back, I guess."

"If a man said that to me, I'd hit him."

Hawkins did a fake gasp. "Sticks and stones may break my bones," he said.

"I'm getting this franchise. Your sissy ass will be out in the cold."

A sigh from Hawkins. "Well, a girl can dream, can't she? Smile, princess," he ordered Ciara.

Mark stomped off, mumbling under his breath. I didn't get a phone number or nothing.

Ciara sat in the front seat on the way home, talking ninety miles an hour.

"The nationals, I made the nationals. We're going to Las Vegas! Hawkins is, like, losing his mind. We have to get all new things ready. Oh my God. I can't believe it. And like now I have the full collection. The dolls and the books and everything."

And me? I was like sitting in the back seat with "the full collection." There were tapes and clothes and furniture, like packaged in these really like old-fashioned looking packages, with tasteful tones of gray and script-ish looking fonts, which like anyone at my agency could tell you was like never how packages looked ever back in the olden days. I was like sitting back there with this stuff, and I was really really really grossed out.

"Aren't you proud of your sister?" my mother asked.

"I guess so," I said. It was late and I was tired, and I hadn't gotten the phone number of one of the cutest brothers I'd seen in a long time.

Ciara went to her room right away with all her new things. I went to the kitchen to get myself some Very Berry Hi-C.

"It wouldn't have killed you to say something to her," Mother said. She slammed her bag into a chair. At least it sounded like a slam to me.

I shrugged.

"I don't like that attitude," she said. She ran a hand across my waist as she walked past me going to the refrigerator. It was gentle, but I could feel the hot currents of anger pumping from her fingers.

"Don't make a federal case out of it," I mumbled.

"What?" she said. "Don't you mumble at me. This is still my house."

"I said," I said forcefully, "Why are you making a big deal out of this. So, she walks across a stage and croaks out a song and smiles. You'd think she'd discovered cold fusion."

"Jealous," she sputtered. "Jealous of a twelve-year-old girl. Shame on you."

I opened some pantry doors. "Where's the Geritol, mother? I think you're getting senile." In the background from upstairs I could hear Ciara belting out a new number in preparation for the upcoming nationals. I couldn't for the life of me find a melody to place the song.

"Don't you think I won't slap you," my mother said.

"Don't you think I won't slap you," I mocked.

"Deneen—"

"Oh, Deneen nothing. The child is out of control."

"Can't you be happy for her? What have you got against her, anyway?"

"I don't have anything against her. And I don't know what *you* see, but I see one pretty miserable young person up there. She's mean and she's sneaky. I caught her stuffing food in her face. The kind of food *you all* don't eat."

"I do not want to hear this," Reina said, picking up her purse.

"No, of course you don't, because then you'd have to do something about it."

"Deneen, I've got this under control, whether or not you believe it. I told you not to interfere and I meant it. Now, I am going to my room before I completely lose control of myself and say some things we'll both regret. Good night." She patted me again on her way out.

"Fine. Good night, then." I wasn't feeling too much in control myself. I was tired and angry and frustrated. A perfectly adorable man had jumped off the hook on me. What was a girl to do?

I went downstairs and fired up that shower and took me another loofah bath.

# Ten

Let's get the preliminaries out of the way:

| | |
|---:|:---|
| *Name:* | Mark S. Layton, Jr. |
| *Date of birth:* | When the angels sang |
| *Height:* | 6' |
| *Weight:* | Under control |
| *Occupation:* | Love God |
| *Cologne:* | Polo |
| *Organ:* | Top of the line |
| *Performance:* | Read on |
| *Comments:* | My head's still swimming and the last thing I want to be doing is sitting here holding onto some pencil. Mark, Mark, Mark, where have they been keeping you all these years. I ain't never had me nothing like that before. |

*Recommendation:*

After which I covered the page with my signature happy faces, plastered with shit-eating grins.

Why be coy? I slept with him. Honey, it was some good stuff, I want to tell you, and I will. Later. But hang on a bit.

At the breakfast table the morning after the pageant, Mother sat in her usual place, hidden behind the *Post-Dispatch*. I tried to engage her in conversation, but all I got was short answers of the "yeah, uh-huh" variety. She was still angry with me because I'd dared say something remotely critical about Good Queen Ciara. Mother could be this way, I remembered. When she was upset with you about something, she'd as soon talk to a traveling salesman as look you in the eye. Once, back in the old hippie days, she gave me the silent treatment for weeks because I'd dared tell her that one of her club ladies, Aunt Marcella, was a gossiping old shrew. This was after the bitch had the nerve to call up my mother and tell her that she had seen me "flouncing myself around Northwest Plaza like a guttersnipe." Aunt Marcella claimed that I didn't even have the common courtesy to greet her in a civil manner, and had, in fact, walked right by her and then laughed at her when she called my name. In the first place I was probably so stoned that I wouldn't have recognized Jimi himself had he tried to pick me up; and in the second place those old cows in Mother's club all looked the same to me. They look like the other uppity old broads one sees at the mall. Last but not least, I, Athena Deneen Wilkerson, have done a lot of things in my time, but flounce like a guttersnipe has never been part of my repertoire. Mother gave me the silent treatment for a month after the Aunt Marcella flap. I figured she'd get over this Ciara snit a lot quicker. She brightened up considerably when the queen herself waltzed into the room, hauling an armload of the previous evening's winnings.

"And just what have we here?" Mother chirped, as bright as a sorority house president on the first day of rush week.

"This is Prudence. She's a nurse." Ciara posed on the end of the table a blonde serious-faced doll, wearing a nurse's cap and a pale blue jumper. "And this is Chastity. She's a teacher." Chastity was the same size as Prudence, only with a plaid jumper, and with a pair of gold wire-rim glasses perched on the end of her pug nose.

"Aren't they adorable," Mother said. "Hortense and Faith have some new playmates."

"Five more!" gushed Ciara.

I figured Hortense and Faith must be some more members of the tribe. At least I hoped so. God forbid there should be any other living things in this house I didn't know about, especially of the little girl variety. And as for cute, well that wasn't the first word that came to my mind. Disturbing would be more like it. Don't get me wrong; I've wheeled my cart around the toy department of Target enough to know that disturbing is a relative term. Let's be honest. In the boys' doll section, most of those creatures are covered with gaping wounds and dripping various forms of green slime or other bodily fluids. Talk about "less than fresh." Nor were these disturbing in the way that Barbie is disturbing, in her perfectly proportioned, miniature white woman way. (And while we're on the subject, why can't those damn people at Mattel, or whoever the hell it is makes these dolls, figure out it's not enough to dip Barbie in the brown dye and give her a hair weave and change her name to Larinka. They got to get Barbie some booty. Give the sister a case of BWA—black women's ass. Get her some nice purple jumpsuits and a few caftans and a headwrap or two. Folks need to stop playing and get real!) The problem with these dolls Ciara had was that they were the wrong size— not in the hips or in the titties—but just all over the wrong size. They were baby doll sized—like those big old beige-colored plastic babies we all had growing up, the kind with the perfect little bloodred painted-on lips and the pinhole cut in the crotch for the water to run out when you fed them their bottle. Except these dolls—Prudence and company—weren't baby dolls. They were supposed to be grown women, I think. Or at least little girls pretending to be grown women. They had been given adult roles—teacher, nurse, anchorperson— and serious adult expressions on their faces. At the same time there was this childlike puffiness about them: ringlets in their hair, frilled panties, and extra pouty lips. They were like the figures in the painter Botero's work: demented-looking little adults who could no doubt do you some major harm if you got too close to them. I thought it was fortunate that I didn't know any actual people like these. The only adults I knew that looked like this were on TV. The Sally Struthers character on *All in the Family* comes to mind.

"We're throwing a big tea party for the new ones," Ciara said.

Before I could suggest that she might be a little old to be throwing tea parties for her dolls, she added, "You're not invited, Deneen."

I thought I saw my mother give her a wink.

Once again I was gang pressed to take our queen to rehearsal. Ciara brought with her Vanity and Intolerance, or whatever the damned things' names were. I asked her as she arranged them in the seat beside her and fastened the seat belts across all three of their disgustingly narrow waists if she didn't think it was a tad inconvenient to be hauling them around. She cupped her hand around each of their ears and whispered something and then they laughed at me. Boy, those wenches sure didn't know who they were trifling with. Let them keep on playing, and see didn't I cut all three of their behinds.

"I was great last night, wasn't I?" Ciara said, not really a question.

"I'll say this for you: you've got a healthy ego."

"Whatever. Did you hear that cow singing Whitney? I tripped her fat butt backstage. All the girls were laughing at her, too."

"That's not very nice. She seemed like a pleasant young woman."

"You *would* like her. You've got so much in common."

I kept having these fantasies that a horde of animal-skin-covered ravaging Asiatic men on large horses would ride up next to my car, snatch her up by the hair, and haul her butt to the steppes and out of my life forever.

Hawkins was a fluttering cache of energy when we arrived.

"So much to do! So much to do!" he seethed, prancing around the way one imagines the head elf does on Christmas Eve at the North Pole. "The trade show next week. The nationals in Vegas the week after. We've got work to do." He ordered me to the shampoo sink and Ciara to a room to get changed.

"You know, I'm not even—"

"Don't start with me, fish," he said as he shoved my head under the faucet. "We gonna cut about half this mess out of here today," he said, and then, "Miss Ciara, put on that gold pantsuit with the high neck. We'll try that, but she just may be too yellow to work it."

Fine, I thought. And while Ciara modeled a dozen different outfits—apparently Hawkins had already spent the morning cleaning out the racks of the better Young Miss departments—he pulled my hair up by the ends and snipped away at it near the roots. The thing was, I actually didn't mind much. I was having to admit that each time he finished I looked, if not better, at least a lot different. I can't say that was a bad thing. All

my life I had been one of those women who found a hairstyle
and then stuck with it until a loving friend took me aside and
told me it was time to move on. For the better part of college
I sported this big huge Angela Davis/Jermaine Jackson Afro
that I thought was real cute at the time, but when I look back
I realize that that hair was rather like walking around with
a giant piece of shrubbery on my head. I was always bumping
into door frames with that hair, and bugs would fly into it and
I'd have to be running into the bathroom to pick them and it
out. In the morning I'd wake up looking like a Conehead, and
I would be a frightful thing to behold, too, except the dude
I would be with would look just as frightful with his nappy
head all mashed down the same way. Since then, it's been dif-
ferent versions of the corporate Deneen. You know, the three
Ps: pressed, parted, and pasted down when it got too nappy.
(All right, so there's only been two hairdos. So what? I've
had two hairdos. Satisfied?) First I had that pulled-back and
pinned-up tight-on-the-back-of-my-head hair that Denise
Nicholas used to have on *Room 222*. I wore it and I wore it and
I wore it and I wore it, and then a friend made a remark about
how long I'd worn it, so I got me that turned under Prince
Valiant page boy hair, just up from my shoulders with bangs.
And I wore that and wore that and wore that. I was letting it
grow out—for God knows what reason—and was just leaving
it in this raggedy-ass ponytail, until Hawkins got a hold of it.
He must be doing something right, I thought, thinking about
that fine Mark Layton, the reeling in of whom I credit partially to my feminine wiles, and partially to Mr. Hawkins
DeAngeles, who the morning of the pageant had transformed
me from a somewhat demented-looking LaToya Jackson to
a marginally seductive Martha Reeves, circa 1964, featuring
a bouffant crowning a circle of eyebrow-length bangs. And

I must have been thinking about Mark—yes, I know I was because Hawkins had just swished into the room and announced, "He called up here looking for you, by the way,"—and therefore I missed the most pertinent comment of the day, which was, "I'm gonna put some color on this mess."

"Who called up here looking for me?" I asked, instead of saying, "You'll do nothing of the kind."

I tried not to sound too anxious, though I had spent every waking moment and probably the better part of my dreams trying to figure out a way to hunt the man down.

"Don't even try act innocent with me," Hawkins said, and just then in the other room I hear Ciara's thin voice quavering the words "if I should stay," and I grabbed Hawkins's arm, and I said, "Oh, dear God! No!"

"What's wrong with you?" Hawkins asked. "Yeah, he called. And let me tell you one thing about Mr. Mark Layton."

At that moment Ciara busted out at the top of her lungs. "And aye-ee-aye-ee-aye will always love you-ou-ou," and I thought, God, please kill me now.

"This is the best song you could come up with?" I asked. "She could do 'Purple Haze.' 'All Along the Watchtower.' Anything but this."

Hawkins was lathering into my hair some sickly sweet-smelling beige goop swirled with reds and a bunch of other colors. "Mr. Mark Layton ain't thinking about nothing but his money and getting him some hootchie. There. I said it. Lord, strike me dead."

"He seemed like a perfectly nice gentleman," I said. I was grimacing in pain, and at one point on one of Ciara's endless Is (that song has more aye aye ayes than "Cielito Lindo"), even Hawkins swallowed extra hard. Aye aye aye grabbed his arm and dug in with my fingernails.

Hawkins pulled himself away and flourished a business card from his smock. "There his number is. There." He placed the card on a high shelf behind the sink. "You want to call that fine-ass nigger, you reach on up there and get it. What you better not tell nobody is I's the one gave it to you. There."

"What are you doing to my hair?" I asked, and Ciara screamed out the big "you" that Whitney stops the show with.

"Jesus, save me from these trifling heifers," Hawkins said, and shouted into the other room for Ciara to cut it and take it from the top.

"And, another thing about that Mark Layton." Hawkins grabbed me under the chin and started dabbing at me with some sort of color stick. "We need something more rusty on these cheeks. And I got two other words for you, little miss, and those are: proprietary information. You know what I'm saying." He grabbed one of my earlobes.

"Ouch!" I slapped his hand away.

"That Negro is trying to do me out of this Dream Dolls contract, which is rightfully mines, and you can ask anybody in the business if Hawkins DeAngeles ain't the next one in line."

I threw up my hands, speechless. Ciara, whining her way through one of the quiet parts of her song, came mincing into the room, looking us in the eye, and cooing out her lines with a lot of trumped-up emotions.

"That's it, sugar," Hawkins said. "Sell it."

"And aye-ee-aye-ee-aye will always," she screamed right in my face.

Hawkins whispered in my ear, "You go out with that fool, everything you seen here, you didn't see it. Cause if I find out, . . ." and he twisted my earlobe some more.

"All right! Shit!" These people were out of their fucking minds around this place.

What Hawkins did to my hair was dye it a color somewhere between dark toast and a dirty camel. Most of it was that color. There were other colors in there, too, everything from blonde to black and some other colors that don't occur in nature. He made little bangs and balled it up into a fez-shaped thing on the top of the front of my head—sort of a Vanessa Williams look.

Ciara said I was retarded-looking. I let her out at the mall, hoping it was International Snatch a Teenage Bitch Day. Forget her nonsinging ass, anyway—I was as cute as I could be. I made my way to the pay phone and dialed up this Mr. Mark Layton to see what was on his fine mind. Hell yes, I snatched his card down. Seeing as I'm a half head taller than Hawkins, it wasn't much of a reach. The faggot stood there tsk-tsking and waving his finger at me and talking about how someone was gonna get him some hootchie, and how I had better keep my big lips sealed shut. I gave the nigger the finger and slid that card right into my bra, right there in his face.

There was no address listed, just Layton Enterprises with a P.O. box and a phone number. I'm looking adorable and about to come out of my skin and what do I get but a damn answering machine. It was the usual "get back to you soon as I can" crap, and I started to hang up on it, but figured, what the hell, I'd leave him a short one.

"This is Deneen Wilkerson. We met at the—"

"Hello, there," that silky smooth voice said. What had been metallic and flat on the tape was as warm and sweet as I remembered it from the previous evening.

"So, you screen your calls."

He made one of those disgusting, back-of-the-throat, male noises and said, "You know, the women, the women."

"Yeah, I do know," I said. "A lot of us women working for collection agencies these days. You can't be too careful."

"Baby, all my business is straight. You hear what I'm saying."

"Whatever," I said. I tried not to say it in the Ciara way, but somehow the word "whatever" lends itself to eye rolling and pseudo-exasperation.

"So what can I do you for," he says to me. And me, standing there in the shopping mall, trying not to feel too trashy, have to hold the phone out from my ear because I can't believe this man has just dropped that old line on me.

"You left a message for me. Remember? With Hawkins DeAngeles?"

"Oh, yeah. How is that ornery old tight-fisted sissy?"

"You got his number—call him up and ask him how he is."

"You're one of them feisty gals. I likes me a feisty gal."

"You wanted something, Mr. Layton?" If I had any doubt, I didn't any more. I knew very well what he wanted. I wanted me some of that same product.

"Say, baby," he says, "I'm sorry I ran out on you last night. Really I am. That pageant thing messed with my head. You know how it goes. What say I make it up to you?"

"Make it up to me? Why, just what did you have in mind?" Just then I pictured myself as any of a hundred characters Doris Day portrayed in her career, hands clasped demurely just below my chin, strapped across one arm a patent-leather handbag whose color matched my shoes and hat. The Doris image was fixing to get into a fight with an image of Hawkins, who was behind me over my left shoulder whispering, "Hootchie. Hootchie."

"Oh, I don't know," says Mark. "I was thinking maybe a nice dinner would be just the thing to make up for my rude behavior."

"Gee, I don't know," Doris says. Me, Deneen, was trying to figure out just which fancy joint I wanted to be taken to.

"What do you say? Just the two of us."

"Well . . . ," and I sighed. "I guess."

"Tonight. How's tonight? Eight-ish."

"So soon?" Doris said, and I was ready to tell the bitch to take a walk. I gave him my address, bought me an outfit, went to find the freshly purged Ciara (tacos, if the breath is any giveaway), and headed home to get ready.

He took me to the Webster Grill. A newer place trying to look like one of those clubby older places, filled with people like him and me—Yuppie and Buppie upstart trash—who in the old days never would have been let into the kind of place it aspired to be. Mark ordered appetizers made from one of those scraped-off-the-side-of-an-ocean-liner-and-comes-in-a-razor-edged-shell things. The sort of thing men order to get a reaction out of us girls.

"Want a bite?" he offered, and of course I did my best six-teen-year-old cringe and said something of the I-ain't-eatin-none-of-that-nasty-mess variety. He chomped on, merrily, plucking ash gray flesh from dangerous-looking shells and swirling it through lumpy briny-smelling sauce.

"Tell me about yourself," he says.

"Well, gosh, there just isn't too much to tell," I responded, and I thought, Deneen, you've got cute hair, and you're wear-ing a cute outfit that you just added an unauthorized charge to your mother's Famous account to purchase (a simple little faux sixties number, short, with slits up the thigh, beige to match my new hair): try and play it smart. Just then the nigger

slurped him up another one of those sea slugs. I figured I'd
be running the show from that point forward.

"I'm just your average very successful, well-educated,
financially independent strong black woman trying to make
her way out here in the world," I said.

I thought he'd choke on that slime ball.

He cleared his throat and said, "All right, then." He raised
his glass to me, I clinked his, took a swallow of Beaujolais,
grasped the reins firmly and took complete control.

"Now, why don't you tell me about you," I said.

"Working hard, working hard," he said, in that way men
say it when they want to make it clear that you couldn't
possibly know or understand anything about hard work,
particularly of the male variety.

"So which are you: a pimp or a drug dealer?"

That seemed to hurt his feelings a bit. Yeah, I was ashamed
of myself for being so fresh-mouthed, but not really that
much. A man like this could benefit from a dressing down
now and then. Let him know who he was messing with.

"Damn," he said. "A brother can't get a break for nothing.
I told you all my dealings were strictly straight up."

"Are they now?" I said, and I leaned in closer to him, eye-
balling him over my glass of wine. Men enjoy this sort of
thing; this leaning up and smiling at them stuff. I stopped just
short of batting my eyes. I might be a tramp, but I ain't no ho.

"I'm a franchisee," he said.

"And just how long have you been in our beautiful
country?"

"What I do is I find the next big thing. I study the market
for a time. I figure out the best way to get in, who do you have
to know, where's the opportunity. I buy in, I build it up for
a couple years. I double my money, and I move on."

"To the next big thing," I said, and raised my glass to him. "To the next big thing."

He ordered the New York Strip, and I had some pork chops glazed with bourbon butter. It turns out the next big thing is the All American Dream Dolls Company, which some guy out in Oklahoma started in his garage. According to Mark, it started out with this guy's mother piecing together handmade dolls for her grandkids. Mom was something of a backwoods feminist and thought it was a good idea if all these dolls were role models of some kind. She gave them stern expressions and careers—albeit traditional ones, like nurse, nanny, and schoolmarm. Word got around about these quirky homemade creatures, and she couldn't make them fast enough.

"This son of hers is no dummy," Mark said. "Now, check this out. A smart girl like you knows the future of this kind of business."

Smart girl like me? I had either oversold the merchandise or was being massively patronized. I couldn't tell which. I work in a business where it goes with the territory to make ordinary fluoride toothpaste seem like a ticket to a teen orgy and where talking down to people is considered a virtue. I had no perspective. Furthermore, at the time of Mark's question I was busy shamelessly sopping up the last of that whiskey sauce with a piece of sourdough bread. I said, "Huh?"

"Vertical integration," Mark answered. "Toys. The entertainment industry. It's all the same thing these days. That's where I come in. You understand?"

I nodded, even if I didn't understand. I did the mental equivalent of kicking myself under the table. Come on, Deneen, I thought. Get with the program. If this guy wanted an airhead, he'd date your sister. Somewhere in my disordered brain I remembered a long talk Mr. Waltershied and

I had had about the future of American business and what that meant for the advertising industry. A card floated into view.

"Like Disney?" I said.

"Exactly! You got your movies. You got your theme parks. You got your merchandise. You got your stores. You got it made! This guy, this woman's son, he sees these dolls taking off. He sees an unending stream of preteen girls—a new crop every year. He's thinking TV shows and magazines and fan clubs—"

"And beauty pageants?"

"Don't sneer, Deneen. Do you know how much money people plop down to get their daughters into those things. Thousands. Per kid. If they can't pay, they get the local hardware store to sponsor her. Just like the Little League."

I rolled that around in my head for a while, trying to equate stealing second base with romping down the runway in a sunsuit. The sad thing was, I could sort of see a similarity. Let's just chalk it up to my at the time still being pretty crazy.

"And, of course, Deneen, you know where the big money is?"

Child pornography? Teenage hookers? I was beginning to think maybe this date was a bad idea after all.

"Television, baby. If this takes off and they start broadcasting these little pageants, there's gonna be some serious money made."

"Yeah, but—"

"Save it," Mark said. "For me, this is a can't miss business. Low buy in, low overhead, low risk, high return."

"High return?"

"Serious money."

I raised my glass to him again. "More power to you, I guess."

I swallowed over my already numb tongue. I had had an awful lot of wine. One really shouldn't give liquor to a crazy person. First of all, when you are crazy and you get drunk, you become convinced that you really weren't that crazy in the first place. The simple-minded crap people say to you—for example, their lame-brained get-rich-quick schemes—suddenly starts to make sense. If I'd had my checkbook, I'd have bought a Dream Dolls franchise myself, right there in the Webster Grill. Then there is the horny problem. Being drunk makes me horny. This was, of course, only compounded by my recently developed sober horny problem. I could have jumped his beautiful bones right there in the restaurant. I did not, and it would have been fruitless anyway at that point. As we all know that other little brain they have down there in their pants—the instincts, we were calling it—works full time, *except* when the subject is money. That's the only time it gets to take a nap.

"So, enough business talk," I said. Mark was momentarily startled. "What does your regular girlfriend think of all this nonsense." And, I thought, Oh, Deneen, they aren't this transparent even on *The Bold and the Beautiful*—TV's trashiest daytime drama.

"I'm not presently seeing anyone," he said, lowering his voice an octave at least, and I cooed, "Ooooh."

We ended up at his place in time for *Nightline*. I did a very sexy striptease to the music of Ted and Pat Buchanan discussing the future of the American judicial system. I was flushed with sweat as I popped out of my bra. Mark grabbed me and rolled me back on the bed. He nuzzled his mustache into the flesh of my stomach.

"I loves me a big woman," he said.

"Can you handle a big woman?"

"Can you handle this?"

He shoved my legs open and started working me with his tongue. Yeah, he could handle me all right. "Shit, yeah!" I screamed. I was moaning and groaning and rocking the bed up and down and hoping he didn't have no neighbors.

I figured I'd better give him some before I passed out. "Looky here," I said. I grabbed hold of his "instincts" and Ted and I both said simultaneously, "We'll be back with some program announcements right after this."

Mark carried on like I was trying to kill him. I might have, cause I was crazy enough—demonstrated by the fact I'm not one likes to get too overly familiar with a man's personal area, but this night his was saying something to me. I talked right back to it, girl, telling it to behave itself and asking it didn't it want to be Deneen's friend.

Mark spun me around this way or that—I can't quite believe my body made some of those shapes—and we were on to the "main course." Could have been the Olympics, was so much bouncing up and down and sweating going on.

"Goddamn it," I screamed. "We're gonna break this damn bed."

"Fuck this bed," Mark said, and I said, "No, fuck me," and he sure nough did. For about the next two hours. No lie.

I finally pushed him off me. "I got to go," I said. "They'll be looking for me."

"I'm not through with you," he panted.

"Another time. Okay."

"You're a wild woman. I like a wild woman."

What I was was a crazy woman.

A mighty satisfied crazy woman at that.

# Eleven

I awoke the next morning with a song in my heart and a swirl of peach-colored hair atop my head. It looked like a bird's nest—spun in one direction and open at the top as if awaiting eggs. Puffy, raw lips, a tongue that felt as if it had spent the night on its own in the desert. I had dragged myself home somehow from the previous night's diversions, and I was a complete wreck. Even if I had had a good time.

As hard as you might find this to believe, I was not this way before the trip to Wisconsin. I was not the sort of woman who hustled up some man for a torrid one-nighter, nor the sort who woke up dazed-looking and hung over in a fright wig the color of a cheap cloth coat. Before Wisconsin I was more the sort who nursed the same cocktail all evening, who dated chastely for months on end, the sort who might at some point down the line submit to a bit of vanilla, missionary-position sex, but only if the C words were at hand, C standing for both condoms and commitment. I was not a prude. I just never particularly enjoyed having some man I didn't really know inserting a body part of his into one of mine. Before Wisconsin I was the sort of woman who considered every move she made, who thought her way through and beyond every possible outcome, who weighed each alternative and who had at the ready a full stable of contingency plans and any number of fall-back positions. Impulsiveness was for fools, I thought, and only chumps bought tickets in the rush line.

I thought too much back then. I know that now. I over-analyzed everything, and down that road lay the madness I had embraced like a long lost sister.

I stood in the basement bathroom that morning, in front of the mirror, stuffing my new almond tresses into the trusty red Cardinals cap. I saw beneath the rough-edged morning-after weariness a sly world-wise beauty, the sort of a woman who in a 1940s film noir would burst into a casino and take on all comers at whatever game was proffered, and I wondered where in the hell this new doll had come from. And what had happened to that other girl, to the mousy one, to that Deneen? Where had she gone?

"What's this?" my mother said to me, fingering some loose strands of beige hair. I sat at her breakfast table munching leftover shrimp toast along with Cap'n Crunch cereal.

"Hawkins is experimenting," I said, happy that I once again merited speaking to.

"Does that color have a name?"

"Something this lovely defies naming," I said. "And speaking of lovelies, where is herself this fine morning?"

"It's almost noon, and your sister—and I assume that is to whom you make reference—had an early call. I'd like you to retrieve her for me. About two?"

"Sure. No prob. Anything else?"

"Nothing," she said, pointedly stirring her already well-mixed coffee. "Except that, well, you were out rather late last night."

I knew this was coming. On the way home the night before I had decided to tell the cow to stay the hell out my business.

Then I remembered that the cow was also my mother, that I was living in her home and on her good graces (as well as from the occasional twenty-dollar bill lifted from her wallet).

"We got to talking," I said, thinking that this old chestnut sounded as good as any. "You know how that goes."

"Well. You're a grown woman. I guess."

"You guess?"

"I don't want to fight, Deneen. I really don't." She smiled the sort of wise and patient smile that one imagines the pope reserves for nonbelievers.

"Then we won't fight," I said.

"As long as we understand each other."

I figured since we were getting it all out, we might as well get it all out. I asked, "And what about Ciara?" I thought I saw her suppress a mild shudder.

"I've already told you: Ciara is my problem. I will deal with her." She took ever the slightest sip of her coffee and returned it to her saucer.

"And if it happens that I disagree with you, or that I think . . ."

"All right Deneen," she said, folding her hands together and leaning in my direction. "How's it gonna be then? I don't know the rules here any more than you do. We're two adult women living in the same house trying to get along. I'm trying to respect you and I know you want to respect me. How do you want us to work this?"

A little more direct than I had expected. I averted my eyes. Apparently she wanted to make like grown-ups. Who expects this from their mother? But after the initial shock, it seemed like a good game plan, at least in my wine-fogged postcoital haze, it did. I played my next card as if it were the last ace in a cutthroat game of War.

"It's a boundaries thing, then," I said.

"And I'm telling you I don't know what it is. I'm also telling you that I'm your mother and I'm also her mother—which you are not. *Mother* means something. Doesn't it? Doesn't it?" She gave me a look over her half-frame bifocals that was somewhere between exasperated and pleading. We stared at each other, like a panel of nerdy contestants on *College Bowl*, each waiting for the other to come up with the correct response.

"Then I'll butt out," I said at last.

"Fine. I guess," she said, more tentatively than I or she would have wished.

"Okay, fine." I took my toast into the study and called work.

"Waltershied, Williams and Caruthers."

"Congratulations. You just won a free ass-whooping, courtesy of yours truly."

"Don't even mess with me, bitch. These white folks is about to run me crazy up in here."

"Any particular white folks."

"Here. You talk to him."

". . . and another thing. Why's it so goddamn hard to keep tomato juice in the refrigerator. I go in there and we're out every time. Don't we got a service takes care of that?"

"Maybe if you didn't drink all the damn juice up—"

"Deneen, where in the hell did you say you were? Skip it. Listen to this: we're out at sea and there are these two sisters—"

"No sisters."

"You got some kind of a problem with sisters?"

Did I have a problem with sisters? "Do you mean *sisters* sisters or *sisters.*"

"Hey, I hadn't thought about that. The way I understand it, them Asians like you sisters."

And I thought for once in his hyperactive life, Walt might

be on to something. Believe it or not—and as terrible as this sounds—these days in the advertising biz one doesn't think about race at all. I mean, when I went into the business I thought I would mau-mau my way in there and knock down barriers that kept African Americans from being sold the same kind of worthless crap everybody else got sold. I would write up these scripts with a lot of very black-looking and -sounding folks talking about getting their clothes clean. One or two of those babies actually got made. Then an interesting thing happened. In the eighties the marketing departments at the big corporations figured out—without any help from me—that there were all these folks who didn't look like the Waltons out there spending good cash money on the shit they made. Most of our clients figured they'd just as soon get them a piece of that pie. These days when we do a campaign, we don't even stop to think about color anymore. We come up with the concept and let the art department figure what it'll look like in *Reader's Digest* and in *Ebony.* But Walt was right. In ads from America for the overseas market, race still meant a lot. Let's face it: only in America do we have what you would call your basic Negroes. America invented Negroes, and the rest of the world can't get enough of us. The rest of the world likes Negroes almost as much as they like American cigarettes. That's the truth. They love *The Cosby Show.* They think Michael Jackson is some sort of a god. They like our style and the way we dress and talk and sing. Can you blame them?

Maybe, just maybe, we might be able to do something with a black woman in a douche spray ad in Asia. Just maybe. I'd have to think about it.

Just in case, I wasn't letting Mr. Waltershied get the drop on me on this one. (Technically speaking, it wasn't his idea anyway, since until I asked him what kind of sisters he meant, he hadn't been thinking about my kind of sisters at all.)

So I said, again, "No sisters."

"Deneen, what the hell is it with you? No blondes. No sisters. So what do we put in this commercial? Albino transvestite midgets?"

"Hey, there you go, Walt. Work with that awhile. Two little red-eyed dudes in dresses in the checkout line of the convenience store."

"Don't fuck with me, Deneen. I got a headache like a sonofabitch and that nutcase Katrina is driving me up the wall."

"You want me to talk with her?"

"What I want is for you to get your ass back here and to get the hell to work on this account. We got a deadline here."

"I been busting my butt on this account for a week now," I lied. He knew and I knew it didn't work that way. One did not spend weeks working on pitches. All you would get was crap, lists of half-baked ideas, warmed-over derivative shit from last year's award shows. What one did was wait until lightning struck—like it just had with Walt and his sisters thing. "I got pages of ideas. Listen to this: we use all black women in the campaign."

"Deneen! I just said that!"

"No you didn't."

"Yes, I did."

"No, you did not. You said sisters. I said *sisters.*"

"Deneen, are you trying to put me in the state hospital? Is that it?"

I could just see him up there, rubbing at the place in his stomach where an ulcer would form. "Admit it, Walt. It makes you crazy when I come up with a good idea—LIKE THIS ONE—before you do. Admit it. You're jealous."

"Are you smirking down there, Deneen? Because I'll tell you what, if you were standing here I'd wipe that smirk off your face."

"You and whose army. Jealous. Jealous. Jealous."

"Oh . . . you. . . ." And I could practically feel him seething through the phone. I had him now. "I'll tell you what, lady. I'll give you the sisters idea, but the proof—as they say out at Betty Crocker's—is in the pudding. We'll see who can develop this baby."

"You're on. Switch me to Katrina."

"You'll be eatin my dust, girlie."

"Waltershied, Williams and Caruthers."

"Tell Walt he's met his match this time. Tell him Deneen said she was—"

"Oh, Lord help me, you done got him all worked up again. And I was gonna get my legs waxed this afternoon."

"And the other thing is, you need to behave yourself."

"Me! Behave myself? You better reconsider who you—"

"Katrina! Katrina!" I slammed the phone on my mother's desk a few times to get her attention. "Katrina, calm down. Now, you know how you get. I'll be back pretty soon, I think."

And it was just at that moment that I realized it was probably true.

"You got to hurry, Deneen. I'm finta do something every-body regret and I don't even know what that is myself."

"Katrina, now, you know your Deneen wouldn't let you do that, don't you?" I used my best soothing voice on her, the one I had to use whenever she threatened to erase all the computer files and quit. Katrina might be air-headed, but she knew where all the bodies were buried in the office. On a raised eyebrow from me she could give an annoying client a half hour runaround that gave me and Walt time enough either to sew up a campaign or think of a killer excuse why we hadn't.

"Here's what I want you to do. Are you listening?"

"Yes, Deneen."

"First, I want you to take your Walkman out. You got it. Now turn it to KMOJ and get ready to let it play."

"You told me if I have this on at work one more time you'd snatch me bald."

"I'm making an exception. But just until I get home, okay?"

"Okay."

"Just make sure you can still hear the phone.

"Next. When you see Mr. Waltershied, I only want you to say this one thing to him. Say 'Yes, Mr. Waltershied. Anything you say, Mr. Waltershied.' Got that?"

"Yes, Mr. Waltershied. Anything you say, Mr. Waltershied."

"Turn on your computer. Open up a new file. Write down everything he says to you so we can talk about it. And every time you feel yourself getting ready to go off on him or anyone else up there, I want you to write me a note right there on the computer screen. I'll call you every couple of hours and you can read them to me. Can you handle all this?"

"Yes, Mr. Waltershied. Anything you say, Mr. Waltershied."

"That's very good, Katrina. I'll be home real soon."

"I miss you."

"You know, I miss you too." I didn't mean to sound as surprised about it as I did. I hoped I hadn't hurt her feelings. It was just then I realized, though maybe not at a conscious level, that I really did have some sort of real life that I had walked away from. In my head another of those locked doors had swung open, was gaping wide, and I could see inside that door there was a land of a thousand lakes, and I had a life in that land. There were people there and I meant something to them. Standing by that door was one of those plastic prize models from *The Price Is Right*, and she was smiling broadly in that toothsome open-mouthed way they do, and pointing with her whole arm at my lovely condominium, considerate neighbors, cherished coworkers and friends. "All this could be yours, if . . ." except I couldn't make out what the "if" was. And then there was that Calvin sticking his head into the scene, waving and looking generally pathetic. Just begging for another letter.

I wrote:

> *Dear Casanova:*
>
> *Yeah, you. Think you hot stuff? Ha, ha, ha. Let's talk about what a real man can do for a woman. Baby, I'm talking about a real man, a man who knows all the ways to make a lady feel good, a man who at least knows there's someone else in the room. Know what I mean? Remember?*
>
> *Hallelujah! I am healed.*
>
> *What did you say your name was?*
>
> *Jealous?*
>
> *Of him? Or me?*
>
> *See ya, I wouldn't want to be ya,*
>
> *Deneen*

Alas, gloating is an ugly thing. (But, why does it feel so good?)

I did not send that letter.

Hawkins had gotten up that morning and decided to do himself up French—an intellectual beatnik look. He was dressed in black with a turtleneck and beret skewed carefully to one side of his head.

"*Sacrebleu!*" he said, snatching the baseball cap from my hair. He pulled and fingered through my bird's nest, clutching his chest as if he were going to faint.

"It was an accident," I said. "Honest, I didn't mean for it to happen."

"Accident my ass. They ought to revoke your license. You a disgrace to womens everywhere." He jumped up on a footstool, fluffing and snatching through my hair.

"I'm ready to *go*. Now!" Ciara said.

"You go on upstairs and pick some outfits out my magazines for the pageant," Hawkins ordered. Ciara gave me one of her million-dollar ferret-faced scowls and stomped up the steps.

"Is it beyond hope?" I asked.

"No such thing," Hawkins said. "You pretty close to the edge, but then I'm Hawkins, after all. My mistake was not spotting you right away for what you are. You one of them low-maintenance gals."

"You are so right," I said, being guided into his chair.

"So tell me all about it."

"Tell you all about what?"

He spun me around. "What you think? Hootchie!"

"I beg your pardon!"

"Must of been some good stuff, judging by the state of this rat's nest."

"If you think that I'm going to sit here discussing my personal life with you, well you can put that thought out of your mind."

Personal life is what they call hootchie on the daytime dramas.

"Suit yourself. I heard it all before anyway." He was raking out my hair with a giant pick and snipping it off at the ends. Every now and then he'd spray something in it. I waited as long as I could before taking his bait.

"And just what is that supposed to mean?" I said.

He hummed something that sounded like "Precious Lord Take My Hand." "I've done many a head in this chair," he sighed.

"For your nosy information, Mr. Layton and I had a business dinner."

"And it was some mighty good business, too, wasn't it girl-friend. Yes, Lordy." He laughed a nasty, just-below-the-tonsils laugh I wouldn't have believed he was capable of.

"If you must know, we discussed the beauty pageant busi-ness." And I thought, take that with your fruity froggy self. He spun me around.

"You discussed what?" He got all up in my face.

"I wouldn't worry myself. None of your 'proprietary information' came up. At least none I recall."

"I have had it up to here with that Negro." He raised up a piece of hair and took a snip at it. "These damn Johnny-come-latelies. Think they can waltz into someone else's terri-tory and set up shop. You don't see me setting up no fried chicken stands, do you? Hell, no!"

Fried chicken! Mark Layton was in the fried chicken business?

I could not ask that question because I found myself in the middle of one of those conversations where my presence was not an absolute necessity.

"Fifteen years I worked to build this up. I started back when these gals around here was twirling batons and getting made up at the Estée Lauder counter. Hawkins DeAngeles brought a new standard to the table. Fifteen years!"

Every exclamation was punctuated by a new spike in my hair.

"You know how when you get to the end of the runway and you do a little wink for your mama and daddy? That was me. That was Hawkins DeAngeles."

I had never been on a runway in my life.

"In the Miss Missouri pageant, I was the first one to use a French braid. Me. And I'm supposed to let some no-account, thick-lipped, chicken-frying dog get in on my action. No, ma'am."

I hadn't noticed Mark's lips being that big. He had, however, tasted slightly of Crisco and secret mixtures of herbs and spices.

"I'll tell you one thing; he might have money, he might have connections, he might be the best looking nigger this side of Hollywood. But what he don't got is Miss Ciara Renee Jones, and you can tell him I said so. Rub his nasty old face in it."

Ciara? My Ciara? This man was staking his career on that . . . that . . . that *thing* upstairs.

"I'll tell you what," he said, whipping me around after furiously pulling through my hair with a large plastic brush. "This one's on the house. But I want you to tell me everything that dirty dog says to you. Every single word."

"Well, I don't know, . . ." I coughed, waving away a cloud of aerosol hair spray, a product I did not know was even legal anymore. He snapped the cap on the spray container and dropped it into my purse. A message of some kind, I guessed.

"We'll talk tomorrow," he said, almost flirtatiously.

Shortly thereafter I was cruising out Highway 40 with the sweetest-looking Tina Turner hair you could ever imagine. Katrina and I could be twins.

"Your hair looks cute today." Ciara said.

I almost swallowed my gum. I eyeballed the wench over my sunglasses.

"No, I mean it. It's sort of . . . sophisticated-looking and everything."

"Well. Gee. Thanks."

"I wish I could do different things with my hair. I tried, but you know how it is."

"You have lovely hair." Which is true, she did. She had that disgustingly soft, spun silk hair that cascaded down from her head like a filmy waterfall. A rich chocolatey-brown color, riddled with the kind of natural red and gold highlights my Tina hair only mimicked.

"I'd like to do something to it, but what I mean is, . . ." she paused, "You know how *she* is."

Could this be happening? Was I about to be having, at long last, a sisterly talk with an actual sister of mine about the thing sisters love to talk about more than anything in the world? I plunged right in.

"Yeah, I know how *she* is all right."

"Oh, Deneen, I knew you'd understand." She reached over and squeezed my arm, squealing with delight.

A break in the action here while I remind the reader who the players in this drama are. Our star, Deneen, is a lonely and confused (somewhat crazy) woman, in the express lane to middle age and not at this moment in her life the best judge of character. Our ingenue is a precocious and spiteful brat, currently going by the name of Ciara. As you may have noted, butter wouldn't melt in her mouth. That our heroine fell into such transparent manipulation need be considered in terms of the circumstances. Having always been, like Blanche DuBois, dependent on the kindness of strangers, and having a sister who was more than kind of strange, one ought to

reasonably expect the lead in this drama to at least attempt
to see the good within said sister. One, like Deneen, would be
wrong. Not only do leopards not change their spots, they have
often been known to invest in having their teeth and claws
sharpened. Back to our story.

"I'm glad we're going to be friends," I said. Ciara shyly
dropped her eyes.

She said, "I'll bet when you were growing up you got to do
whatever you wanted."

"Ha!" I laughed, tossing my Tina Turner hair in a mature
sisterly way. "Mother was just as strict with me as she is with
you." And, out of some unbidden sense of parental loyalty,
I added, "But you know she's only looking out for our best
interest."

"Right," Ciara said. It seemed perfectly innocent at the
time, but thinking back, that "right"—punctuated with a smile
that highlighted her canine teeth—was as crisp as a fresh head
of iceberg lettuce.

"We're lucky to have such a caring mom." I threw that in,
feeling sisterly and daughterly and all around just a great gal.

"Lucky, lucky, lucky," said Baby Sis.

We chatted the rest of the way home. Ciara asked me
about my job, and I told her, and I asked her about her little
friends and the things she did for fun, and she told me. This
sister business wasn't so bad after all, I thought.

Then we turned the corner onto our street.

"Deneen. Can I ask you a big favor?" Ciara said this in a
cross between singsongy and whiny. She even batted her eyes
at me.

"Of course you may, sweetie." Whenever I remember back
to this moment I would like to slap this particular Deneen
until she was unconscious.

"My friend Carrie I told you about? Well, she's having a sleep-over pool party. You-know-who says I can't go because Carrie's parents are out of town and everything, so I was wondering if you wouldn't say that you and I were going on an overnight trip, like up to Chicago or something, and then I could, like, go. Just like all my other friends?

I took my sunglasses off and looked real hard at the wench. My mouth hung open like I was waiting for someone to spoon some oatmeal into it.

"Have you lost your mind?"

"Come on, Deneen. Her older sister will be there. She's like sixteen. It's not like anything could happen."

"No!" I said. I stared her down, then went to open the car door. She reached over and grabbed my arm.

"Are you sure?" she asked. She leaned into me, looking at me up from under her eyebrows.

"Yes! I can't believe you even asked me this."

She grabbed me again. "I mean, are you really, really sure." Her expression made me feel as if I was in the middle of a 1950s suspense movie. I returned my sunglasses to my eyes and fled toward the house, clutching my plastic grocery sack in front of me and sneaking peeks back over my shoulder the same way blondes like Kim Novak and Tippi Hedrin did when they were on the lam in those Hitchcock movies. All I needed was a gauzy pastel scarf and I'd have been perfect.

A return engagement with Mark erased this ugly episode from my memory. He had ordered in pizza—which we made quick work of. Then he made quick work of me.

"I want to try something unusual," he says to me. Me, a woman with Tina Turner hair, stuffed into a skin-tight offwhite minidress. What would give him the idea I'd want to try something unusual?

We did one thing he called the Pretzel and another thing he called the Layton Lollapalooza. That one had me flapping my wings, and I was practically clucking like a chicken, too.

In between sessions, we lay there and talked for a while.

"You wouldn't happen to know where a girl could get a good piece of fried chicken?" I asked him.

"Ha!" he laughed. "That spiteful old dog."

"So you would know."

"Yeah, I own a couple of franchises. I told you—I'm diversified."

"Diversified, are you?" I tickled him in his side, and he pushed me away.

"You see I'm doing pretty well." He indicated with an out-stretched arm his fine fine home. It was right out of a designer catalog, the sort of thing a girl could more than get used to. "How bout you?" he asked. "You like living with your parents?"

"It's just my mom, actually. And my sister, Ciara."

"So? Do you like it?"

I realized I could not answer his question. Where, after all, did I live? My clothes and my car and my everything else I owned in the world lived in a townhouse five hundred miles away. It had been a while since I had seen or thought much about any of those things. I had been contentedly coming and going from someone else's house, most of the time acting as if I owned it myself. I was ensconced in various routines— eating and sleeping and watching my regular shows and getting my hair done. It sounded like a pretty good life to me.

"It's okay, I guess." If I betrayed any ambivalence, he did not pick it up. Instead he asked:

"Ciara—she's the one in the pageant, right?"

"Yeah. She's the one."

"Damn, she's something else. If I had a couple girls like her—hell, if I had one girl like her—I'd have this deal sewed up."

"So, you *are* a pimp."

"Don't give me that, woman." He did some extra cozy cuddling that kept me from slapping him upside his head. "You just don't understand business. That's all."

"Hey!" I tweaked him on a nipple. "Don't forget who you're talking to here. I work in a business that was founded on human exploitation. But that don't mean I have to like it when it's happening to my own flesh and blood."

"Have you thought that maybe *she* just might like it?"

"You can't be serious."

"I don't see anybody dragging these girls out there making them sing. My girl, the one that was the runner-up, she can't wait to get on stage. It's what she lives for."

"You don't know much about twelve-year-old girls, do you?"

"I know they like to wear nice clothes and win prizes."

"What they like is to have everyone on earth pay attention to them. Especially people of your persuasion. You all should really should be ashamed of yourselves."

"So what you're saying is Ciara is too stupid to figure out what's happening to her? Ciara and your mother, that is?"

I was once again in the middle of one of those conversations with some man pretending he didn't get it. I decided I didn't even believe them anymore. It was the goddamn end of the millennium, for Pete's sakes. I slung myself on top of him, thinking that if the idea that women weren't putting up with this shit anymore hadn't sunk in yet, maybe I could fuck it into him. I whipped him up and sat on it and started riding up and down and giving him my lecture about how women were sick of all this shit, and that included walking up and down some gangplank and having dirty old men grade you like you were a side of beef. He didn't have a response except for a whole lot of that sexy moaning and panting he does.

About eleven I toweled myself off and announced I needed to be in at a respectable hour. He laughed like there was something funny about that.

I drove home from where he lived way out in Chesterfield feeling about as alive as I had felt in my entire life. I rolled down the windows and let my maintenance-free hair blow around my head just the way it was supposed to. There were stars that night, and I looked from my window and imagined new names for the constellations: the Vulva of Venus. Cassiopeia's Clitoris. Life could be so simple and so wonderful.

A person did not need responsibilities—such as mortgages or car payments or jobs to go to or any of that other mess. A person needed to have someone to pay those bills for her, and buy that food, and then to find herself a man who could put the Pretzel and the Lollapalooza on her. That was what life was about. I can't really tell you that at that moment I thought there was anything crazy about me at all. To the contrary. I think that just then I might have gotten as close to sane as an adult person can get in this world. I think that deep down inside we all want to be taken care of. Somehow, in our mixed-up and backwards world, belonging to someone has become a bad thing. And though I realize now that for me having someone of my own might not ever happen the way I wanted it to, I also know that companionship is not a bad thing to want, nor is the disappointment at not finding it something to be easily dismissed.

I believe I could have gone back to my mother's right then and there, packed my things, and said see you later. Except . . .

Except, having spent the last several hours working up an appetite, I had stopped in the kitchen to assemble myself a snack of those chicken nuts, potato chips, and dip. I had settled myself in at the table for a quick scarfing session when I had the feeling that someone was watching me.

I turned around to see Ciara huffing and blowing into what I first thought was a clear balloon. She filled it to the size of a dachshund's torso.

"Mark, Mark, Mark, where have they been keeping you all these years. I ain't never had me nothing like that before." She quoted, right out of my sex diary. My *private* sex diary.

"You little bitch," I said, and started after her. She circled to the other side of the room and stuck a pin in the condom and popped it.

"I'm going to that party," she said. She slung the spent rubber in my direction. "And you're gonna wish you'd helped me get there."

I shoved a chair out of my way to snatch her upside her head.

"Problems down there, Deneen?" my mother called.

"Nah na nah na nah nah," Ciara taunted, and then bounded up the steps toward her room. Mother met her at the top. Ciara was as cool as a bowl of lime sherbert.

She said, "Sissy and I were just discussing some of her hobbies. They sound like so much fun. I think I'd like to try them!"

"Oh, I'm so glad to see my girls getting along." Mother walked by me on her way to get her regular nightcap of a microwaved glass of skim milk. She encircled me with an anemic little hug, which I barely noticed, since my eyes were glued on my sister. Ciara did one of those obscene open-mouthed tongue-wagging head-lolling gestures that your least mature National Basketball Association players do to enrage their opponents. I pointed my finger at her, but couldn't find the words. She swished her hips out of my view, simpering at me over her shoulder.

That did it. I had had it with the demon seed, and this time she was going to pay. Whatever sense I had recovered thus far took the express train back to vacationland.

I waited until I was absolutely sure everyone in the house was asleep. I got the sharpest pair of scissors I could find and I let myself into my sister's room.

# Twelve

It was never my intention to cut off all my sister's hair. You must believe me. I admit that for a moment there when I saw her locks—splayed out around her on the pillow like a feathery halo—I really thought I would shave her bald. I was tempted to, anyway. I touched her hair and found it as soft as I had imagined it would be. It had that fine satiny texture that my hair has for about ten minutes after I leave the beauty parlor, and only if the wind isn't blowing and the humidity is below forty-nine percent. Some of us got blessed and some of us got hair like horses or rams or other unpleasant farm animals. I knew women who poured so many chemicals on their heads that what remained were crispy hard knots, women who spent a year's savings and their vacation time traveling across country from salon to salon, women who had resorted to surgery—trying to get themselves just one little hank of this spun sugar my sister had crowning her head. Right then I hated her for that hair more than for anything else I could think of.

She turned to the side, sleeping soundly. She was warm, the way children are in sleep, and her breath was coming in peaceful waves. Prudence and Faith and Temperance clustered around the scene, protective, like so many fallen and bloated angels. I resisted the temptation to gather them together and arrange them into the types of pornographic tableau that are featured in *Penthouse* magazine. Too obvious. Too trashy. Instead, I reached into my sister's mane of lovely lovely hair, lifted a section, and with the scissors snipped a tiny collection of strands, close to her scalp. I left them there to be combed out in the morning.

Shame on you, Deneen, you might be saying: a late thirty-something-year-old woman violating a child in the night. And, as I think of all the things I did over the course of my crazy summer, I have to admit that this is the one I am most ashamed of. At the time, however, I felt nothing remotely re-sembling shame. I was angry, I wanted revenge—for the name calling and the snooping and the dirty looks, for the curlers she'd borrowed without permission, and for the general downright hatefulness I had been privy to.

And in waiting for my trespass to be discovered and for the hysteria to begin, I created for myself a whirlwind of nervous anticipation, the same kind the mother of the bride must create when preparing for her daughter's wedding, or the astronauts have waiting for the next morning's launch. I closed myself in-side that whirlwind, anticipating the moment when a handful of liberated hair would convince my mother just how terribly sick her other daughter was.

I lay on my bed that night in a hot swarm of rage. At first it was junior high school rage—or at least the kind of blinding anger I recalled from my days at Hazlewood East. It took me quite a while to remember that I did not, in fact, have to worry that tomorrow morning Ciara would meet Rhonda Dalke at the lockers before my bus arrived and tell her that she had been told by Pat Thomas that I had French kissed Stevie Thorogood under the bleachers after last night's football game. The truth was I didn't much care what she had read about me, nor about the fact that she thought she could blackmail me with the information. Fat chance. I was a grown woman. If I wanted me a little hootchie, well, it didn't have nothing to do with anybody in this house, and the first amendment said I could write about my sex life anytime I damn well pleased.

No, what I didn't like—what I have never liked—is when a trifling wench like her thinks they're gonna play games with me. Back in college there was one of these vixens, and she thought she would play me for a chump. She was one of those always coming by to borrow a blouse, or stopping in to copy today's lab notes. Hey, I'm a generous sister. (Just ask Mr. Mark Layton.) But then this bitch turns around and starts whispering about me behind my back. "Did you see Deneen's hair, all mashed down in the back this morning?" "Her thighs are looking mighty big these days." "She better start wearing a bra on them big floppy titties of hers." The thing was, she was saying these things to *my* girls. She was saying them to folks she knew was gonna turn around and tell me. The bitch was playing games with me.

I fixed her behind good. I bided my time, though. Waited until I could really set her ass up. The next semester we had three classes together, and honey, she thought she had a good thing. I gave her copies of my notes—hell, I even typed them up for her. She quit going to class altogether. What she didn't know was that half the shit I put down I made up just for her, and when it came time for finals, her behind flunked all three classes. It was good-bye Macalester for that wench.

You can ask anybody at Waltershied, Williams and Caruthers; Deneen don't play. I will treat you fair and pro-fessional and courteous, and I would even take the shirt right off my back for you if I thought a little extra break might help you. But don't mess with me. I don't like it.

And I don't care if you are family.

I sipped my Diet Dr. Pepper the next morning waiting for the big blow up. It didn't come. That morning and the next morning after I'd given her a second going-over, she came down, her hair already brushed, and we sat there with our various breakfasts and I—like the vice president of the Hair Club for Men—eagerly waited for the subject of hair loss to come up. It never did. My mother had this thing she would do sometimes in the morning—she would get up from her breakfast and perch herself on a stool. She would gather Ciara next to her gently with one arm and then with the other pull a brush through her hair. Mother did it that second morning. Ciara closed her eyes and indulged her, submitting to the brush the same way an old family dog would. At the end of the routine mother always pulled the loose hair from the brush, balled it up, and then lit a burner on the stove and incinerated it. I watched her eyes closely, looking for a missed stroke, for some sort of closer examination, anything that would indicate a sign of concern. None came. Over the burner the only slightly larger wad of hair exploded with sparks the way it always did and drifted away into nothingness.

Humans, of course, lose many hundreds of hairs a day, or that's what I've been told. Actually, I remembered that fact from an ad campaign I worked on years ago for some rather caustic shampoo/conditioner combination which was claiming that it could "stabilize" damaged hair. As mammals, our bodies are for the most part hair machines, and it made sense, of course, that my mother and Ciara weren't going to notice the odd extra strand or two in the brush. A different technique was called for.

The next night I found Ciara in her room, gangly in her summer nightie, arms in front of her, hair stretched out behind her, as if flying. I gathered that hair in a bundle and cut an inch off the ends.

The following morning my mother was in one of her upbeat moods, one of the particularly obnoxious ones she gets into where she can barely contain her joy at being part of this world.

"My girls are looking exceptionally lovely today," she announced.

I said thank you, and Ciara did her coy number where she turned her head to the side and put her open hand up to her hair to fluff it. Except when she started to fluff she found her hair was in a higher place than she remembered it to be. A troubled look crossed her face.

Bull's eye!

But the look quickly passed, and I knew right then what the problem was. It was that teenage malfunction where in your brain there is some sort of aberrant logic circuit that explains away things that to normal people (adults) are alarming or troublesome. Things such as, what on earth could possibly be in the secret sauce at McDonald's to make it that color, and not being able to figure out how it might be possible to remove a sock without using the other foot. It's the same circuit that allows them the endless watching of MTV.

Realizing I was up against a formidable foe (and just because later that same day the weasel gave me for no good reason an extra dirty look when I passed her on the stairs), I ramped the program up a few notches. That night I went into her room and with my trusty scissors indiscriminately snipped out whole clusters of hair from around her head.

The next morning—the fourth morning of what I like to call Operation Beauty and the Beast—I got myself to the breakfast table extra early and sat there, coolly munching on a bowl of Peanut-Butter Cap'n Crunch cereal and a pint of Ben & Jerry's New York Super Fudge Chunk ice cream. From up in her room I heard a scream and I was immediately transported to heaven.

"What on earth?" Reina exclaimed. Ciara ran down the stairs, shrieking as if her drawers were on fire.

"Mommy! Look!" Ciara held out her brush and her hands. Packed full, it was, with her formerly magnificent tresses.

"My goodness," I said. "What ever has happened?"

"Mommy!" Ciara cried and folded herself into her mother's arms. For a second there I actually felt sorry for her. She, after all, was having the ultimate bad hair day. Mother pulled up through the hair, here and there freeing a strand that Ciara's brush had missed.

"Well, I never," Reina exclaimed. "Deneen, come look at this. What do you suppose?"

I sauntered over and felt around the troubled scalp. A few healthy brushes from Ciara had already disguised my handiwork.

"You know," I told them, "I've heard this can happen to people when they're under too much stress. Or when their diet is poor. Are you eating okay, sweetie?" I fronted enough concern to staff weekends worth of disease telethons.

"Yes," Ciara whimpered.

"Well. It must be stress. I'd take her to the doctor if I were you."

"Do you think so?" Mother asked.

"Just look at her. You can't be too careful about these things." To be honest I was pissed off because for the most part she still looked terrific, every bit the beauty queen she was. I decided it wouldn't hurt to gild the lily. I leaned toward my mother conspiratorially and whispered, "You know what it's like when they're at this age."

"I'll call Dr. Guilden, I guess."

Mother pivoted her head back and forth between her two daughters as if we both had some sort of a problem. I shook my head sympathetically in my sister's direction. Underneath Ciara's pouty whimpering I could see the beginnings of the realization that she was on to me. I've seen enough palace intrigue films to remember that though I might be the queen of the gameswomen, my darling sister was made out of more or less the same stuff. Watching one's back was always a good plan.

To tell you the truth, by the morning of the fourth day of Operation Samsonette, I had mostly lost interest in the whole affair. I had lost my pique, but it was more than that. To be honest I could never understand perverts and con artists who took advantage of children. It really is like shooting at the proverbial fish in the barrel. Where was the sport in that? Those sickos are just afraid to play in the big leagues with the rest of us.

Granted there is something a little specious about a woman who spent four days giving her baby sister unauthorized beauty treatments, lecturing perverts, and I admit I was a little over the top. All right! My behavior was mean and hateful and sick. And I would have been harder on myself had I not by morning four replaced my anger with a heartfelt belief that what I was doing to Ciara was really for her own good. I be-lieved—and believe to this day—that there was something seriously wrong with that child. She was undernourished—almost certainly bulimic. She was manipulative and mean, a cutthroat competitor, the kind of person who would trip a fat girl to win a beauty pageant. And on top of that she was as close to tone deaf as she could get without causing nerve damage in her listeners. I believed and I convinced myself roundly that "restyling" Ciara's hair would sound the alarm bell that needed to be sounded in order for my mother to take action.

So as Reina set up a doctor's appointment for that afternoon ("Yes, today. It's life or death, for God's sakes!"), I knew that my sojourn with the scissors had reached its end. I had extracted my revenge. And though I found it bitter—as are all such victories—I leavened it with the possibility that Ciara might actually get the help that she needed.

During those four days, I was also having to keep things copacetic on the Minneapolis front. Katrina, being the trooper she was, had taken my advice to heart and had plugged herself in and tuned Mr. Waltershied out. According to *her* he would storm out of his office every twenty minutes or so and she would spin around to the computer and type up each and every word of his tantrum. According to *him*, Katrina was being her usual vague self; though he couldn't figure out how, while ignoring him, she still managed to get done what needed doing. He didn't have a clue that it was really me long-distance pulling both sets of strings.

I decided that in addition to wrapping up this douche spray account, now was as good a time as any to clean up the loose ends that never get attended to on one's desk. Each of us has one of those separate and permanent "in" boxes full of stuff that, were we paying attention when they'd crossed our desks in the first place, we'd either have said "no" to, filed, or thrown into the trash can. I told Katrina to go get mine.

"You got an invitation here to a Chamber meeting—"

"Dump it."

"Here's an offer for a free software upgrade from—"

"Dump it."

"Meeting with Mr. Waltershied, tomorrow at 3:00."

(Which tomorrow? When was that?)

"Dump it."

After we finished with mine I had her wait until Mr. Waltershied stepped out to lunch and then go get his.

"Deneen," he says to me a day or so later. "I can't believe it. I'm actually getting some work done around here for once. I'm getting letters answered, all my filing's done. Say, maybe you should think about staying gone."

"Don't forget our little bet," I reminded him. I said that to keep from cussing his lazy ass out.

"Bet? You and me made a bet?"

"Sure did. You remember, we bet that whoever came up with the best idea for the douche spray ad—"

"Do you have to say douche spray, for God's sakes, Deneen—"

"Douche spray, douche spray, douche spray . . . would get taken by the other one to lunch at *510*."

"I would never make a bet like that."

"But you did. I was on this very phone. You were sitting there pacing around your desk, yelling into the speaker phone much like you are right now. Oh, and by the way, douche spray, douche spray, douche spray!"

That made him pick up the regular receiver. I can't stand talking to folks who do other things when they talk to you. "Works every time," I said.

"Deneen, you know and I know that a person can't win a bet with you. Why would I even bother entering into such a deal?"

"So, what you're saying is you don't have any ideas for the douche spray campaign and that therefore I win by default."

"I said no such thing. I got pages of ideas. I got ideas until I'm using the extra pages for toilet tissue. And there was never a bet. No. Bet."

"Let's hear em. You go first."

"Okay, Deneen, check this out. Two sisters—"

"Sisters, not *sisters* sisters, right?"

"Yeah, yeah, yeah, yeah, yeah, we been through that. So these sisters, I see them on a cruise, you know, resort-wear, blue skies, shuffleboard. Lots of brothers in them dashiki deals. They start talking to each other about, you know, whatever in the hell this stuff does, and the one says—"

"Hold the phone, there, Buster. Just a sec. What do you mean "whatever in the hell this stuff does?"

There was a big pause on the other end of the line.

"Mr. Waltershied?"

"Don't pick at me, woman. You know, the stuff. Whatever in the hell you buy this stuff for. That's what these two chicks are talking about on the cruise. And so the one gal says—"

"Hold up. Hold up. So what it is you're telling me is we're billing this million plus account, and you don't even know what the hell the product is for."

There was another long pause.

"No. Of course I don't. How in the hell would I know something like that? No!"

I had to sit there for a minute. I took the phone from my ear and gave it a good hard look.

"Boy (I almost said 'nigger' but I caught myself), you're telling me you been married twenty-something years, got two teenage daughters, and you don't know about douche spray."

"Hey, Patty and the girls got closets full of this shit. Boxes and tubes and puffy shit and bottles. What do you expect? I'm going up to my thirteen-year-old and ask her to tell Daddy the fine distinctions between different kinds of tampons?"

"We were not talking about tampons. But let me explain the whole thing to you right now."

"No! Deneen! I don't want to know. I swear to God. One more word and I'm off this phone. I mean it."

"But this is not a dirty topic, Walt. All it is, is two basic kinds of—You stop that humming. Stop it!"

"*You* stop talking about . . . it."

"If we can't talk about *it,* how is it we're supposed to write a commercial about *it?*"

"Let me remind you, young lady, that this is advertising. Not sex education. And the day we actually have to have anything to do with the shit we sell is the day I leave this business."

He had a point there, I guessed. I had done campaigns for all sorts of products I couldn't care less about. Some of those products were useless and one or two were downright deadly and evil. I had done *political* ads, for heaven's sake. For vile antihuman cretins, no less. It had never bothered me before.

Still, there was a different issue here. There was an important point, even if I couldn't quite put my finger on it yet. I only knew that it had to be possible to do this campaign the right way—whatever that was—and that it was worth figuring out, and that if anyone was going to figure it out it was going to be me, and that I wasn't going to let it be watered down or ruined due to this bastard's ignorance or rush to turn it around.

"In that case, I win," I said. "I guess we'll be going with my ideas."

"We haven't *heard* your ideas. AND THERE IS NO BET!"

"Okay, here goes. Now you know how sometimes during a heavy flow—"

"Nope. Deneen! Uh uh! No way."

"Well, if you don't want to hear my pitch, I guess I'll have to do all the work myself."

"Fine. Fine, Miss Smartypants. I'll tell you what. You want to bet? How bout we bet your job on it? How bout that?"

Oops. Hoisted on my own tampon, as it were.

But you know my motto: Never blink, even when you're bluffing.

"My job," I said. "Sure. You're on."

"Enough screwing around. We got big bucks on this. I can't afford to futz around. I want you in my office. Here. In person. End of this month. I want the whole thing laid out. And I expect to have my socks knocked off."

"Excuse me, but that doesn't sound like a bet. That doesn't even sound like deal." What it sounded like was a threat.

"You want a deal? Okay, here's the deal: OR, you come home now and we get back to work. Now. Today. Like we always do."

"Walt."

"Don't 'Walt' me, Deneen. You know what I think? I think you're playing possum."

"You don't understand."

"Deneen, you think everybody else is dumber than you are. You think nobody pays attention to anything but you. I think you had a little setback and it scared you."

"Don't you bait me, Mr. Waltershied. Katrina had no right—"

"I think you're chicken, Deneen. I think—"

"You go to hell."

I hung up the phone on his ass right then and there. Just who did he think he was talking to? I'm not his child. I'm not some flunky either. I'm a grown damn woman. A vice president. I'm responsible, and I get the job done. I'm respected all over town. I pay my bills, and, and, and.

And I *was* hiding out at my mother's house in the suburbs of St. Louis. I had hair that just the day before had been dyed auburn and styled into the same hairstyle Goldie Hawn used to have on *Laugh-In* in 1969. I spent my evenings having wild sex with a man I hardly knew. I had just the night before mutilated a child's hair with a pair of pinking shears.

I spun around in the desk chair and threw my head back. I opened my mouth and released a long breath, slowly, my body sagging deeper into the chair as the air rushed from my lungs.

What *was* I doing here? How had I let this happen to me?

I wish at that moment I could say that I saw inside my head the doors flying open and the three-by-five cards exposed to the light of day, but that would not be true. The metaphor had, in fact, died right there. It was now just me and my problems that I did not want to think about. And an enormous, ponderous sadness.

"Deneen. Come with me, please."

"What, mother?"

"To the doctor's. Please."

"Oh. I mean, sure."

Ciara had stuffed her hair into some sort of oversized fedora and was wearing a large pair of sunglasses. I couldn't remember that anything had been wrong with her eyes. My general remorse about my entire life embraced her.

"It'll be all right," I said.

"Like you could care," was her answer.

Dr. Guilden's office was in a high-rise on Brentwood Boulevard. Mother and I waited in the reception room while he gave her the once over.

"I just knew it would be something," my mother said.

"What do you mean?"

"Ciara. She's not an easy child, you know."

"Say more," I prompted. We were finally going to get to the heart of it.

"Nothing," Mother replied. "It's just this pressure, is all. This pageant mess. This trip to Las Vegas."

"You can always take her out of it."

Mother looked at me over the top of her glasses. "We must not be talking about the same child."

"You know how I feel about—" I started to say but she raised her hands to remind me I was headed across an agreed-upon boundary.

She sat there fidgeting with her purse, leafing through a magazine that she grabbed from the coffee table—an old issue of *People*. This was a new side of her for me, this nervous fidgeting. She had never been the sort to let anything seem to get to her. Even when my father left her, she had rallied right away with a nonstop series of parties and club events. Back in those days she was the sort of woman who looked at life as some sort of grand parade. Sometimes one of the floats got a flat tire. You parked it, and the rest of the rank kept stepping. These days she was more like an ancient majorette. Marching had gotten old, the costume had become threadbare, and her arms were just plain tired of keeping things spinning.

"She'll be fine," I said, patting her arm.

She rifled violently through a six-page spread that my agency had lost the bid on and then slammed the magazine down on the end table. "Deneen, please. The child's healthy as a horse."

"She is? Why are we here?"

Mother straightened the magazines she had strewn, and I watched her worry turn to scorn. "The demon probably cut that hair out herself," she seethed.

"Mother! I don't think so. Ciara?"

"We are here, my dear oldest daughter, because I'm an elementary school principal and old habits die hard. In my business a sick child equals pay attention. We're here because every now and then in my haste I forget who I'm dealing with."

I looked at her incredulously. "I don't understand."

"She's been stealing from me, you know. Cash. Right out of my purse. Forty dollars here. Forty there."

That much. I hadn't taken that much, had I?

"Well, you know, mother, maybe—"

She raised her hands to stop me again.

We sat there a while longer, mother's scorn turning to something like humiliation. I was swimming in my own moral confusion. There was a little part of me that felt bad because some of the things mother fretted about were not, in fact, Ciara's fault. There was a big part of me that was thinking how awful it must be for her to have a child who could do such terrible things. That part teamed up with the part that couldn't help throwing in her two cents worth.

"You know she throws up," I said.

Mother turned toward me, took in a deep breath, pointed her finger at me ready to let loose. Just then, Dr. Guilden came out and signaled us to come over.

"She's fine. I have a vitamin there for her to take just in

case." Ciara stormed toward the office door, pulling mother behind her. She made a face that would warn off vampires.

"Thank you, Dr. Guilden," mother called.

"A trip to the beauty parlor wouldn't hurt her," he whispered to me in the same stage whisper he probably used with his nurses.

Hawkins was booked so we ended the afternoon at another salon in Clayton. The stylist would show a cut to mother who, if she approved, would nod her head and then pass the magazine to Ciara who would scream, "No!" and throw the magazine at me. (As if I had anything to do with it.) About five-thirty she settled on a swept-off-the-top-of-her-head pixieish look—the kind of hair Julia Roberts had in *Hook*. Ciara simpered into the mirror like the star of a discount shampoo commercial.

"I'm so glad we were able to get it fixed," I exclaimed, and I even managed to sound enthusiastic about it.

Mother rolled her eyes at me and mumbled. "Don't you get it, woman? The demon's been angling after this haircut for six months." Mother set her teeth and pasted on an expression that let it be known there was to be no further discussion of hair in her household.

All the way home Ciara kept flipping that hair around and running her fingers through it. It was cuter than ever. It really was.

There is no God.

She turned to me, stationed in the back seat like the baby I was. She narrowed her eyes at me, puckered her lips, and blew me a kiss.

# Thirteen

The next morning mother pulled her car up by the curb in front of Hawkins's house and announced she had some things to straighten up on her desk at school, and she would be back to get us in a few hours. I had sat up late the night before waiting for creative lightning to strike. It hadn't. I had come charging up the steps at what I thought was a decent late morning hour—say, 11:15—only to discover it was really just 8:30.

"Let's go, Deneen," my mother had ordered, and I, in my sleep-deprived, addled state, had complied. It wasn't until after she left that I realized that, without wheels or a purse, I was hostage at Hawkins's house, and with Ciara, no less. My sister and I had been left at the baby-sitter's. Ciara skipped up his walk and rang the doorbell.

I thought we were going to have to take old Hawkins to the emergency room. I really did. He lay back on the sofa in his living room, gassing in and out with these little breaths, fanning himself with throw pillows, and just generally carrying on.

"Are you going to be all right?" I asked.

"Lord, I've been good, haven't I? I stopped smoking like you wanted and I stopped looking at them nasty magazines. Why this? Why me? Why now?"

Ciara traipsed back and forth in front of him, modeling her

new hair. She would stop now and again to caress the mop the way women used to do in hair spray commercials.

"It is kind of cute, don't you think?" I prompted, not needing to be doing CPR on a man wearing a sports coat covered in yellow and black squares. He looked sort of like an upright checkered cab.

He moaned. "Cute! What do cute have to do with anything?"

Ciara popped her gum, rolled her eyes. "Have a cow, will you," she said, in her vacant valley voice. "Everyone has short hair these days. Get used to it."

Hawkins got up and reached out to touch the hair. He approached it as if it had been smeared with dog poop. He mustered enough courage to reach in and raise up a handful in my direction. "Does this look like pageant hair to you? Don't you even try to answer that."

Ciara groomed her hair back into shape with her fingers.

"It can't be that bad," I said. Could it?

"How in the name of Jesus did I get my business tied up with some ignorant heifers like this," he said, apparently to someone living up in his ceiling. "Look around this room," he ordered. He pointed to the fifteen or so pictures of big-teethed, jewel-crowned women who decorated his walls. Honey-colored, coffee-colored, sepia, beige, red gold—and there were even one or two girls who must've been just plain white girls up there. A whole range of ages, too, from pre-teens to somewhere in the twenties—though it was hard to tell underneath the makeup.

"Look at my girls," he ordered, "and then tell me do the words 'big hair' mean anything to you."

On closer inspection, in addition to sparkly tiaras of various magnitudes, each woman had been topped off with massive quantities of bouncing and behaving hair. Serious hair. We're talking hair with wings and tunnels and curlicues and balconies. We're talking hair that not only demanded you notice it, but the sort of hair that might set up its own separate ticket booth and concession stand.

"Hair!" Hawkins shouted. "Big hair!" He was heaving in and out and frothing at the mouth.

"Now, Hawkins," I said, easing him back onto the sofa. "In *Vogue* and in all the big fashion spreads, this is what the girls are wearing—this boyish, Peter Pan look." Ciara moved through a whole range of poses, acting as if someone were actually snapping her picture at the rate of seventy-five shots per minute. She pouted her lips and formed her mouth into seductive-looking Os. She jutted her hips out, angled her narrow body, and made her eyes vacant and wide.

"This ain't Paris. This ain't New York." Hawkins ticked those off on his fingers. "Hell, this ain't even Minneapolis. This is Missouri. You take your interfering behind over to the mall and take a look at the hair on the women. Big hair, and lots of it, too."

Me? "I had nothing to do with this hair," I said. Which was technically the truth. If it were up to me the wench would be bald with pimples.

"It was you and that Layton character," he said, pointing a well-manicured finger in my direction. "That hootchie must have been mighty good to stoop to a dirty trick like this."

"Hootchie!" Ciara screamed. "Ha! Ha! Ha! Ha! Ha!"

Hawkins gave her a dirty look. She was subdued. She was at that moment, in fact, getting nervous. In her fetching but devious head she was beginning to imagine her crown being slipped onto some other girl's mane.

"Maybe we could fluff it up or something," she said,

flummering it with her fingers and thrusting her arms out like a showgirl.

"Didn't leave me much to fluff, did you?"

"Her idea," I said, pointing at my sister.

Hawkins checked his watch and sighed. "We get started now we can do a weave, I guess."

"No!" Ciara screamed.

"Baby, come here," Hawkins reached his arms out to Ciara, guiding her down beside him on the sofa. "Baby, I can't take you into the nationals with your hair looking like this. I can't do it to you or to me. I got what you call a reputation to think about. A reputation means something in my business," he said and then glared pointedly in my direction. "But I'm mostly thinking about you, sugar. Old Hawkins just couldn't stand the thought of all that work you did being for nothing. Do you understand?"

"But I can win," Ciara said resolutely. "I know I can."

"You are a pretty and talented and smart young lady. But I'm afraid you don't know nothing about business. Bidnez. That's B. I. D.—nez. I'm sorry, you don't. I do. That's all there is to it. Now what we'll do is we'll put a weave in, starting right about here." He indicated about a two-inch section of the front of her hair where it was the longest. "I got some nice hair in just the other day—not quite as nice as what you had—but it'll match just fine. We'll run it down just to your shoulders. So we can give it some volume. Oh, you know what, Deneen. I was thinking the other day, we could do this for you! They're doing this thing now where you cornrow and then arrange it into all kinds of fountains and decorations and mess."

Sounded good to me. He reached over and felt on my head.

Ciara snatched his arm right back. Heaven forbid I should get any attention.

"I don't want a hair weave," she pouted. "It'll look stupid and everybody will know."

"Oh, so on top of everything else, now you want to insult a person. For your information, Miss Thing, St. Louis and its vicinities are chock full of all kinds of folks got people thinking what's on top of their head is theirs, when what's up there is really mines. You know that gal they got doing the weather on Channel 7—brownskin girl?"

Ciara and I nodded.

"Bald as a beaver."

"No!" we gasped, simultaneously, mouths agape.

"Yes, ma'am. Head all covered with naps, look like dots on rice."

"That's amazing!" The man did do good work, then. That Marcy Jones-Jameson looked like a million dollars on the air. She had this picture-perfect upswept hairdo that blossomed at the neckline into a froth of soft swirls. Who knew?

Ciara patted at her own naturally beautiful hair. She was heartbroken. Poor thing. The new cut was perfect for her. Overnight she had gone from a gangly, storkish creature with a fountain of hair into a mature, blossoming young woman. She had been ready to give up that other image of herself since I'd been home, ready to try something new. Here he was, dragging her right back.

I held my peace. There were important lessons for her here. Everything has a cost, some things cost more than others, and a lot of shit out there ain't worth what you pay for it in the first place.

"Can we make a deal?" she asked, eyes cast coyly down at her lap.

"That depends on the deal," Hawkins replied.

Two shrewd operators from way back. I'd like them on my team when we went in to pitch the car companies.

"I'll do the showcase with my hair like this—"

"No! Uh uh."

"You didn't let me finish." She swatted his hand as if he were a naughty boy who'd tried to feel under her blouse. "If it goes okay—which it will—then . . . we'll talk." She batted her eyes.

Their negotiating was fascinating. "We'll talk" was code for we'll have round two. It was like watching a cat stare down a crocodile.

"You talk like this showcase wasn't nothing but a little toss-off sort of thing. It might not be a pageant and you might not be getting no trophy for it, but it's where I get to show off in front of my colleagues and it's still my professional name on the line."

"Come on," Ciara said. She squinched up her nose like the old pro she was. "I'll make you look good. You know I will."

"All right then, Miss Hollywood. Here's how we'll do it: Tomorrow you go on out there with this little bit of frizzle frazzle you got on your head." He mussed it and she recoiled. "If the reviews aren't absolutely top of the line, we do it my way. Otherwise you can take your half-bald self on out of here for good."

"Hawkins!" Ciara simpered, cuddling up next to him. "Don't be such a fussy wussy." She snuggled his neck. I hoped he had his anti-venom kit handy.

"Get off me!" he ordered. "Let's get them dresses fitted." He swatted her behind, shooing her on down to the studio. He leaned over to me on his way out and whispered, "If she grow any more titty in the next week, we can all kiss the Dream Dolls goodbye."

The showcase was more or less the local pageant professional's trade fair. Ostensibly a fashion show, the evening was where the local sponsors and promoters and coaches got together informally to gossip, show off their wares, and scope out the competition for the upcoming cycle of pageants. The gown designers hawked their latest creations and the hairdressers their latest flips and swirls and topknots. The showcase was also the time to give your latest discoveries—the hot young contestants of tomorrow—their "maiden voyage," to borrow an unfortunate phrase.

Strictly for the pros, this was a hush-hush, private affair, held discreetly in the ballroom of a downtown hotel. Hawkins's crowd eschewed the hoi polloi—the hot-comb and family-van suburban rabble—who traveled from pageant to pageant with a carload of bucktoothed daughters, looking to catch a break as Junior Miss Feedcorn. According to Mark—who'd checked this out before laying down his first dollar—the showcase crowd was "the big boys." The high rollers. The folks who found the girls when they were young, groomed them along through the petites and the juniors, and then shepherded them all the way to USA, America, Universe, and the World. Mark says that on Miss America night, the smart money in Vegas knows exactly who is behind those girls up there, and that they bet accordingly. And in keeping with his theme of vertical integration, he says that these folks not only front the girls, but that "the real big boys" own the rights to the local and state pageants as well.

Layton Enterprises had three girls in the showcase. We had talked about it in bed the night before—in between a little thing he called the Shanghai Sling and another little thing he called Mark's Mystery Move. Just recently slung, I was a bit fuzzy headed at the time, but I do recall him telling me that his approach to the pageant game was going to be to "repackage the merchandise."

"I been reading the fashion trades and looking at some of these hot young actresses," he said. "The trick, as I figure it, is to get ahead of the curve a bit."

Mark said he was going with a smarter, more elegant, high-glamour girl, girls like the ones he had placed in Ciara's Dream Doll pageant. There was definitely a different look about them. They stood out onstage that night like Rembrandts at the starving artist's sale.

I asked him, "Don't you think that, really, what people want is more of what they always have? Simpering. Perkiness. Lots of All-American-girl hair and teeth."

"Well, some of that," he told me, "is just your basic showmanship. That sister of yours, she's got showmanship coming out her pores. But some of it is a matter of taste. And tastes change. You're in the marketing biz. You know the drill. You got to have the product ready *before* the public knows it wants it."

Products. Is that what these girls were? I thought about it and I realized I couldn't really come up with a better classification. Entertainers? Not particularly, not most of the ones I'd seen, and certainly not my sister. Models? Not in the garment district sense of the word. Nothing they wore was for sale. The audience sure wasn't filled with department store buyers. Public relations? In one of the big national pageants one of the women—tottering on her high heels in her skin-tight swimsuit—referred to her chosen occupation as "public relations consultant." I had always assumed that that was a euphemism for hooker. "Product" seemed as good a word as any to me, even if I couldn't quite put my finger on just what it was that was being sold or to whom.

On the one hand, I could think of Ciara as a product, as some sort of commodity, out there on the shelf, designed, programmed, and packaged to turn a profit. A product I could ignore, the same way I ignored things such as drain openers, low sodium condiments and gourmet cat food. Products were not things I regularly had to be annoyed by, to fret over, to worry about—except at my job, of course, and there they were more or less just screws, bolts, and widgets—the pieces one had to use to make the machine work. So she was a product. But this wasn't just some box of cereal or a container of douche spray. This was my flesh and blood, my mother's other daughter, my sister. Product seemed, at the moment, more inappropriate than ever.

"It's a crock of shit," I said. "Those poor girls."

"Your heart is bleeding all over my luxurious satin sheets. Those poor girls? My good woman, a lot of these girls aren't the least bit poor, and very few are what you'd call stupid either. This is not a hobby, Miss Deneen. While the rest of em are out there running their butts around the shopping mall or sitting on their behinds watching TV, these young women are out pursuing goals. By the time they get to college, a lot of 'those poor girls' have earned enough to pay their way through, and the really good ones—like your sister—pay their way through graduate school and beyond. 'Those poor girls'— even the runners-up and even some who don't get that far— walk off those stages and into careers in public service, in the entertainment industry, in business, in *your* field. Don't talk to me about those poor girls."

"And out of the kindness of his heart, a nice fellow like you just opens his wallet and—"

"And don't get sanctimonious. It's a business. I'm a businessman. It's a business where there's decent money to be made. It's above board and perfectly legal. Yeah, there are some sleazebags out there—just like in every other business. They set up these tinfoil and streamers operations in some gymnasium and take Joe and Jean Suburban for fifty bucks so they can see their princess up on the stage. And so what? Grandma gets some nice pictures, and everybody goes home happy. The stuff I want to do—the stuff your sister is already doing—is a high-class, national industry. I bring the girls to the marketplace. With any luck, someday soon I'll own part of that marketplace."

"Girls to the marketplace. Sounds like a pimp to me."

Mark, at that point, rolled onto his back, bent one leg and crossed the other knee on top of it. "This from a woman who works in an industry that hires cartoonists to sell cigarettes to children. What's the going rate on those ads these days?" he asked. He snuggled into my side.

I had nothing to say. I knew that advertising wasn't the world's cleanest business. For that matter, was there any such thing as a clean business? People were always blowing this cigarette crap in my face. Always pointing out the wretched excesses—the black communities filled with tobacco and liquor ads, the zit-cream commercials with their false promises of clear skin and a happy social life. I couldn't deny the reality of such transparent excess. I also worked in an industry that donated its time and energy to informing people of public-health crises, such as AIDS, and social problems, such as domestic abuse and safety in the home. I worked in an industry that was regulated up the butt, an industry where you had to be extra careful, because any seemingly false claim or damaging reference could land you in court for the rest of your life. I shoved the nigger's tickling hand from my range.

"There are degrees of evil," I said, massaging his arm, ready to return to his best topic—sex.

"Evil! That's rich, Deneen. Does Hawkins DeAngeles seem like an evil man to you? Does he?"

I shrugged.

"Hawkins DeAngeles may be an exasperating obnoxious old faggot, and he may be trying to stand between me and a potentially lucrative business deal, but he is not an evil man. He would never do anything to hurt your sister or any of the other young ladies he works with. That's true of everybody I've met. It's a business, but it's a *people* business. Think about *that.*"

I did think about it, as I watched Ciara hop up and down off a footstool for her final fittings for the showcase. Hawkins tugged at the hem lines and pulled and pinned fabrics. "Good girl," and "You are just so precious," he said, and other such things. And while, sure, it might be better to be fussed over for being witty or intelligent or altruistic, I had to admit that my sister's life could be much much worse. I knew women who at Ciara's age had days filled with rage and fear, hiding from molesting relatives and abusive parents. Girls who went to work shelling peas in a factory to help put food on the table. I knew a woman who at Ciara's age was engaged to a man who expected her to bake perfect pies, wear frilly aprons, and come to his bed dutifully when called. I myself had been a plump, taciturn thing, whom nobody paid any attention to. I thought about the way Hawkins had made me feel the half-dozen or so times he had done something to my hair. (We were sticking with the auburn Goldie Hawn thing for the time being.) He was bitchy and a spiteful old gossip, but there was not an angry bone in his body. He dipped my head in the shampoo sink, teased me out with one of his trusty tools and made me feel like a million dollars.

Ciara came out in a simple white shift, sleeveless, with a round neck and a black cameo choker. Jackie Kennedy might have worn this very outfit.

"Boo hoo!" Hawkins howled. He plucked at the dress just above her ribs. "See how funny it's hanging? My little girl done grown up on me."

He ripped out a side seam and fussed with the material. "Stop that, fore I slap some sense in you," he ordered. Ciara was enjoying herself, thrusting out her brand new assets. She shot me a glance, and we actually laughed together—I think for the first time. We averted our eyes quickly, embarrassed, it seemed, that we had shared a real moment.

"No more pageants for her," I said.

Hawkins waved that away with his hands. "Miss Teenage America, here we come."

About then Mother blustered in, breathless and flushed. She flopped down on a love seat, next to me. "The weekend at last. This summer school is about to kill me. Thank God, only a week to go."

"All the Jones women in my home. I am truly honored."

"Can you fit me in, sugar?"

"Mother!" I said. "Your hair looks terrific."

Hawkins offered her his arm and escorted her toward his salon as if she were to be presented at court. "Consider the source," he said. Mother smirked and behind her back I gave them both the finger.

"Telling!" Ciara sang.

I pointed her in their direction, indicating she should go ahead. I dug into Hawkins's huge magazine basket. He subscribed to all the big beauty rags, and to all the trade publications as well. I checked out the competition—the ads, mostly, but the women, too. The glossies were filled with the usual Herb Ritts-esque glamour stuff—gaunt, pale, hard-bodied young men and women, seemingly in the throes of orgasm over whatever the product was. Boring. The only thing remotely interesting were some older ads I found for Benetton—horrific images of packed refugee ships, dying AIDS patients, and exploding car bombs. I liked them, but as of yet hadn't figured out what they had to do with selling casual preppy clothes. But at least they were interesting.

I turned to the trades. God, I could practically see these ads in my sleep. From quarter pagers to cross-the-fold spreads, we were all of us doing SOS, the same old shit: big picture of the product and some cutie pies that supposedly had been using it. This was the heart of business for Waltershied, Williams and Caruthers. If it wasn't stuff for the beauty industry it was farm implements or industrial-size bottles of catsup or mayonnaise. We did a whole campaign last year—a big biller, too—for a company that made some sort of goo to be kept by the stove in restaurant kitchens and used in the place of butter. "Don't tell the customers!" was my tag line, and I featured this big fat chef peering out the kitchen door at a table full of satisfied diners. We inset a bottle of the crap, lit in such away that it looked like a carafe of wine. I usually assigned such boilerplates to one of the green kids, someone fresh out of school. That, or to some old-timer we were carrying until retirement. Problem was there was so much of this kind of work. Industrial spreads were our bread and butter. Literally.

This Far East account could change that. Done just right, the campaign could open the door for us to the big leagues.

We'd be out of these trade rags and bidding on those Super Bowl accounts and on the TV sweeps campaigns. There was an awful lot riding on a can of douche spray.

And I was blocked. Still. I sat there beside a basket filled with every women's magazine in the world. I had some idea about sisters, and I knew I was supposed to be selling douche spray. In my mind I tried to mash it all together, like in a blender or in a cement mixer. I made lists in my head, I free associated. I came up empty.

Ciara snatched the magazine off the top of my pile— open to one of those black-and-white, semipornographic underwear ads.

"Thinking about your boyfriend?"

"Excuse you. I might have been reading that."

"I don't see any words on this page." She tossed the magazine back in the basket. "Who is your smelly old boyfriend anyway?"

"I don't have a boyfriend. I have friends. A number of friends. You wouldn't know them."

"He's probably some smelly old garbageman. Or a homeless person. That's who you do it with, isn't it? Homeless smelly garbage people."

I picked up another magazine and ignored her.

She got right up in my face. "You and your garbageman. You probably go to some parking lot, and you take off your clothes and you let him stick his nasty garbagey thing right up in you." Her breath smelled of stale grape gum. I gently turned her head away from mine.

"Don't you touch me!"

"Don't you get in my face!"

"You're so nasty. The things you do." She stalked back and forth in front of me, arms crossed, seething. She was as unpredictable as a swarm of bees. There was no telling what would set her off.

I sighed and laughed a little laugh. "You know, Ciara. There's nothing wrong with sex."

"What did you say to me?"

"I said there's nothing wrong with sex. There's nothing wrong with people having sex. There's nothing wrong with *me* having sex."

"I'm telling mother you said that to me."

I pointed her in that direction again.

"You're not even married."

"You don't have to be married to have sex."

"Especially if you're a slut."

I stood up and leaned up over her. She met my eyes.

"Your mother's under the dryer now," Hawkins said. I had not seen him come into the room. He pulled Ciara away from me. Our eyes kept contact as she got dragged away. "You go sit with Mama," he ordered me, quietly.

I waited until my breath came even. I found Mother, feet up, draped in a mauve-colored wrap, hair rolled and sealed into a pale pink bonnet drier that droned almost soundlessly atop her head. I sat in a chair beside her.

"Hi, baby!" she chirped grabbing my hand, holding it and shaking it. Whatever tension she had brought from school had been rinsed away. A simpy smile sealed her lips.

"How you doing, Mama?"

"I'm in heaven. Can you tell?"

"It's good to see you relaxed."

She inhaled and exhaled in a long sigh. "I'm slowing down, Deneen. I really am. It's harder and harder to go into that school every day and do the best for my kids. They need so much."

"I know you work hard. Time to think about retiring?"

She gave me a "get-real" look, brows raised, bottom lip turned under.

"You could. Mr. Jones left you some money." There was insurance, I knew, as well as a pension of some kind.

"It's not the money, Deneen. Well, part of it's the money. I've grown accustomed, as you might have noticed, to my creature comforts." She patted the inflated pink bonnet and laughed. "I could quit right now and we'd be okay. But whatever would I do with myself?"

"You could rest. Travel."

"Let's not forget our Ciara."

"Can't forget about her. There's always boarding school." Mother and I both laughed at that.

"Can you imagine? No, my baby's got to stay with me." She looked at me wistfully. I smiled back at her, nuzzled her hand with my cheek. Where was this woman when I was growing up? I would like to have known her.

"The thing is, Deneen. I'm a working woman. You know that about me. You're one, too. I don't know what I'd do without my work."

"You're tired, though."

"That's the point, sweetie. You get tired. When you get to be my age, you'll see. But you keep on keeping on. Don't you?"

I put my head on her arm and wept. She rubbed my head and told me it was okay.

"I'm going home, Mama."

"You ready now? You seem like you are."

"Yeah. I am."

She pushed me up to meet her eye. "Say, tell you what.

Stay a couple more days. Come to Vegas with me for the pageant. Please? It would be something we could do together."

How could I say no?

The lobby of the showcase hotel was abuzz with people huddled in groups, whispering, guffawing, sipping cocktails. It was the sort of event where there couldn't possibly be any actual conversation going on because everyone's eyes were darting around the room to see who else was there or who it might be better to be seen with. People waved at Mother and beckoned with their hands. I was in no mood for networking—especially when it was someone else's net that was being worked.

"Deneen, I really should go holler at Mr. What-cha-ma-deal."

"Another time, Mother." I dragged her into the ballroom to the spectator's gallery.

I spied Mark across the room, buttonholing a powdered-faced matron in peach chiffon. I found out later she was Phyllis Randolph Clark, a former Veiled Prophet Queen and one of the grand dames of the local pageant scene. I winked at him, and he did one of those steamy things with his eyeballs that people do when they know where each other's ticklish spots are. I thought it best not to head over there with Mother. Part of me didn't want to be embarrassed and part of me didn't need the competition. Reina is, after all, just another woman.

Hawkins had given us strict instructions as to how we were to behave at the showcase. We were there, he said, solely as escorts of a minor child. Our function: Like the swells seated above the riffraff in the boxes at some squalid turn-of-the-century burlesque house, we were to be quiet, privileged observers. There was to be no hooting and hollering for any of the participants.

As if.

The evening had all of the chummy false informality of one of those TV celebrity comedy roasts. The emcee—a man who is now a well-respected anchorperson but who I remembered from my childhood as Toggles the Clown, host of *Toggles Playhouse*, local home of the Three Stooges—introduced each of the coaches and sponsors as being dear old friends of his. The insiders—who literally sat inside a roped-off area of tables ringing the runway—laughed at private jokes and called out comments to each other across the room. The rest of us smiled pleasantly, kept our applause to a minimum (as suggested) and, if they were like me, tried to figure out who was or had been sleeping with whom.

The coaches and sponsors called out their girls one by one and they paraded out just like the products Mark suggested they were. He had brought his three girls from the Dream Dolls pageant. They were just as they had been that night: of a different character—pretty, but like orchids at a rose show, not quite fitting in. He might be a visionary, but I heard an awful lot of whispering and mumbling from the rank and file.

Ciara was part of the conventional fare. She, along with four other young women Hawkins showed, walked up and down the runway in the outfits he had selected.

"That girl," Mother whispered to me about a buxom brownskin woman in a sparkling evening gown, "is a contender for Miss Missouri. She'll be in the top five this year. You can bet your house on it." Mother looked at me over her glasses as if she expected me to run out and call my bookie.

Ciara was currently Hawkins's youngest girl. (He refused to work with the "Little Miss" crowd—the 3- to 8-ers. He said you just couldn't tell at that early age—they could very easily grow up to be dogs. Look at those child stars. What kind of investment was that?) She did everything she was supposed to. I could tell—I'd seen the routine enough. All the skips, all the simpering, all the demure shrugs.

It just didn't work. She was a disaster. The long legs, the more sophisticated hair, the sprouting mosquito bites. She was out of sync. She was almost as bad as Bette Davis in *What Ever Happened to Baby Jane?*

Mother and I went to find Hawkins at the end of the evening. Impeccably dressed in a tuxedo—one did not dress "out" for the showcase, I was told—he greeted his colleagues and threw back his head in laughter at their jokes. I met his eyes and waved. He waved back, and I could see he was filled with disappointment. Though Mother insisted, Ciara refused to go up to him, even to say goodnight. I could tell that from behind her sunglasses she was giving us the evil eye. I wanted to slap that pout off her face.

I watched while the next afternoon Hawkins used what appeared to be a cross between a soldering iron and a hot glue gun to attach a new head of little-girl hair to my sister. Ciara breathed heavily as if she were about to cry, but she did not, would not.

"All better!" she simpered when he had finally finished. Over that big fake smile her eyes were as cold as steel.

She flounced up the steps and Hawkins leaned into me with the most serious expression on his face I had ever had from him.

"We got one week of this little girl shit left. Thank God Almighty." He pointed at Ciara's sprouting chest and said to me. "You tell your mama to find something to tie them titties down with, you hear me?"

# Fourteen

What I told my mother was true. I was ready to go home.

It wasn't so much that I felt better. I can't really say I knew how I felt, to be honest. Those closed doors and filed-away trouble cards were—I can now admit—everyday denial, just as my therapist said. Like the rest of us here languishing at the end of the twentieth century, I had turned denial into an art form. There was so much that warranted ignoring— always another nation imploding or another house filled with a crackhead's neglected children. Why not pop a movie into the VCR or head out to the mall where you didn't have to think about anything? Why not?

I could tell I was ready to go because I was filled with the same stomach-tingling anxiety I felt whenever I had been too long in a hotel on a business trip. I wanted my bed—the one I had broken in. I wanted to walk to the refrigerator in my bra and panties and drink orange-flavored sparkling water directly from the bottle.

Hawkins, stinging from Ciara's cool reception at the show-case, put all other projects on hold and was sequestered with the ice queen, attempting to recover the child within. He would pick her up at 8:00 A.M. and return her late in the evenings, often well after dark. Not even I was to be witness to the transformation. She would come in dragging her sports bag, too tired even to pick a fight.

"Remember what I told you!" he would yell up the steps. She would raise a hand behind her. It appeared to me she was signaling defeat.

I didn't care about the rehearsals, but I did miss the impromptu beauty treatments that came during costume changes. I would return to Minnesota with the hair I had, the hair he gave me for the showcase—a blunt cut, modified twenties/flapper look, with cute little parted bangs. According to Hawkins, this was the kind of style that would look great "even if your lazy ass don't take care of it and lets it get all mangy." I promised him I would look after it, and hoped he was right in case I didn't.

I realized that the direct approach would not help me find the solution to my advertising dilemma. I knew—had known since the first time in my life I wrote anything even remotely creative—that one could not will an idea into existence. You could sit and stare at the blank page until your eyeballs dissolved and not form an intelligent thought. An idea had to come to you.

So I waited. Something would happen. (Before the deadline, I hoped.)

There was no need to call the office. My meeting with Mr. Waltershied was set, and there was no further need to dissemble or stall.

I browsed my mother's bookcases. Again. I washed and ironed what few clothes I had.

I guess I was rambling around noticeably, sighing, throwing myself onto the furniture.

"You're at loose ends," Mother said to me.

I shrugged.

"Looking for something to do?"

I shrugged again.

"You could come to school tomorrow morning and help out around the office. We can always use an extra pair of hands."

I could think of nothing I'd like less than spending a hot July day in the office of Marvin School. By now, Mother had no doubt spread the word among the women who populated her school that her daughter was around, needing love, compassion, support, help, and whatever other aid and comfort a building full of dedicated nurturers could dish up. Even under normal circumstances one could hardly get in the door of that place before the mothering began. I could just hear her: "My baby, Deneen!" "My poor angel!" I felt smothered just thinking about it.

"I'll find something to keep myself busy," I said.

"You sure? I wouldn't want to worry about you."

Which was just enough of a motherly thing to say to have its proper effect. The next morning I got up feeling good and guilty.

I dropped her off at school, borrowed her car, and met Mark for an early lunch in the lobby of a downtown office building. The building was gray-pink granite, undistinguished looking. Mark claimed to have a "branch office" in it.

"They got a nice little soup and sandwich place down about three buildings," he said. He took my elbow in that way men do when they want other men to know you belong to them. A few suited business people also braved the summer heat, passing us on the sidewalk, walking purposefully with blank expressions on their faces. Mostly the street was deserted, and I missed the skyways of Minneapolis with their lunchtime hustle and bustle.

Mark suggested the chicken-with-wild-rice soup, so I ordered that. We sat at a small table overlooking a concrete plaza ringed with flags. Mark dug into his bowl, lapping it up, praising it as if I had made it myself.

"How's that sister of yours?" he asked between slurps.

"Same as ever," I responded.

"Shame about her hair," he said, shaking his head. He sounded disingenuous to me. He picked the label off his bottled drink. There was no disputing that this was a handsome and elegant man, chic in his navy blue pin-striped suit. And I realized that I had never seen him in the daylight, that I had only been with this man in shadowy restaurants and auditoriums, or in the quavery candlelight of his condo late at night. Here he was. About as polished and perfect as it is possible for a human being to get. Me, I sat there stuffed into an old jumper I had packed for scuffing around Door County. I felt like last year's model after the new crop of cars appears in the showroom. There's something about a man who looks as well-groomed as Mark did that always makes me feel shabby and cheap, but this day my inadequacy was especially acute. At that lunch I felt like a ne'er-do-well relative, come downtown for a free lunch with a prosperous and tolerant uncle.

Say something to him, I thought. But the only thing I could come up with was, "You look terrific," so I said that, trying not to sound too much like my sister and her friends impressing the cute boy on the school bus.

"You're just trying to make me blush," Mark responded, and he did blush just a bit, too, his rich brown coloring warming with the red to an almost burnished copper tone. Mark gazed back at me across the table and something about his eyes made me as uncomfortable as the tight and frumpy blue jumper, divided as it was down the middle with, not a crease, but an insistent wrinkle from being stuck too long at the bottom of my suitcase. He reached out and folded one of my hands into his.

"You're something else," he said. "You really are."

What was this? What was a man like this doing, taking my hand in his and dropping a line like that?

"I really mean it," he added. "I mean, we don't know each other all that well yet, but I am quite smitten. Quite."

Smitten? In all my years on earth I had not heard that I had caused anyone to be smitten. And a darling man like this? Then one of those voices started talking—"Deneen! Deneen!" it said, and I told it to shut the hell up. Just look where your big mouth has gotten me now.

This was supposed to be a hobby. I was supposed to have worked my way through a dozen or so of the finest men in the lower Midwest. I was not supposed to have found Mark Layton. Smittening was nowhere in the program.

"I . . . I have to go," I said.

He asked me if we were getting together that night. His puppy-dog eyes were damn irresistible. I said sure, and then I felt guilty for once again not having responded to provocation from a man. I could not think of a thing to say to him. The best lover I had ever had tells me I had smitten him, and me, a professional copywriter, I was absolutely speechless. The voices had abandoned this sinking ship like so many opportunistic rats. Perhaps I had scared them away. Perhaps they had locked themselves away in one of those now-unneeded rooms in my brain, saving their deviant hectoring and encouragement for my next period of loss and despair.

Leaving me here with this man, smiling—simpering really—
appearing, no doubt, crazier than I had ever been back during
the recent times when I was the most out of my mind.

So I said, finally, "You really do look good."

That a girl, Deneen. Pander. Cultivate the obvious. It's
your life's work, after all. I turned to walk away and saw from
the corner of my eye that he blew me a sweet soft kiss.

He had not, by the way, returned my compliment.

Mother's guilt had penetrated, reaching its intended target.
Despite the potential for being mugged by a houseful of
mothers, I did stop by Marvin Elementary on the way home.
Marvin is an ugly mud-colored building, designed in such
a way that there is no telling the location of the front door.
I remembered that there was an entrance off the parking lot
near where they keep the dumpster.

"Can I help you with something?" a man asked me. He
had on a blue shirt with "Wally" stitched over the pocket.

"I'm looking for my mother."

Another man, "Smitty," said, "You're kind of a big girl
to be lost, aren't you?" Both of them—sitting there with
their feet propped up, holding sections of the *Post-Dispatch*—
laughed those nasty nasal laughs that men have.

I was not in the mood to be teased. I had had more
impressive men than these fired for much less.

"My mother is Dr. Jones. I believe she's the principal here."

Wally snapped to attention and gave me meticulous
directions to her office. Both men were suddenly very busy.

The office swarmed with activity. I didn't see Mother
around anywhere, so I asked the secretary if she was available.

"Please have a seat, she's in a conference just now."

"Actually, my mother said that there might be something

for me to help out with here in the office. I had some time so . . ."

"Just a second."

The secretary called someone named Phyllis from the back room. Next thing I know I'm stapling together the school newsletter.

I got assigned a helper—a yellowish mixed-race girl named Alicia.

"Let me know if she's any trouble," the secretary said. Apparently Alicia had been sentenced to school service as part of some sort of plea bargain for an incident in the cafeteria.

"What do we do?" I asked her. Alicia had the job down to a science. She collated the papers into a neat stack and then handed them to me for stapling. We established an easygoing, mechanical rhythm.

"We're a good team," I told her. She beamed.

We worked in silence. Phyllis kept bringing out more copies to replenish the stacks.

I found the work in some way soothing. However simple, the job had its own mindless urgency. It became really important to me that I get the staples in just the right place in the corner.

My mother's office was busier than a bus terminal. Children came and went, some placid, some in full tantrum. The phone rang constantly. Mother came out and waved at me in a way I thought was a little chilly.

"That's your mama," Alicia said. It was not a question.

"That's right," I responded. This girl impressed me with her directness and coarse intelligence.

"She's mean. She don't let nobody get away with nothing."

"She can be pretty tough when she wants to."

"You live at her house?"

"Yes," I said. I didn't add "for now" or "for a little while" or "temporarily." The poor girl had enough troubles without having to try to sift through somebody else's tangled family dealings.

After we finished the last of the handouts, Alicia said "Bye," and was escorted away to another work site. I imagined her spending the rest of her life in some form or another of penitent servitude. I stretched my limbs by the office window.

"Who's next out here!" my mother called.

A chubby brown thing raised his hand. As cute as he could be. He had huge dimples in his cheeks and he covered his mouth, giggling. I could see he was the dickens.

"Tony, Tony, Tony," Mother said. "Come on in here and sit your ornery self down." She could barely hold back her smile. She winked at me as he passed.

"Does it ever stop?" I asked.

"Keeps the blood pumping," she said, patting her heart. "I love it."

Who could imagine what a little fellow like that could do to end up seeing my mother. All I heard before she closed the door was, "This had better not be the same old . . ."

God bless her. God bless them all.

I found the activity exhausting. The ad agency was hectic, but it didn't run with this kind of frenzy and emotion. Out the window I saw that there was a small park across from the school.

"Tell my mother I'll see her later," I told the secretary.

At some point the park had been well cared for. Leftover patterning of gardens showed through the half-assed mowing like the ghost image of a woman's face that had not quite been painted out. Pentimento, artists called these reminders of what had or might have been. The playground equipment here had once been cheerful, bright colors, shiny and slick. Now everything was weeds and rust. This could happen to a neighborhood so fast. People who cared moved away. Doors stayed locked, and people stayed locked behind them. A section of busy Page Avenue bordered one end of the park. A diesel truck rumbled by, and I tried to imagine what it had been like here when this play yard was full of bright young life, bubbling and hysterical.

I remembered, then, that I had played here myself. My father brought me here—I couldn't have been more than five years old. I had bounced on that middle horse and slid down the slide when the colors of its handholds were rich red and deep blue. Daddy and I had come down here to pick up Mother, who was then a young teacher at Marvin. We were early and had waited here until she cleared her desk for the day.

That memory felt distant, as if it were from an episode of a sitcom as opposed to a memory of my own life. This, of course—St. Louis, my mother, my sister, all of it—was not my life anyway. I had made a new life for myself. By choice, by force of will. That new life existed five hundred miles away, in a different landscape entirely. Prairie instead of rolling hills. Frame houses and not brick. Other parks besides this one from my distant past. My life was in Minnesota, not here, and I wanted it so bad just then that an ache set up in my chest and tears brimmed over my eyelids.

Was this my moment of clarity and sanity? Well, maybe. I don't know. I don't think I even believe in such moments, I don't believe that in one second we are one way and in the next we are somehow different. Life is process. We morph and change in slow motion, bloom and decay, stretch and shrink, forget today that which yesterday we'd have given our lives to defend. Me, I only know that just then I was done with my . . . hiatus. I was going back to my life, home.

A bag lady came and sat by me on the bench. I had not noticed her and did not see where she had come from. Her powerful earthy odor overwhelmed me. She had her bundles neatly bound in twine.

"Apple?" she asked.

"I'm sorry. I don't have any . . . ," I answered, but then realized she was offering me a piece of perfect-looking fruit.

"No, thanks. I just ate."

"Suit yourself," the woman said—one of those things that was just like what my mother would say. The woman might have been an Indian or Asian woman but was dirty to the point that I couldn't tell.

"They're giving em away over at St. Stephen's," she said. "I got lots."

I nodded. She ate her apple and the one she had offered me. She ate all of it: core, seeds, and all.

"Gotta go home," she said, and then she ambled away with her two-wheeled cart and her packages.

I agreed.

Mother and I had dinner outdoors on the terrace that night. We weren't expecting Ciara until late. Mother made a fruit salad. Despite my lingering craving for real foods—such as Double Stuf Oreos or Kung Pao chicken—I decided to eat her chosen fare and be pleasant about it.

"These are delicious cherries, Mother. Where did you get them?" I thought I might buy some myself, seeing as how cherries were not completely a health food—they had sort of a trashy reputation and were the kind of "good for you" food you could feel virtuous about eating a whole box of.

"At the grocery store," she answered, bobbing her head as if I had asked a stupid question.

"Any particular store?" I prodded, laughing, realizing I was in the middle of one of those conversations people have when they become overly familiar with one another.

"Schnucks," she answered. She smiled, daring me to ask her another question. This was Mother's don't-talk-to-me-unless-you-want-to-talk-about-something-important mood. She would pretend to be doing the sort of thing she was doing right now—reading a catalog or fussing with her cuticles or picking at her salad. What she really wanted to do was to have a heart-to-heart, but she wanted me to be the one to come up with the topic. Damn, it had been a long time since I'd played this game. Back to the old days of the puffy, un-healthy Mother and the taciturn and surly Athena. She, afraid to alienate me by prodding, me not willing to give her the satisfaction of opening the door to a real conversation. Did some things never change?

And we had topics. Plenty of them. We needed to talk about my leaving. Oh, sure, I'd told her that day at Hawkins's house that it was time for me to go home, but we needed to talk about what next, about how we'd go on as mother and daughter from here. I did not know how to begin that con-versation. And, we needed to talk about Ciara, about her ridiculous beauty pageants, and about her nasty attitude, and about how sick she just might be. But, talking about that was off-limits, Mother and I had agreed on this. That rule was a big part of our new mother-daughter relationship—the status of which we didn't seem to be able to talk about either.

Mother, I'm leaving you again.

Mother, will you call? Can we talk? Often?

Mother, what becomes of us now?

Instead: "Now that's the Schnucks up on Manchester, right?"

She finished chewing another mouthful of pineapples and peaches and grapes. She looked me right in the eye. "They're all over, Schnucks, and every one of them has cherries this time of year." She proceeded to list a half-dozen locations.

"There's another one. You know, just before you get to Highway 40 up on Lindberg where Shneidhorst's Restaurant is. They built one up in there."

"Shneidhorst's is on this side of Highway 40."

"Well, you're just wrong about that, my dear."

"No, I'm not. And it isn't. It's been on this side forever, as I recall."

Mother rolled her eyes and looked away.

"Look, Mother, I drove by there yesterday. I saw it. How many Bavarian gasthauses could there be around here?"

She rested her fork on her bowl, folded her arms and smiled. "I have lived in this city for sixty years. You, you're off in the frozen tundra for half your life and now all of the sudden you're the expert on the St. Louis area. Far be it from me to get in the way of an expert." She swept a hand as if shooing away a bug. "This side it is."

I balled up my napkin and threw it on the table. "Let's go. Right now. I'll prove it to you."

"There's nothing to prove, sugar. I believe you. I'm just a forgetful, ignorant old colored woman. Put it out of your mind."

"Come on." I pulled her chair back from the table and set her catalog aside.

She fussed with some plastic to cover the little bit of the fruit salad we hadn't eaten.

"This is ridiculous," she laughed.

"Let's go. Let the flies feast."

I drove up there and showed her that I was right.

"Oh, no, Deneen. That's not Highway 40. That's Interstate 64. That's brand new. I guess Mother was right." And then she mumbled, "As usual."

Don't make me slap you, I started to say. Instead I kept driving up Lindberg.

"Where are you going, girl?"

"Just be patient."

"None of us has time for foolishness." I did not point out to her that as a woman killing time until her real life resumed, I had nothing but time.

I exited on Page and drove over to the frozen custard stand.

"Deneen!" Mother gasped.

"Now, Mother, a little frozen custard never hurt anything. It's just ice milk and natural sweeteners." Actually this particular brand tasted like they made it with pure butter fat and bags and bags of sugar, but telling her that wouldn't have helped my case.

"Well . . . I guess I could have a little dish."

I got her a mini and had them scoop a few fresh strawberries on it. I got me the triple turtle praline, onto which they smothered caramel and chocolate and candied nuts. I figured if you're gonna go, go large.

Mother spooned up her treat and giggled as if it were the most evil thing in the world. "You're corrupting me," she said. Otherwise we did not talk.

We strolled around the ice cream stand, which was old-fashioned looking, strung with yellow lights, looking much as if it belonged at a lake resort or in a small town. We scanned a corkboard papered with community announcements. Baby-sitter needed, '87 Dodge Truck for Sale, Bake Sale,

Rummage Sale, Spiritual Guidance. There was nothing there either of us wanted. The lights of Page Avenue seemed festive for some reason, in all their strip mall splendor. We gobbled down the rest of the custard and strolled to the car and headed home.

Later that night, Mark had wrapped himself around me spoon-fashion, breathing deeply and making a slight whimpering noise the way he did when we cuddled, in the wake of "the act."

"I'm going home next week," I said.

"Four days of you in this bed. I may not live."

"No. You didn't hear what I said. I'm going home. To Minnesota. Next week. Monday."

"Oh," he said. "I forgot." There was a dejection in his voice I had not anticipated.

(I know what you're saying. Deneen! Have you lost your mind! The man is smitten. SMITTEN! But, what was I to do? A long-distance relationship—I was still trying to figure out short-distance relationships. Going back to my old life meant giving up part of the new, didn't it? So, I tried to do it like a big girl. I really did.)

"My mother and I are taking Ciara out to Las Vegas on Friday for the Dream Dolls finals and then I'm going to go on back up to my place." I sat up and, though I did not want to be done with the evening, began to gather my things. Mark rolled onto his back.

"So that's it, then."

I started to slip into my panties, but collapsed against him on the bed. "How in the hell do you guys do this."

"Do what? Slip on your drawers and say see you later? You slip on your drawers and say 'Later.'"

234

I curled back down beside him on the bed, weeping. He put his arm around me and rocked me. "You didn't have to be so damn nice," I cried.

"You prefer I was some slick-headed bastard who slapped you around?"

"It'd be easier to say good-bye."

"I like you, Deneen Wilkerson. I done got used to you."

I was silent. Was I supposed to say thanks? Was I supposed to bat my eyes and act surprised? None of this was in my script. I guess, to be honest, there was no script. Maybe that *was* the lesson.

"Who says you have to go? Lots of jobs around here. Lots of places for a woman like you. No. You don't have to go."

I took a deep breath and extracted myself from his arms. "I don't think you understand. I'm not looking for another opportunity or an offer from you or from anybody else."

He crossed his arms and smirked. "So this was just one of those summer camp kinda things."

I turned from him. "If you want."

"Woman, you about a lie." He laughed. It sounded bitter. I slid into my blouse. He pulled me down next to him.

"I don't know who you think you're fooling," he said.

Neither did I, but I knew that if I could just get to the door I'd be fine.

"You want to play like you're just one of these alley cats out here, slinking from Tom to Tom. You know what, sugar, you wear your heart on your sleeve."

"I should get on home." I mumbled that into a chest that was moist from my tears. He held on and so did I.

"Want me to do the dirty work. Figure I'm like all these other dogs out here who would be just as happy see the back of you so I can take up with the next one."

"You got women beating down your door," I sniffed.

"Oh. You want to change the subject. Nah! I don't think so. We were talking about poor Deneen and how these doggish men just keep messing her over."

"I'll just be going now." I didn't move.

"How do you think I feel? I'm enjoying a good thing with a lady, and I think she's enjoying me and just when it's really getting real, she rolls up out the bed and says 'See ya!' How am I supposed to feel?"

"Well, you knew I had a life and a job and a house some-place else."

"Fine." He pushed me off him. "That's just fine. Go on then. For now." He fluffed up the pillows and pulled the comforter up to cover his legs and stomach. He was smirking as if he knew something I didn't. I gathered myself into my clothes and tossed at my hair.

"I'm sorry," I said. The words sounded as thin and limp as they were.

"I'm not saying good-bye to you, Deneen."

I picked up my purse and fished out the car keys. I took a deep breath, summoned up my best poker face and turned to him.

"Well. . . ." I gave him a false smile and an anemic wave. He mimicked me. I turned to go.

"Deneen. See you out in the desert, sweetie."

I kept moving, heading toward my car, headed toward home. I kept moving, and I tried not to laugh or cry, even though I wanted to do both, even though I wanted to go back. I kept moving. Sometimes if you keep moving, things have a way of working themselves out.

# Fifteen

I sat next to Mother on the flight to Nevada. Ciara, hair bundled and curled into an intricate do-rag, sat behind us beside Hawkins. Underneath the incessant white noise of the engines I could hear him hectoring her with reminders and suggestions. I figured out that another young woman on the early morning trip was also a contestant. Similarly topped with curlers, she had the same snotty-nosed teen-beauty-queen edge to her that Ciara did. Every half hour or so, one or the other girl would feign an excuse to walk by and check out the competition.

When not crazy, I am a marginally nervous flier. I was counting on mother to chat me through the takeoff and landing parts, at least. Instead, that old sister got her down two of them Chiclet-sized airline pillows and one of their regulation blue army blankets and took her a nap.

Las Vegas was everything I'd hoped it would be and worse. I had been to the Indian casino outside of the Twin Cities and been properly stunned. Mystic Lake was your basic, warehouse-sized structure, duded up with a few neon lights and chandeliers. It could have been a discount store except that, instead of being filled with inexpensive merchandise, it was wall-to-wall jam-packed with slot machines and blackjack tables; and every table and every machine was occupied. No sooner did some bleary-eyed loser vacate a stool before the rube behind her took her place. The beeping and clanging and flashing of the machines at first had annoyed me, but eventually became hypnotic. The polyester-clad blondes of Minnesota did their darndest—twenty-four/seven—to see that at least one generation of Sioux would have a nice new car every year and come home to the latest in ranch-style luxury.

Minus the Indians, Las Vegas was Mystic Lake times a million. There was a bank of slots right there at the end of the jetway. Slot machines were, for that matter, everywhere and rather than looking like a swollen-up dime store, most of the casinos had been tarted-up and gilded as if the city were one oversized and continuous World's Fair. There were pyramids and temples and Polynesian villages and circuses and lights that literally turned day into night. And enough gushing water to quench the thirst of a small nation.

The pageant was held at a tired, sand-colored hotel that had become a feeble and rather tattered old uncle amidst newer and livelier cousins that sported their own volcanoes and tigers and exploding pirate ships. While in the process of thematizing itself to match its gaudier competitors, this relic maintained a thriving business catering to the needs of conventioneers and hosting events, such as the National All American Dream Dolls Pageant. The marquee welcomed the contestants as if they were visiting royalty.

Hawkins took Ciara away to practice for the production number, do some preliminary competition and "get to know the other girls"—which is, I believe, code for reviewing the good sportsmanship rules and hearing the consequences should there be any cat fights. With them out of our hair, I thought mother and I would go sightseeing, maybe find that Liberace Museum or go out to Hoover Dam.

Mother emerged from the bathroom wearing the gaudiest gold-encrusted blouse I had ever seen. It was printed with what looked like a lion's face, but was so swirly and overly stylized I couldn't tell what it was. Did I mention the blouse was black? She had donned an old fishing hat with a pink rabbit's foot pinned to the back like some vestigial tail.

"What is this?" I asked.

"My lucky outfit. Girl, let's go before them machines cool off for the day." She grabbed a decorated toolbox that was the sort of thing one might find at a sewing bee. This one had a section full of moist towelettes, a rubber glove, and one of those rubber index fingertips for counting cash. If I hadn't known any better I'd've thought we were going on some sort of perverted picnic.

"Maybe I'll just stay in the room and read," I said.

"Don't be a fuddy-duddy."

We took a cab and drove a couple of blocks down to Circus-Circus where mother had heard "the money poured out like the machines had been greased." Inside, everything was loud pink and blue and yellow. Mother found a change trolley and filled up her toolbox with dollar tokens and ran over to what was essentially a merry-go-round of slot machines. She must have had seventy-five bucks worth of dollar tokens.

"You know, Mother, this is really just a racket." I started giving her my speech about how she would be better off back in the room flushing her coins down the toilet.

She dropped in three coins. Three bars came up and around eighty dollars in coins plopped out.

"He-a-ay!" she hollered, like she was in the audience at the Def Comedy Jam or something. Another sister behind her turned around and said, "Go on, girl!" They gave each other a high five. Apparently they all know each other in these places.

"You try it, Deneen."

I dropped in one of her fake circus dollars and pulled the handle.

"Big money!" she shouted. I got a blank and a bar and a blank. Above my head a man let go of a swinging trapeze and flew across the room to the ankles of his partner.

"You take yourself someplace. You're giving me bad luck." She shoved me off the stool with her hips.

"How long will you be here?" I asked.

Mother checked her watch. "I don't know. I'll be in this area right around here. Let me know when it gets close to four."

As she spun out of sight on her carousel, I saw another three bars pop up on her screen.

It was ten o'clock in the morning.

I opened the casino door and the same kind of heat blasted me as when I opened the oven door to baste a turkey. The temperature on a sign I saw was a combination of three numbers I did not know was possible on Earth. Following the crowd, I ran to the building next door. Another casino.

I soon discovered that in this city one could travel this way for miles—popping out the door of one casino and into the door of the next. And there was a steady stream of us cattle who did just that—moving up and down the street in some sort of glitz-inspired trance. At several points, moving sidewalks captured you and delivered you to the heart of another pleasure palace. I had never seen buildings of this size. Some of them went on for blocks, and it was all so . . . pleasant looking, really. None of it seemed any more tawdry than your garden-variety suburban shopping mall.

And what had I expected, after all: gun-toting mobsters and their ladies? White-tuxedoed double agents with

Eurasian beauties dangling from each arm? What I got was middle America, in all of its hip-hugging stretch-panted bee-hived cowboy-hatted glory. That, and the rest of the world, too—clutches of Asian tourists spinning prayer wheels at a shrine in front of a faux Roman forum, a gaggle of German teenagers on the lam from blackjack-happy elders. The whole world was in Las Vegas—thousands and thousands of us. Truckloads of money glided by me on the casino floors. Down-on-their-luck gamblers leafleted me with ads for "in-room" entertainment. Faces I recognized vaguely from TV or the movies wandered past, some seeming as stunned as I.

Several hours later, limp and dehydrated, I wandered the bowels of a smoked-glass pyramid. I had come to the end of the line, it seemed, no casinos beyond this one I could see. It was as far as I was going, anyway. I was delirious from thirst and could not look at one more fake temple or ersatz golden palace.

All the women in the pyramid appeared to be Cleopatra or Nefertiti—jet-black hair straight to their shoulders. They all had these terrific figures and were wearing the sort of silky pajama-type outfits such as are featured in the more chaste sections of the Victoria's Secret catalog. I snagged a woman pushing a change trolley.

"Could you tell me where a person could get a drink?" I asked.

"Got ten bucks?" she answered.

I rolled my eyes. This damn city. They practically charged you to pee. In Las Vegas what wasn't a casino was a pawn-shop. I fished out a pair of wrinkled old Lincolns.

She winked at me. "Take this roll of quarters over there and start dropping em in that poker machine. They'll pour so much liquid in you, you'll wish you had a hump."

"Thanks," I said. I walked to where she had indicated—a bank of poker machines backed up against a bar that was tricked out as if it were a barge on the Nile River. It was quiet over here. Apparently the video-poker crowd came later in the day.

I dropped in a quarter and hit a button. I didn't even play poker in real life, so I wasn't sure what the protocol was. I knew that it involved some sort of flush or sweep and that it worked better if you had a cigar. I pushed a button that said "draw" and waited for the results. A bell dinged twelve times, the machine flashed and a handful of quarters dropped into a bin. I must've done something right.

"Good girl," Cleopatra said, leaning over the bar. Cleo sounded much more like Asbury Park than Cairo. "What can I get you?"

I shrugged. "Surprise me?"

She came right back with something sweet and orange-juicey. I couldn't tell you what it was, but it sure did hit the spot. I drank it down like it was going out of style.

"Kinda slow around here," I said.

"It'll pick up." She leaned over the machine so the flanks of her hair paralleled her face like blinders. "Draw two," she ordered.

I did. The machine buzzed to indicate what a big loser I was.

"Damn!" Cleo said, and then patted the machine next to me to indicate I'd better give up on mine. I slid right over. "It'll pick up in an hour or so. Folks sleep in out here. They start working the machines real good after their lunch settles. You're a first-timer, aren't you?"

"Me?" I dropped another quarter and hit some more buttons. No bells this time either. I shrugged. "Yeah, this is my first time."

"Yup. I can spot em. You get your regulars come in—the ones come out two or three times a year. You get your driving-through-to-see-Grandma-in-Arizona type. What brings you to the desert?"

"I came out for a beauty pageant."

Cleo looked around as if someone were trying to put something over on her. "Excuse me, uh, toots, but between you and me, ain't you a little long in the tooth, if you know what I'm saying. No offense, or nothing."

I laughed. "I have a twelve-year-old sister. Not that I'm exactly a hideous old beast, thank you very much." Closer inspection revealed that she'd been around the track a few times herself. Fine wrinkles of the kind that are barely masked by the best makeup mapped her skin in tributaries and rivulets. A good set of teeth and a tight chin had served her well the last few years.

"Put it out of your mind, doll," she said. "And might I add that you are wearing the hell out of that sun dress. Looks like a million dollars on you."

"Well, thank you, ma'am." I raised my glass to her and drank down what little was left.

Cleopatra snatched the dregs. "Let me freshen that up for you." She brought me back a brand new one with a couple of toothpicks of fruit in it.

I said "thank you," and added, "As long as we're passing out compliments, that haircut really flatters you. Not so good on some of these other girls, but it's perfect for you."

Cleo grabbed the top of her head and lifted it up about six inches. "Get with the program, girlfriend. It's a wig. You been in the desert sun too long." She laughed like a hyena and called to a man at another machine, "Hey, Joe. You want another?

"Right back with you, sugar," she said to me.

I dropped in a few more quarters. Sometimes I would get something and sometimes I would not. I think I was breaking even, but it was hard to say. I *was* feeling rather light headed. Perhaps I had had too much sun.

"The wig's made from real human hair, though," Cleo said. "Costs an arm and a leg, and we have to buy em ourselves. Try this!" She handed me a glass of something blue and cool looking. "It's a new thing we been working on back here."

"What's in it?" The drink tasted fresh, like pineapples and bubble gum mixed together.

"You don't want to know. Drink up. So, a beauty pageant, huh?"

"All American Dream Dolls. It's a new one."

"New ones, old ones. SOS, you know what I'm saying? Business as usual."

"You sound like a vet, Cleo."

"You kidding me? See all these girls around here— schlepping drinks and hauling change with their tits hanging out of these dime-store costumes—all these broads in here are veterans."

"No!"

"The problem is, where do you go with it? You invest your whole goddamn life in trying to get some judge to score you a ten. You get some tens. You get a couple thousand bucks. Then what?"

"I don't know. You go on to college, I guess. Get married."

"Marriage! Don't even get me started on that scam. You married, doll?"

"No."

"Smart girl. Me, I'm what you call a three-time loser. Which is to say I married losers. Three times. You meet these guys and it's all lovey dovey and hearts and flowers. Once that dick cools off, you find out what the guy really wants is somebody to scrub the damn toilet and pick up a six-pack on the way home from work. Who needs it!" She waved her hand at me and went and got Joe another beer.

"How you doing?" she came back and asked, pointing at my blue drink. I tapped the rim to indicate she should keep em coming.

"You seem a bit on the cynical side, Cleo." She tossed back her head and laughed. She had that sun-worn, deep brown skin color that some white women get in warm climes.

"Let's just say I'm practical," she said. "I got two boys— fourteen, sixteen. Anthony and Joe Jr. They both help out around the place and got jobs to pay for their own shit. They're good boys. I'm lucky that way. We manage okay. I figure I get these boys grown up and hopefully headed out of this crazy city, and then me, I'll figure out what the hell Diane's doing with the rest of her life."

"You're Diane. I'm Deneen."

"Deneen, you're an independent woman, so you know the score, am I right?" She handed me another drink.

"You're right," I said, and took a big sip. The room took on the soft, padded feel that had lately been so familiar to me. Since I had worked so hard to lose this feeling, this would definitely have to be my last blue thing.

"I'm thinking a real estate license or maybe a nail salon. I got a couple years to play with it."

"You'll do fine," I told her. She would, too. She had that land-on-your feet look about her.

"Look, it's getting busy over here. I gotta hustle. Set that glass up here when you're done."

"It was nice talking with you," I said.

"Same here. Good luck."

I scooped up my quarters from the tin tray where they had landed and stuffed most of them into the pocket of my sun dress. It looked as if I had one really long and lumpy breast. The rest I set on the bar for Diane.

"Thanks, doll," she said. "And say, Deneen!" she called, as I turned to go. "Tell that sister of yours to go take a physics class or something."

"Yeah, sure." I waved to her.

I made my way somehow out of the pyramid. I had a man who thought he was King Tut hail me a cab to run me back to the hotel.

Chilled air filled the room, once I'd found it. I tossed my-self onto the satiny coverlet and fell into one of those semi-conscious dream states where I was perfectly aware of the progress of the sun in the sky outside the window and of the rhythmic beating of the seconds on the clock. At the same time, impossible things happened: Katrina came into the room with Calvin.

"Look what you've done to him!" Katrina exclaimed, in a voice that was both angry and full of zest. She stepped aside to display him like a prize on a game show. He was sallow and thin, wasted to the bones.

"I didn't do that," I said. "It's that disease. Don't you understand?"

They waved their fingers at me. "Very bad," they said. "Very bad."

Then it was Mr. Waltershied. He had on a jacket covered with what I thought were fishing lures, and bandages taped to his face. On closer inspection it turned out his coat was covered with tampons and the bandages were really sanitary napkins.

"These products are great, Deneen. Think of what I've missed. Why didn't I know about this earlier?" He had a spray bottle in one hand and a squirt bottle in the other.

"You shouldn't have those," I said. "They aren't for you. You shouldn't even be touching them."

"Look at her," Ciara said. "Like a big old whale. Covered with all that nasty money."

"Deneen, sweetie," Mother said. "Get up and come to dinner with us."

"Huh?"

Ciara picked up a handful of quarters and pelted me with them. "I can just imagine how you earned these," she whispered.

"You forgot to come back for me," Mother said. "Good thing that that Double Diamonds I was working jammed. I'd still be sitting over there."

I was groggy, and I had a bad headache. Mother ordered Ciara to see if Hawkins was joining us for dinner. With her rubber index finger she paged through a stack of bills.

"How'd you do?" I asked.

"Well I was up about nine hundred dollars at one point. I hit two triple sevens in a row on that carousel."

"Nine hundred dollars!"

"Sure thing. I cashed out of there and thought I'd go try the Double Diamonds. It was just starting to come back up, when it broke on me. Looks like I'm up—let me see—five fifty on the day."

"Nine hundred dollars!" That was three car payments. My

mortgage was almost nine hundred dollars. She waved her hand at me to indicate it was nothing.

Hawkins had a "business meeting" with some of the Dream Dolls people, or so he told Ciara. He could very well be cruising around out there in one of his outfits looking to get picked up.

We ate at a buffet in the hotel where there was a choice of steak and every other food on earth or prime rib and every other food on earth. I had the prime rib.

"What did you do with yourself all day, Deneen?" Mother asked.

"She went out and earned those quarters," Ciara cackled and then made some obscene sounds with food in her mouth. Mother gave her a dirty look.

"I just walked around," I said.

"Sure is an interesting town," Mother said.

"Interesting is not the word for it. You know—"

"Doesn't everyone want to know about the pageant?" Ciara asked. "Well, I'll tell you. First we had a sharing time where all us girls sat on the floor and told where we were from and what our favorite colors were and what we wanted to be when we grow up. Then this one old lady came in and she's supposed to like be the lady who invented the Dream Dolls and she told us how pretty we were and all sorts of stuff like that. She was really sweet, like somebody's grandma or something. And then we went over the rules and everything, and they told us how they wanted us to be extra good sports and how no matter what happened, we were supposed to keep on smiling and cheering. They were like 'you girls are all winners already' and junk, and I'm like, yeah, right. And then we worked on the big opening production number. You want to hear it? Okay, good. It goes like this:" She pushed back her chair and started in.

> *American Dream Dolls, they're the ones*
> *They make your playtime so much fun*
> *American Dream Dolls all the way*
> *Brightest thing in the brightest day!*

Two tables down a red-headed girl got up at her table, waved at Ciara, and then the two of them proceeded to give the dining room a stereo version of the wretched song. I thought about putting my napkin over my head.

> *American Dream Dolls, hey, hey, hey,*
> *They're the best things in the USA.*
> *American Dream Dolls, the very best,*
> *They're heads and tails above the rest.*

The song continued for several more verses with various oo-ing and aah-ing parts thrown in for good measure. By the time they finished, four or five more of the little robots had joined the group. They hugged each other and squealed and bowed. Some diners actually applauded. I put my hands in front of my face on the off chance someone might know me here. My hair was doing its best to challenge Hawkins's just-run-your-fingers-through-it rule. I had satin comforter marks on my face.

Wouldn't you know it, there, across the restaurant was Mark with some sweet young thing. I smiled, waved, rolled my eyes and pointed to my sister. The ardor in his eyes seemed to be directed at me, and I hoped he was prepared to get stabbed. Sweet young things generally did not like being upstaged. I diverted my attention before the big scene went down.

"Well, that was embarrassing," I said.

"Oh, oh, and then, later, we do this other number. It goes like this—"

"We'll see it tomorrow afternoon," Mother said, calmly placing a hand on Ciara's arm and anchoring her to the chair. Thank God.

"Anyway, then they interviewed each one of us and asked us a lot of important questions like about homeless people and junk and then up in front of the judges we all got to do our songs or whatever. Then we got to change into our play-suits and walk on the runway. And then it was all done. Fun, huh?"

"You've had a very busy day," Mother said.

I bit my lip. I rubbed my hands together and put them over my mouth as if I were praying. I couldn't contain it. I had to say it. "Doesn't sound the least bit fun. It sounds obnoxious and silly."

"Deneen!"

"Mother, that song they have those girls singing is nothing more than a commercial for that old lady's toys. A bad commercial, at that."

"Oh! Mama! Did I mention that I get to hold Prudence during the opening song? Only ten girls got picked to hold dolls and I'm one of them. So, Ha! Ha! Ha!"

I sighed. Ciara sat with one leg extended behind her on the chair, bouncing up and down on it, picking at her food. I caught her eye.

"Can I say something to you?"

She crossed her eyes and kept bouncing and picking.

"I'm serious. I hope you'll listen to me. I know we haven't gotten along very well. I take responsibility for my part of that. I think we should go home. Tonight."

"Mother, is she still drunk or what?"

"Ciara! Deneen, I don't think this is the time."

I closed my eyes and pressed on. "I think what we should do is go pack our things and thank Hawkins for all his trouble and get on the next plane out of this place."

Ciara rolled her eyes, rolled a finger around her ear and started humming the American Dream Dolls theme.

I closed my eyes again and kept talking. "I think this pageant stuff is giving you all the wrong messages about women and all the wrong messages about yourself. I think Mother has made a terrible mistake by getting you involved in this."

"Now, see here, Deneen—"

"I think it's not too late. And I think we should go. Now." I left two quarters on the table and set the trend by heading for the door.

"Get some rest," Mother said to my back. "We'll be up as soon as Ciara finishes her steak. We've got a full day tomorrow, and she needs her strength."

In the room I paced back and forth, livid with anger. How had it come to this? How had a perfectly ordinary suburban woman like my mother been sucked into such a lurid and disgusting business? Here we were, thousands of miles from home, in Hustle City, USA, a city full of get-rich-quick schemes and fading beauties. Here my mother had swallowed hook line and sinker someone's bait about the road to hap-piness in America. Drop in a quarter, pull the lever, and your troubles will be over. Strip to your underwear, tell your problems to Geraldo, march down that runway brave and bold, and, whatever you do, keep smiling for the camera.

Maybe Reina Wilkerson Jones had no standards, but one of her daughters did. Mother might not make a stand, but I sure would. Right here in this big pink hotel, I would. I would make both of them realize the error of their ways.

I sneaked down to the gift shop and bought an imitation Swiss Army knife.

"You're rather quiet this afternoon," my mother said, coming in from a brief run on the machines.

"How'd you do downstairs?"

"This is a tight old joint here. After the pageant I want to go downtown to the Union Plaza. I heard they're loose, loose, loose in there. Come with me?"

"Sure," I said, knowing that on my mother's little slot sprees I was as extraneous as an appendix.

"She's all set!" Hawkins cheered, bursting into the room with Ciara, still wrapped in her bathrobe. He was clad in his regulation performance day tux, shaded behind a cool pair of dark glasses.

"Now, Mama, I want you to get her into her playsuit. Be careful of this hair. Don't forget to tie down the you-know-whats. Miss Ciara, I will meet you backstage in fifteen minutes from right now. Sync."

"Sync," she simpered, teeth already Vaseline coated.

"Ladies, you are witnessing the birth of a queen. I can smell that Dream Dolls franchise now." He swept from the room in a whirlwind of cologne.

While Mother got to work on the breast binding, I got to work on the doorknob.

"This feels funny. All pushed in," Ciara whined.

I loosened a set of screws that were on the metal frame that held the lock.

"Hawkins says that after this pageant we go on to the teenager's competitions. He says they can be as big as I want. The bigger the better. He says we can even pad them if we want to."

If Mother responded, I didn't hear it.

There was another screw that was on the door handle itself. It was tight and I had to lie on the floor to get a good purchase on it.

"Is there a problem over there, Deneen."

"No, mother. I'm just checking something out here in the bathroom." With just a tweak of elbow grease I loosened that baby up good.

"Careful with my hair."

"I'll just slip this over your head. Put your arms up."

The handle was good and loose. One hard yank and it was history.

"There. Now let's get a look at you. Deneen, come and look at your sister."

I'd seen enough of my sister to last me the rest of my life, thank you very much.

"Spin around for us, baby. Make sure there's nothing hanging off you."

"Mother! Hawkins will triple-check me downstairs. I'm gonna be late."

Mother gathered her into her arms, careful to avoid mussing her hair. "Make me proud," she said, planting a juicy smack on her ear.

"I will." Ciara wiped the smooch away.

"Now, scoot."

I stood blocking the hallway to the door.

"You're in my way," she said.

"I know."

"Get *out* of my way."

"I'm doing what our mother should have done a long time ago. I'm putting a stop to this bullshit right here and right now."

"Yeah, right." She tried to storm past me. I pushed her back onto the bed.

"Mommy!"

"What in God's name is the matter with you, child. Put that knife down."

I had forgotten I still held it from my handiwork. I tossed it over on the dresser and pushed my hands up my arms as if I were rolling up my nonexistent sleeves.

"I will not let a member of this family go down to that auditorium and display herself for a bunch of dirty old men like she was some kind of a burlesque house stripper."

"Move!" Ciara tried to race past me. I grabbed her arm and put her in a hammerlock and threw her on the bed.

"Ow!" she shrieked.

"I mean it," I said. "I'll snatch them extensions out your head before I let you out this room. You think I won't?"

Mother reached over to me, a pleading look on her face, trembling as if she were afraid I'd shove her, too. I would have, I think. Ciara stood by the bed, unsuccessfully trying to hold back the tears that were ruining her makeup.

"I'm not playing anymore. I'm taking a stand about this kinda shit. You, little girl, need to learn some other lessons about what being a woman is about, and we're starting today. Right in this room."

"God, I hate you," she mumbled.

"What did you say to me? You better talk big you got something to say to me."

"I said I hate you!"

"Ciara!"

"That's right. You heard me. I hate you and Mama hates you and Hawkins hates you and everybody hates you. You're almost dead, and you don't even have a husband. That's because who would even want you."

I dropped my eyes in shame.

"That's enough, young lady."

"Look at her. Cow! A big old cow. I hate her. You're just a sick fat old ugly cow that nobody even wants. I wish you'd never come home. I wish you were dead."

"Ciara!" My mother slapped her hard, right across the face.

She screamed and ran from the room, slamming the door on her way out.

The doorknob fell off behind her.

# Sixteen

"Oh, my! Oh, my!" Mother wrung her hands, pacing in place. "Oh, my, what in the world?"

I was still where I had stood in my futile attempt to block the door. Still looking at the floor. I felt as if I were the one who had been slapped.

Mother grabbed her purse and headed for the door. Then she set her purse on the bed and patted her hands up and down my body as if frisking me for weapons. "Oh, my!" she said. "My babies. My baby girls."

She picked up her purse. She put her arm around my waist and walked me to the bed. "Now you don't pay her any mind. She was upset." She fumbled for her room key. "Now you sit here quiet and I'll go make. . . ." She was breathing heavy and making a mess of the usually organized inside of her bag. "Everything will be all right," she said. "Just fine."

I sat there on the bed, still looking at my shoes. I wanted to be back in that basement, back in St. Louis. Back with Oprah and Sally and Jerry and Montel and my other friends. I did not want to do this anymore. This or anything else, for that matter.

"Deneen!" Mother screamed. "Deneen, look." She held up the pieces of the door handle.

"Uh oh," I said. As flat as a runny pancake, I said it.

"Well, this damn hotel," Mother said, throwing it on the floor. She shook with exasperation, so frustrated she was practically vibrating.

"Help her, Deneen," the voices said, and I thought, "okay," and I rallied a bit.

"Let me try and fix it." I figured if I had had the wherewithal to take it apart, I probably could put it back together.

I pushed back in the long metal piece that slotted through the hole. It slid right in, but seemed awfully loose, as if there was nothing grabbing hold of the other side. A sex joke occurred to me just then, involving Calvin Junior, but it seemed monstrously inappropriate, so I shooed it away and have subsequently forgotten it. I pulled the metal piece out again and eyeballed the hole. It seems that whatever there was that was supposed to be on the other side of this contraption had fallen off when the door was slammed.

So much for my pile of screws.

"We'll have to card it," I said.

"Card it?" she asked, and I started to say to her, "You know, it's like when some nigger you went out with in college borrowed a bunch of your records and you want them back so that the new bitch he's doing can't enjoy them and you go to his room and use a credit card to break in." I didn't tell her all that. I just told her to get out her VISA.

Which didn't work. The little flipper was set at such an angle that the card couldn't get around it.

There was, of course, nothing remotely resembling an old-fashioned coat hanger in the dump. They had the nerve to actually have what looked like real wooden hangers. How inconsistent. If they were going to be shabby, at least they could be shabby all the way.

"Call the desk and tell them to get us out of here," Mother ordered.

So I did.

"Hello, this is room 724. We're in the tower. Yes, we're stuck in our room.

"Mother, they're laughing at me."

"Give me that phone."

"They hung up."

"They're gonna find out who they're messing with now." She dialed that phone in such a way I was afraid she would punch through the keypad with her fingers.

"Front desk! This is Dr. Reina Wilkerson Jones in room 724. We're trapped in our room and—

"Don't you laugh at me.

"Listen, let me tell you something. Somebody had better—

"Hello!

"Hello! Damn this hotel, Deneen. Next time we're staying at the Mirage."

She slammed the phone down and flopped herself down on the bed.

"So what do we do?" I asked.

"Do I look like I know? Right now is one of them times I wish I was still smoking. I really do."

I stood there at the end of the bed, useless, hands folded around my trusty Swiss knife, wringing it as if some sort of genie might appear to solve all our problems.

"Sit down, Deneen," Mother ordered.

I did.

I rifled through the card box in my brain searching for an answer.

"I could try and—"

"Don't talk, Deneen."

I didn't.

I ran the sheath of the knife back and forth across my skirt as if I were trying to start a fire.

"Sit still, Deneen."

So I did.

Mother removed a pillow from beneath the coverlet and lay herself all the way out. She placed her ankles shoulder-width apart and turned her palms to the ceiling.

"Breathe in," she sighed and took a long, deep inhale. She slowly let the air out and sighed, "breathe out."

The tension left her body. She looked as peaceful as a new-born, her rhythmic breathing raising and lowering her boxy chest as if she were a boat on a gentle sea. She could be dead, I thought, laid out here in this room in her little linen pant-suit. Tasteful jewelry, just the right amount of makeup. It was sweet and touching and tragic all at the same time. A few tears leaked from my eyes. More than a few, really. I blubbered like Dorothy in the witch's castle in Oz.

"I know what to do," she said. She rifled the hotel direc-tory and punched in some numbers on the phone. "I didn't spend forty years in the public school system for nothing.

"What are you blubbering about? I swear, child, I'm gonna put you in Malcolm Bliss when we get home.

"Hello, maintenance, this is room 724. We have a repair problem that's rather urgent. Can you send someone up?

"It's a problem with the door handle.

"Yes.

"Yes.

"I know how hard you gentlemen work. Your name was?

"With a G? Yes.

"Gerald, should I call in someone from outside? A locksmith? A carpenter?

"At least an hour. Well, as soon as you can would be appreciated. Thank you very much.

"He said it'll be a while. His entire staff's tied up with the pageant."

"I guess we'll miss it."

Mother sputtered. "Hush, girl. Twenty minutes ago, according to you, wasn't none of us going to no pageants."

I looked away, ashamed. "I'm sorry, Mother. I know how much this meant to you."

"Oh, Deneen. To hell with the damn pageant."

"I beg your pardon?"

"You heard me. I said 'to hell with it.'" She slid back and oriented herself against the headboard, filling in behind her with pillows. "I don't suppose there's even anything on TV to watch."

"I'm confused, Mother. You go through all this rigmarole and carry on about how precious your baby is, and then you get out here and say you don't care about it. I can't believe it."

"First of all, sweetie, buying three tickets to Nevada and booking a hotel room is not rigmarole. Running an elementary school, now that's rigmarole. Also, I do not—as you so elegantly put it—'carry on.'"

I gasped. "You do so. You fuss over her like she was made of porcelain."

She waved her hand at me. "I fuss over all my babies. Ciara. All five hundred of them at school. I fussed over you."

She never did. She never oohed and aahed and bragged about me and bought me everything I ever wanted. At least not that I remember.

"Explain this to me then: Why beauty pageants? Why something so backwards and so degrading?"

"It's not degrading if you win."

"Sure it is. You just get better prizes."

She shrugged. "Whether or not you believe this, darling daughter, I am not some reactionary, out-of-date piggish person. As you well know I have been a member of women's organizations my entire adult life. And I haven't been sheltered by some man or in some institution. I don't need a lecture from you."

I slammed myself down on the end of the bed. "Then why are we here?" I pounded the mattress for emphasis.

"I'm here trying to save my child's life!" she shouted and looked away from me, out the window toward the lights of the strip. "The world is eating our children alive, Deneen. It doesn't matter that we live in a nice house in Kirkwood or that I have a good job. I'm around young people every day— all kinds of them from many different backgrounds. And I lose one or two of them every day as well. My boys and girls. To the streets. To crime. To drugs. My hand to God, Deneen, I will do anything and everything to keep that young woman whole and safe and sane, do you understand me?"

"But a beauty pageant?"

"Anything. And I didn't choose the damn beauty pageants. Ciara did. Over the years I have spent a pretty penny putting the whole world in front of that child. All the choices: dance lessons, tennis, swimming, art classes, violin, piano, karate. You name it, she's done it. I wrote the checks and prayed to God that something would catch her fancy—that she would choose *one* thing she liked doing, and that maybe she would get so involved in it, she'd have half a chance to grow up. This is what she picked, Deneen. This was her choice. So here," she held out her wrists to me. "Slit them."

I reached out and stroked her arm. "I didn't know."

"Well. Now you do. Are you happy?"

I shook my head. "It's hard to reconcile, Mama. I think it's . . . wrong. I still do." I dropped my eyes from hers in shame. "You know, that door didn't just break. I unscrewed it. I wanted to trap her here so she couldn't go." I lowered my eyes again and waited for my mother's rampage.

Mother threw back her head and laughed. It was one of those deep belly guffaws. She covered her mouth with her hand and wiped away a few tiny tears. "Oh, Deneen. Did you really think you could keep your sister from getting to that pageant? Did you?"

I shrugged, felt foolish.

"Deneen!" she laughed some more. "She would have made a new door. She would have tied your clothes together and climbed down the outside of the building. She'd have killed you and me both and used our bodies as trampolines."

"I guess you're right."

"You guess? You surprise me, sweetheart. I'd have thought you'd have figured her out by now."

What was to figure? She was a child. Like all the children out there. A little more spunky, perhaps. A tad bit more ornery. I told my mother that, too. "She's just a girl," I said.

"There's no such thing, older daughter. I've known thousands of children over my life and every one of them broke the mold. Ciara is no exception."

"How's she different?"

"Come on, Deneen. You've spent enough time with us. You know what she's like. You tell me."

"She's cheerful. Friendly. Enthusiastic."

Mother shook her head and laughed at me derisively. "You must have her confused with the local Girl Scout leader. That sort of mistake a person could live to regret. Come here." She beckoned me to come sit beside her up by the headboard. She drew me up close to her.

"It isn't very easy for me to say this. You're my daughter, too, and you're the only person in the whole world I can tell this to. You're the only person who I *would* say this to.

"I love my daughter. I love both my girls. I'm glad I had you. And I thank God that my baby is healthy and alive. But I'm afraid I have to say that Ciara is not a very nice person." She turned her hands up as if appeasing God.

"I never thought I'd hear myself say that out loud, but I've known it for a long time, almost since the day she was born. If she weren't my flesh and blood—if I didn't have to know her—I wouldn't want to know her. Do you know what I mean? Can you understand that, Deneen?"

"But mother," I sniffed. "What happened?"

"Are you asking me did I have something to do with it? Probably, and so did her dad before he died. But not very much, really. Deneen, your sister came out of the womb kicking and screaming, scrapping and mad at the whole world. I would feed her sometimes when she was a tiny thing, and she would look up at me with the most hateful looks you could imagine."

"So she has a little attitude problem."

Mother slapped my arm. "This is not a little attitude problem. You don't need to protect me, and you know you don't need to protect her. Deneen, she's everything you've said to me she was: manipulative, sneaky, aggressive—you know the list. She steals. You've said all those things yourself."

"Mother, I have to tell you something. Ciara didn't take that money from your purse. I did. Look." I took from my bill-fold a crumpled piece of paper where I'd kept track of the amounts I'd borrowed. Sort of.

"It's not the money, Deneen. Do you think I'm worried about some damn money? I've got enough money to last me the rest of my life. Here:" Mother opened her own wallet and threw a wad of her fresh winnings in the air. "You don't get it, Deneen. Mother is treading water here, trying to keep her head up. Forty years of children, including you, and I've finally met my match."

She started crying. I sat on the bed beside her and put my arm around her.

"It'll be okay," I said.

"You think so," she laughed through her tears. "I hope you're right. I have these nightmares that one day soon the phone will ring and it will be the Secret Service, and they'll have caught her in some billion-dollar scheme to kidnap the president. They'll be calling me up and asking me have I seen the first lady.

"Don't laugh. She's perfectly capable."

"So what do you do?"

"Do?" Mother sighed. "I try to stay ahead of the ball, is what I do. She's a crafty one. Just when I think I've got her boxed in, she finds another loophole. I compromise, Deneen. Like these pageants. I hate them every bit as much as you do. The aggravation. The expenses. You'd scream if you knew how much I'd spent. But I smile at her and hug her and tell her how pretty she is and how smart she is. She plays along with me. Most of the time. God help me when she stops."

"It's a lot of work for you, Mother."

She rubbed her brow. "Yes, it is. All children are. I did it right once, though." She turned toward me and grinned.

"I wouldn't be so sure," I sobbed.

"I'm sure. I am."

"I haven't been a very good daughter. I stayed away so long. I come home and I'm just a mess."

"You are not a mess. I've seen messes, and you are not one of them."

"Well my life is, then."

"Well? Go fix it, then. It's what we do, us Wilkerson women. It's time to go on back home now and take care of it."

I nodded. A mound of tissue gathered amongst our legs on the bed.

"You aren't afraid I won't come back? I was gone so long the last time."

"I knew you'd come back. When you were ready. Or when you needed me. You can always do that. I know you will."

"Life is just so disappointing sometimes. You know?"

"I know."

"You're always telling us to eat all our food up so we can join the clean plate club. I always did. There was a building up by where we used to live in Spanish Lake—an old roadhouse, I think it was. For years I thought that was the Clean Plate Club. I never understood why I didn't get to go in. Some days it's one disappointment after the next."

"Oh, Deneen." Mother gathered me in again. "That silly old story."

"Mama, I just want to know that someone will love me someday. That's all."

"We do. And we will."

At that very moment, down in the auditorium, Miss Ciara Renee Jones was on the stage, proudly representing the young women of Missouri. Her hair was puffed out from the side of her head like a pioneer woman, adorned around the face with curls made of what was left of her real hair. She was giving her all, belting her heart out, singing, "I will always love you," hands raised, pleading, toward the ceiling in the direction of my mother and me huddled above her on the bed.

Gerald from maintenance came and repaired the door. Mother and I stayed where we were. There wasn't anywhere we particularly wanted to go.

# *Epilogue*

I am back in Minneapolis now. Home, or something like it, I guess.

Ciara did not win the pageant. She made it to the top ten and got an award for being the "perkiest." She simpered and cheered for the others and, at least according to Hawkins, did not scratch anyone's eyes out or trip any fat girls. All the way back to the Midwest, she simmered like a stewpot full of neck-bones and butter beans, plotting, I knew, as to how she would become even more beautiful and more talented and more whatever else was needed to get to be the one wearing the crown next time. I am glad I am not in her way.

Hawkins stayed cool through the whole affair. He painted out the finger marks on Ciara's cheek from our mother's slap. By the time Ciara scraped away the foundation and base, the hand print had faded and all that remained was a memory and pain of the kind that bears fruit at some later date. Hawkins awaits news on the Dream Dolls franchise. He assures me it's looking good. How he will fit running a pageant in amidst hair appointments and the general mayhem that is his life, I can only guess. He told me that the Dream Dolls people were impressed with him, but then added, "You know how those old queens are. You got to bend over for them just to get a glass of water." I told him I would rather not hear about such things, thank you very much.

Mark asked after me, Hawkins reported recently, and I played it off real casual.

The men, the men, the men—always asking after Deneen.

Since I left St. Louis, Hawkins has cut the extensions from my sister's hair and allowed her to unbind her breasts, preparing her for the preliminaries of some "Teenager of the Year" pageant. He is going to "bring her up slowly," he told me. These pageants were not the kind you just walked into and walked out a winner the first time. You entered over and over again, and you kept working at it until finally it was your turn.

He told me the plan when we went for a stroll on the Strip—the evening after the pageant. We walked past volcanoes and palaces and tigers and assorted vendors passing out catalogs full of available naked women. I told him I didn't think my sister would ever be happy as an also-ran.

He blew it off. "I worked with gals a lot more high strung than Miss Ciara. They think they the Queen of the May, all these gals. Think the sun rises and sets on their beautiful behinds. Well, they got another thing coming when they join the House of Hawkins."

"You're gonna whip her into shape, huh?"

"Or die trying."

"Good luck."

We stood and watched an Elvis impersonator hustling people into a decrepit old casino, the kind with the old one-armed bandits in it. Elvis called me little lady and swiveled his hips in my direction a few times. Hawkins told him to swivel his nasty butt on down the street someplace else.

I steered us back toward the hotel.

"I'm going back to Minneapolis tomorrow night," I told him.

"What you want to go back to that ugly old Minnesota for?"

"I've got a job there," I said. "And a house. And friends."

He took me by the arm like he was an old uncle or something. "Who in their right mind would hire a trifling thing like you?"

"I'm very good at what I do."

"Yeah, you would be, I guess. Stubborn as you are. Got somebody waiting for you up there?"

"You mean like a man?"

"Unless there's something else we ain't talked about." Eyes over those glasses again. The fool.

"There was someone for a while. Not anymore."

"So go on. Tell Hawkins what you did to run him off."

"If you must know, the nigger had the nerve to tell me he thought he preferred men."

"Ha! Suppose he thought that made him special. Was he cute?"

"Sort of. And why do you care?"

"You don't know nothing, do you? What I'm saying, girlfriend, is take a look at these men walking up and down this sidewalk here. Your boyfriend would find a lot of company out here."

"You mean all these guys are gay?" I whispered that in case anyone was listening.

"Did I say that? No. What you said was your loverboy was attracted to men. A lot of us are. Men and women both, and some of us more than others. It's been that way as long as I've been around."

"Since the dinosaurs," I mumbled. He pinched my arm and told me not to be a B. I. T. C. H.

"What hurts is, he lied to me for so long. He couldn't even be honest with me about it."

"Sit down over here a minute. Come on." He directed me

to a bench in front of a casino tricked out as a riverboat. "Let me tell you something about the world we live in, my darling. As far as a lot of folks are concerned, being what I am is about the lowest thing you can be. There's many a liar out there, and the ones they lie to the most are themselves."

"The man hurt me."

Hawkins punched me in the arm. "Big strong girl like you. You bounced right back, didn't you?"

I nodded and shrugged at the same time.

"Do me a favor. Be a *really* big girl. Don't turn your back on the boy. It's a hard time for the brother. A friend like you could save his life."

I told him I'd think about it.

Mother took me to the airport as soon as we collected my things from her house. We were saved from a teary farewell by my darling sister who whined about how far we had to walk to the gate. Ciara decided to play-act a big emotional scene by pretending to hug me and plant big fake smooches on me and telling me how sad she was to see me go. I surprised her by wrapping my arms around her as tight as I could and giving her a real kiss on the cheek.

"I'll be keeping an eye on you," I whispered in her ear.

I waved good-bye to Mama, and the look on her face told me that the hug I had given my sister was the best thing I could have done for both of them.

I rolled into my office the next morning without a clue about the douche spray ad. If my head was to be served on a platter, I figured I'd rather have it done sooner than later. I breezed by Katrina, not even stopping for her puppy-dog-like I-missed-you mugging.

"Here I am," I said to Mr. Waltershied.

"Oh. Deneen. I was just thinking, you know, how you're

always going on about how we need to be up front about what these products do. So I had this idea."

No "Welcome back, Deneen"?

I had an idea myself. I had the idea that maybe I, too, ought to think twice about the way I used women to sell other people's crap. I was no better than the rest of them. But such was my business, after all. My business was what paid the bills, was what I was good at, and was what I liked doing more than anything in the world. Life is always about compromises, isn't it? Everywhere one turns.

"You with me, Deneen?" Mr. Waltershied said. "I'm ready for your pitch."

I didn't have a pitch. All I had was a head full of questions and a wish that I could guilelessly put a tiara on my own head and wave to my adoring subjects.

At the same moment I flashed back to the Benetton ads. Once again the proverbial lightbulb appeared. I'd have the agencies send me every black actress and model in their books. I would assemble a rainbow of women, from blue black to high yellow, from teenage to ancient, from tiny petite to refrigerator size. I'd pose them in front of the camera and tell them to do absolutely nothing. No smiling, no mugging, no fury, no tears. Just show their simplest, most serious selves. Every commercial would show a dozen or so women, and at the end would come the product—in its Asian packaging, of course. Across the screen, also in the appropriate languages, would be the words "For Women." That's all.

Did it come off? About as well as such pseudo-feminist claptrap could. The client loved it, and they're showing those commercials across the continent of Asia. People got half the message, at least: they can't keep douche spray in stock in Singapore.

It's the other half of the message that worries me.

The ad agency now has more business than we can handle. In case you're interested, the letterhead reads: Waltershied, Williams and Wilkerson. W cubed it is!

All in all, while I may not be healed, I am at least a lot better. My hair looks great, nappy or combed, just the way Hawkins promised it would. I fly down to St. Louis every six weeks or so for a maintenance job.

And to see Mother, of course.

And then there's Mark. Yes, there's still Mark. What can I tell you? The man was, after all, smitten.


So what was this all about? What was the point?

Self-indulgence?

Buppie exhaustion?

Midlife crisis?

Fit of pique?

My preferred version: I fell off the bike and I got back on. Some new ground may have been broken (except I'm not sure I believe in new ground).

There are, of course, questions. More than I care to answer—assuming I had any answers, which I don't. What I would like to know is: Why did I have to be crazy to really enjoy sex for the first time? And why is Katrina considered a slut because she dresses in a way that flatters her beautiful body? By the same token, why is my sister five hundred miles away prancing around on display considered a model young lady?

Every time I circle in on what seems to be an answer, it dissolves in a puddle of contradictions.

What's a girl to do but get on with her life? I'm

comfortable, safe, relatively happy, healthy. Lovely, if I don't say so myself.

Even so: many days I feel like a first-class passenger on the *Titanic*. The food's great and the accommodations are terrific, but just look what's on the schedule for tomorrow night. That's how life is, I guess. What can one do but stock up on floatation devices and hope for a seat in the lifeboat?

There's one other thing I should tell you. Katrina was busy, and I didn't have the money for a cab, so guess who I called to pick me up at the airport?

Calvin.

Of course.

The two of us are talking. No biggie. Just friends. Just like Hawkins said. You know how it goes. Being a black woman these days, you've got to develop a strong sense of irony.

Other books by David Haynes
available in Harvest paperback editions
from Harcourt Brace & Company

*Live at Five*

*Somebody Else's Mama*